THE 12TH LETTER

JACKIE HOVORKA

J&J Ranch Productions

ISBN: 978-1-68433-164-2 (Paperback); 978-1-68433-854-2 (Hardcover)
PUBLISHED BY J&J RANCH PRODUCTIONS
www.JJRanchProductions.com

Printed in the United States of America
Suggested Retail Price (SRP) $19.95 (Paperback); $23.95 (Hardcover)
THE 12TH LETTER is printed in Chaparral Pro

Dedicated to my husband,
Sgt. Robert "Johnny" Hovorka,
who always stays positive, supportive of my work,
faithful to God, and is the most amazing man I've known
since I lost my grandfather when I was still young.

Special thanks to the Warrior Bonfire Program
for their continued support!

THE 12TH LETTER

PROLOGUE

GALVESTON, TEXAS
PRESENT DAY

Thousands of shortened lives laid dead and scattered everywhere on the desolate landscape awaiting their resting place in the ground, most without names and anyone left alive to mourn them. But someone had to bury them. And that was how it went, on and on for days; strangers being buried by strangers.

When I first arrived in Galveston as an angry and damaged thirty-year-old war veteran, there was so much I didn't yet know. How could such a beautiful ocean bring unimaginable chaos and loss as it did when our country's worst natural disaster hit Galveston? Yet in the hurricane's aftermath, hope and kindness still prevailed.

Before learning about the island's tragedy, I only knew of pain, devastation, and death being brought on by people with no goodness anywhere to be found. And I hated life because of it.

Funny how God can orchestrate miraculous events in your life to prove you wrong; things you never imagined possible.

CHAPTER 1
July 2000

The last rays of the sun disappeared behind drifting grey clouds and swaying palm trees. Another late afternoon rain shower was coming. As the wind began to howl and the temperature dropped to a more comfortable eighty something degrees, I stopped my bike on the street to let its engine idle down.

My new neighbor was on his driveway finishing off the last coat of wax over his pristine bay boat. The older man paid no mind to me. He was too busy rubbing the same small spot on the starboard side. I seriously thought the idiot could potentially rub the paint off of it if he continued on like that. But then the meticulous man stopped his ministrations and frowned up at the inclement sky as angry clouds gathered.

With a shake of his head, the guy threw his wax mitten over the boat's stern and stormed away towards his house. His home was more of a cottage, but still an older structure like the rest on the road. Although it had been updated recently and had a new crisp banana colored exterior, it still had one flaw – glossy painted steps.

In the man's haste to take cover, he lost his footing on those slippery wet steps and almost tumbled over backwards. With a few foul words, he surprisingly managed to upright himself again just in time to dash through the front door. He missed the heavier drops of rain, but his boat did not. Oh… that sweet specimen of a boat he had just made spiffy became totally soaked.

I lifted the visor on my helmet and continued to sit there and admire the gorgeous Skeeter with its twin-engine, center console, and blue flecked paint. What I wouldn't give for something like that one day. Someday. But would there ever even be a *someday?*

I began to laugh a little at that thought and at my neighbor. I did have a few drinks at the bar, so the man's stupidity seemed funny to me at that moment. If he cared so much to keep that boat perfectly clean, why not put it under a porch or buy a boat cover? Duh.

The warm rain continued to pick up as it showered all over my arms. Then, Galveston's ocean breeze lifted the precipitation up and pushed drizzles of its best skies onto my face, too. I wiped at my eyes and looked around the street at the rest of the Skittle-colored houses and the tropical front porch decorations that only a lazy beach town could pull off correctly.

The rain continued on, cleaning and cooling the hot roads and rooftops all around me. It was nice. Serene almost. But then suddenly, almost eerily, the elemental display stopped. Warmth began to surround me again as the sun peeped out from behind the clouds.

I took a deep cleansing breath. The air was full of moisture, so salty and crisp. Just how I liked it. Oh, I was definitely getting an itch to fish in the vast water where that blessed rain had originally come from. It was a nice reminder of where I was.

I loved the ocean way more than the freshwater lakes and rivers from where I grew up. But even at that moment, a linger of doubt hung in the air. Why did I leave Pittsburgh? Why did I choose Texas? Maybe I didn't think that one through. Maybe that was the dang point.

I shook my head and drove my bike up onto the rocked driveway of my temporary residence.

When I put my bike's kickstand down and moved slowly off of it, I took a second to glance up at the old structure before me. It had a different façade than the rest of the houses on the street. Where the other properties were modernized with fresh colorful paint and energy efficient double-pane windows, my abode had old brown paint peeling off the sides and crooked shutters next to cracked windows.

However, the dilapidated house reminded me of myself. I wasn't as old as it was, of course. But, I was just as worn out as each board and nail was that the poor house relied on to hold its shambled-self together with. So, basically… yup, I could relate.

I stood there transfixed and still staring up at the old soul before me. How much had this house gone through in its one hundred years of existence? Was it more than what I endured in my five short years of military service?

When I realized I was swaying from the alcohol, I decided to make my way towards the porch before I passed out on the dang lawn giving my neighbor a reason to laugh back at me.

The first of the three steps on the porch seemed ominous. I squeezed tightly on the thin handrail to help pull me up. I thought about the other man slipping, even with his real and perfectly functioning legs. Thankfully, my house's steps had been replaced a few years back with metal treads instead of wood. It looked tacky, but it gave me more confidence to try to go up them while they were wet.

My prosthetic limb was partly why I debated taking on a renovation of a house with over thirty steps inside and out. But I didn't have a choice if I wanted work in Galveston. Most of the older houses on the island were built up because of constant flooding.

As I labored up the steps, I wondered about how long it would take me to renovate the historic home. There was a lot of work to be done on it. Randall Gaines and his wife didn't give me a deadline. They just hoped they could get it done at a budget price. And I was their man. One thing my grandfather gave me that I appreciated, unlike his daughter, aka my mom, was that my grandfather gave me his time.

When I was growing up and during my summers off from school, he would take me to his job sites with him. He taught me all the tricks of the trade on how to renovate houses. I enjoyed those days. I loved the greasy breakfast meals, endless coffee, and the good humor between him and his contractors.

One large stride across the narrow porch and I walked into the house. I closed the front door behind me and took off my helmet. Oh, it felt good. The cool air inside was blowing directly onto my face then. A tide of gratitude for the invention of the air conditioning system crossed my mind. Thank God the previous owners had put a unit in. It wasn't the hottest part of the day and I did love all things ocean, but not the temperature at night if it meant I slept in a pile of my own sweat. I endured that pathetic existence enough while I was overseas and had to sleep in a hooch out in the field.

I scratched at my short beard and inspected the foyer. The previous night when I first arrived in Galveston and walked into the house, it was already too dark. I couldn't really see much. But I was tired anyway. I knew I had plenty of time to assess the project later. All I cared about was finding a bed. Too bad the only furniture in the house was located up another flight of stairs.

For a moment, I let my eyes focus on the rips in the sunflower wallpaper. The yellow flowers were faded, almost blurry, but they were uniquely designed having been painted by hand. I imagined that the house had been a beautiful Victorian home at some point back in time. Almost like in those magazines my sister-in-law would flip through and show my brother.

I could begin to picture the house's potential. I knew that a fresh layer of wall paper, buffed and waxed floors, and a few new coats of paint would have the place better than it ever was before.

As I stood there, a musky and damp smell hit my nose suddenly. My stomach turned. I leaned over and let my elbows rest on my knees. My head began spinning. Closing my eyes didn't help.

I took some breaths and my thoughts went back to my fifth drink at the bar an hour before. And of that cute blonde that I turned down after all her heavy flirting. I still didn't know why I didn't take the bait. Bring her back here. Possibly enjoy something for a change. I could have used the distraction.

Ahead of me, the tall staircase to my room loomed. I switched on the grimy pendant light hanging from the ceiling above me. Mentally pushing myself along, I began to head up the first few steps of the staircase. Each creaking sound below my feet reminded me of my grandfather's old house. A memory of my brother, Jed, and I running all over his house as kids came to mind. It was the sound of the wood's give and take that always gave us away. Grandma switched us every time we ran in her and my grandfather's home.

As I continued up the stairs, the sounds made me feel like an intruder. I looked up ahead. In between my pathetic shallow gasps for breath, I spoke aloud, "I know, old house. I don't belong here yet, but I will. You'll appreciate me here… in time. Now, just let my drunk-self make it up these stairs, please."

My mood began to change as exhaustion came over me. I began to curse the steep stairs as I fought between the alcohol induced dizziness and the pain to my thigh from my prosthetic.

Thankfully, I managed to make it to the top. But barely. Truth be told, I probably had too many drinks. But maybe I didn't care anymore.

The funky smell from the downstairs area had seemed to subside when I got to the landing on the second floor. Was it maybe mold down below? Not a good sign.

Stumbling through the doorway of the first bedroom off to the right, I tripped over an oddly placed antique chair. Falling without anything to stop me, my left knee hit the floor hard. Fluid white heat traveled up my right thigh and into my hip. Crying out in pain, I rolled over onto my back and kicked the chair. I hollered out, "Ugh!!!!" A few of the seashell pieces on its leg fell off and shattered beneath it.

Now, I was fully pissed. I was tired, aggravated, and hurting. Or maybe I was just freaking ashamed of my weaknesses. I felt useless and weak, and I hated it! I hated me. I hated everyone. And now I hated the house.

I summoned up the strength to try to pull myself up from the floor. However, my fingertips slid across something strange - a lifted edge of one wood panel. I tried pushing it back down, but it stayed lifted a quarter of an inch. Out of curiosity, I let my fingertips skirt the old wood until I felt a gap just big enough for two fingers. I pulled up on it. With not much resistance, I easily raised the entire plank.

I reached behind me for my duffel bag and pulled out my handy flashlight that I always took with me in the field. I turned it on and lowered it as far as I could into the hollow space below the floor. It probably was just an old board that hadn't been replaced with rot below it. Most of the people on the island loved to keep the existing buildings fastened with the same useless and rotting materials. A sentimental nuisance in my opinion.

The flashlight managed to illuminate an area of about five by five feet under the floor. "Huh?" I said aloud. The original builder must have built the second floor with a vacant space measuring at least one foot larger than usual between floors. I wasn't sure why. I questioned if it was just my impaired vision after all the drinks I had at the bar.

I shined the flashlight more to the left of the space. To my surprise, I saw the corner of what looked like a square package covered in a blanket. Was this a hiding spot for someone to put things between the floors?

I lifted the item up and removed the waxy, brown material that covered whatever the object was. I shined my flashlight on its protective wrapping. It was some kind of leather, not a blanket.

I set it aside and dusted off what was remaining in my hand. It appeared to be a journal of some sort.

I opened it very slowly to keep it from tearing. Inside, I saw curvy, almost too pretty of letters gracing the first page. I read a little of it…

The heat here in Galveston is more than I expected. One cannot get away from it. As soon as I wake and put on my habit, I am drenched in perspiration. It is nothing like my home in England. There are a few moments after six o'clock when I am free of my duties and mass when I can walk out on the veranda and let the ocean breeze cool my skin. It is in those moments that I wish I could hear God's voice again. A reassurance that He has not left me. A comfort that I really was called to do His work here. But still, no voice and no replies.

I flipped to the next page.

I am saddened that we continue to receive more and more children as the plague continues. Sweet, pitiable children. Orphaned because of the fever. Just yesterday, a new young boy was brought to me. He is only about eight. He does not recall his name because of the trauma, but he is a tough spirit; he has already started up quarrels with two other boys. Fists and all. God give me the strength to help him.

I decided to continue. I flipped to another page. This time, I pulled a little too quickly on the old paper. The top corner tore from the binding. An ornamental quill fell out of the book onto the floor next to me. I picked the quill up and squinted to see what it was made of. Its pearly shimmer was intriguing. I set the old pen down on the floor and flipped the pages of the book again and continued to read.

The woman talked about losing two of her orphans to some kind of plague. It was the same virus that killed their parents and brought them to the convent's orphanage on the beach, away from the well-populated areas. A plague? An old diary and a quill? This had to be a nun who had already passed.

I closed the diary, set it down by its quill, and laid myself prone onto the old pine floor. My head was still spinning. I couldn't shake the feeling that something about that nun reminded me of Emily. My stomach knotted up as I saw Emily's face again from the day I shipped out overseas. But the sadness was a pretense because she left me for another man while I was in Somalia.

Emily, the girl of my dreams in high school, had been my everything. I remembered us both on our first date. She wore her hair in a low ponytail accentuating her beautiful neck. The whole night, I had wanted to kiss her and run my fingers down the soft skin below her chin.

I was late bringing Emily home that night. Mr. Brooks, her stepfather, waited by the door for us and immediately yelled at Emily. She dropped her head down and walked right by him. When she got to the door, she turned around and blew me a kiss. It was the best kiss I had ever experienced because it was the first kiss I got from an angel. Or so I thought that was what she was. Just a false sense of security.

I opened my eyes, still remembering how she had me fooled for years. I sighed and looked over at the diary. Not even recognizing my own vodka-soaked voice, I spoke aloud, "What am I going to do with you now, old diary? Your owner is obviously dead and, being a nun and all, she had no descendants for me to bring you to, so…"

I picked up the diary again and read a section about how that nun had been struggling with her faith lately. She mentioned a few things about missing someone that was still back in England. A few more sentences about how at one point she thought she was doing the right thing, but not anymore. It all resonated with me. Afterall, I did the same thing. Deployed to another country and then came back home to nothing. I lost everything.

"Okay, Ms. Nun," I conceded. "I'll put your diary back and leave it to rest with your secrets." I scratched at my cheek noticing my beard was getting too long, but then I paused. "You know what, Ms. Nun?" I spoke aloud again towards the old book. "I'm gonna leave you a message. No one will see it anyway. Hope you don't mind. And if you come to haunt me… whatever."

I laughed at myself and picked up the pearly quill. "Ink. I need ink. Dang." I turned the quill over in my hand and moved it down to the paper to scribble nothing at all, of course. But it was a gut reaction to do that anyway. To my surprise, ink flowed easily out onto the page of the diary. But after all this time?

I brought the quill up closer to my face. "How is that even possible?" I shook my head, lowered the odd pen, and started to write.

Dear Miss Nun,

I know it is crazy and you will never read this, but my name is Trey Reynolds. I used to write letters to someone. Heck, I used to even write short stories when I was young. I enjoyed writing. Not so much anymore. But anyway, something about what you wrote got to me. We are, or I guess you'd say, we were, a lot alike. We both left our countries to go to another place to help others. I carried a rifle as a United States Marine, you carried a cross as a servant of God, but we both spent much of our time helping children who lost their parents and we both later began doubting our choice of profession. Because in turn, we lost everything we loved.

I don't know why I'm writing in this diary. Maybe it's therapy. I'm angry a lot. I pretty much hate everything and everyone. My psychiatrist said I should write down my thoughts and even try going back to church. Nah, no church for me. Miss Nun, I've been through too much and seen too much on my tours in Somalia… I just don't care anymore. The liquor is my release. Yup, I said it. I drink a lot. After all, it is the great year of two thousand that everyone says will be our best year ever since we survived the tech fear.

So anyway, I'm going to put your diary back, leave it in peace, never touch it again, have another shot of that vodka Ms. Alexis, the bartender, sent me home with and… I don't know. Goodnight, Miss nun… Or Margaret. Sister Margaret, right? Goodnight, Sister Margaret.

And by the way, that ugly seashell covered chair in this room takes up too much space, so I tripped over it and broke it. If it's yours, I'm sorry but I may have ruined it. But you can't blame a man with one leg, right?

I closed the diary. I put it and its old quill back in its place before I passed out right there on the hard, but thankfully, cold floor.

CHAPTER 2
Stormy West

Screams and shards of glass were everywhere. A baby's cries echoed through the chaos. Freshly blown sand had built up against what was left of my Humvee as crimson colors sprayed all over its smashed door. All around me was movement, but my eyes couldn't help but focus ahead on the barren landscape. Suddenly, the baby was gone. In fact, everything was gone that my senses could detect. Yet something was still there… always there.

I woke up in a pool of sweat. Blinking quickly and breathing hard, I looked for something to focus on. The seashell chair was what my eyes finally decided to land solidly on. That ugly thing actually brought me comfort at that moment. I shook my head and reached down to below my right knee. My leg was tingling, but it was still missing. Even though I lost it, I sometimes felt the pain where it should have been. The doctors called it a phantom reaction or something like that right before they said it was a miracle that I only lost one limb.

The light of the sun barely showed above the shrubs outside the large bedroom window, but it was enough to make my head hurt worse. The glass panes needed to be replaced soon. Like much of the house, they were a century old, so the heat from outside managed to easily seep through and warm me quickly.

I wiped a bead of sweat off my forehead and studied the sash windows. I couldn't deny, they had a nice look about them. The muntin framed design was separated into eight even sections. It reminded me of the chicklet candies my grandfather always gave me after church, my reward for sitting still through an hour of watching people pray for nothing. Like an innate sense of ritual, I still did what was expected of me. That all ended after I went to war.

Checking my watch, I noticed it was later in the day than what I would have liked. I had planned to make use of the rented dumpster outside to clean up a little before it got too hot. I rubbed my face. The deep scar above my unruly beard gave me pause. Just another reminder of everything, but also the reason why I kept a beard. Late nights, short days, and facial hair were nothing like what I was used to after several years in the Marine Corps. My, my, how things can change.

I put on my prosthetic leg and headed down stairs to sit on an old kitchen chair while I debated the final measurements on the cabinets in that space. I thought of how it could be nice to add an island for more of a work area. I started to draw it out in my mind and possibly run over to the hardware store where Mr. Gaines had an open credit line for me, but then I froze up. My hands began to shake. Screw it, I needed some food, and I desperately wanted to get my mind off that baby's cries and Private Johnson's face.

That was my latest ongoing nightmare.

****

Several blocks over and just a quick ride on my motorcycle, I was already entering the bar I had been to the afternoon before. The short, freckled woman, Alexis, was behind the counter laughing with the customers. She slid shots down to a few college frat boys. The tallest of the three had red hair and sunburnt skin. He downed his shot without a second thought. The guy next to him with wide rimmed glasses studied his liquor for a moment.

I sat down on one of the shiny bar stools away from the party goers, away from everyone. But then Alexis, who must have remembered me from my drunken spell the night before, hollered out, "There he is, everyone!"

I exhaled and began wishing I had tried Warf's Pub next door instead.

Alexis was a great mixologist but an annoying bartender. She gave a mirthless laugh and said, "It's Sergeant *Whatever*". With her chin raised high, she waved her dainty hand above her head for more drama. "He has yet to tell us his name so that's the name I gave him."

Finally, in a lowered voice, she added, "But we'll leave him alone."

Alexis leaned over towards me and tapped at her cheek with a mischievous grin. And then… there it was. She raised back up and blurted out, "But! He's a Purple Heart Vet. So, everyone, give Sergeant *Whatever* a warm Anchors Aweigh welcome!"

Pretty much all the bar patrons lifted their glasses and yelled, "Cheers!"

I blew out the hot air that was burning my lungs. I didn't want all this. I wanted quiet. Not this. I cleared my throat. "Can I get my usual, please? And I'll take another of those hot dogs, hold the extras this time," I instructed. "Had indigestion something fierce last night. And please no more of the announcements about me."

The vexing woman smacked her ruby red lips. "Sure thing," she half-heartedly reassured me and turned on her heels with her fluffy hair spinning with her.

Instead of continuing to throw daggers at her in my mind, I looked around with a sober perspective at the small bar. Anchors Aweigh Bar wasn't fancy, but it had a unique and relaxing setting that I admired.

The Christmas lights that strung randomly from the ceiling were a nice touch against the room's dark eggplant colored walls. Behind the counter, the lights dangled over the liquor bottles and accented the beer selection. For an establishment that wasn't known as a sports bar, it had over sixty beers on tap.

Off to my left, the red headed college boy yelled out across the bar at me, "Where did you serve?"

I eyed Big Red and didn't answer.

The boy with glasses shoved his red-headed friend. "You don't mess with them like that."

Big Red rolled his eyes at Glasses. Alexis looked at me and then at them. "Somalia."

The third college kid with them and the smaller of the group, added, "I loved the trailer to that new movie coming out. The one called *Black Hawk Down*. Have y'all seen the trailer yet? It's about Somalia."

Glasses and Big Red laughed at him and then picked up their second shot from Alexis before walking off to play pool.

Thank God.

I felt a tug on my shirt sleeve. A man with more stress lines on his face than me sat down beside me. "Somalia, huh?"

I wanted to get up and leave. But something in the guy's knowing eyes kept me in place. I replied, "Yep."

The man was even bigger than the annoying college kid with the red hair. I watched this stranger take a sip of his milky alcoholic drink that must have splashed onto his outdated hippie hairdo before he had walked over to me. The white drippings from his drink clung to the longest strands of his kinky hair.

He noticed me staring and added, "I was in Desert Storm. Army, 1st Calvary Division out of Fort Hood… here in Texas. Anyway, I'm Larry Wheeler," he said sternly and reached out his right hand.

I shook it. The man still had the typical strong military grip. "Nice to meet you, Larry. I'm Trey."

Larry sat down beside me. "Why Texas? And why does the bartender know so much about you? You come here a lot?" he asked and called over to the bartender, "Another, please, beautiful." He lifted up his empty glass.

She smiled coyly. "You and those White Russians, Larry."

The older guy grabbed the remaining cherry from out of his glass right before she reached for it. "Well, you do make them the best I ever had," he added as a taunt.

She smirked. "I highly doubt that."

When Larry looked back at me, I decided to reply, "I guess you can say that. Had trouble keeping my job after I got back from overseas. Too many nightmares at night and too short fused towards the living during the day."

"Yeah, I know. Been there." With those words, vacant eyes looked over at me. Yeah, he had been there. I bet he had many stories he could tell me about. Instead, Larry lightened the mood back up. "But why Texas, Trey?"

"I love the ocean and…" I gulped down the smooth liquor. "…because of the good disability benefits."

"I hear ya. Cheers to that," Larry said and lifted up his glass. The thick milky concoction he was drinking made me wonder how he didn't get sick from drinking just one.

We tapped our glasses together. "Cheers," I returned and we both went back to drinking.

At Larry's feet, a German Sheppard peered up at us. Larry lowered a treat to the dog's mouth before sitting back up to stir his fresh drink. Soldiers shared only so much emotional stuff. We both knew we had reached our stopping point.

My eyes moved from him to the television behind the bar. The Houston news anchor, Jordynn Randall, started his reporting on his next haunting story. This one was about Galveston's most famous home, Bishop's Palace. I leaned forward to listen, but it was too loud in the bar to hear the entire report.

I watched the images on the screen to gauge the details the best I could. Ghosts and other scary stories were all I used to read about as a kid, especially if it had something to do with pirates and their escapades on the mainland. Everywhere I went when I was a kid, the libraries would be void of any book pertaining to that subject matter after I cleaned them out.

The bar's cook, Steve, brought out my hot dogs and then followed my eyes up to the television behind the bar. "No manches! That is on tonight? I love that kind of stuff."

I frowned. "What? Old houses?"

He pointed at the broadcast. "No, fool. Ghosts."

I popped my knuckles and went back to cradling my drink. "You really believe all that, Steve?"

"Heck yeah, carnal. It's one of my favorite reasons to live here. This whole island is haunted," he swore with an airy sound in his voice.

I remembered meeting Steve the night before through a fog of loud music and many drinks. I had thanked him for the excellent cooking. Steve had laughed and replied that there was nothing special about making hot dogs. The only thing he required was that the owner of the bar stocked Nathan's hot dogs for him to cook.

"Still, it's better than MREs," I remembered saying and we both laughed.

Steve and I hit it off the last hour of that drunken night. Come to think about it, that must have been when I spilled my entire military history onto him and Alexis.

The short Hispanic man turned and headed back to the kitchen as another image popped up on the tiny television. It was a picture in black and white of an old house called the Sampson's Manor. It was triple the size of the house I was remodeling.

Did the reporter say the house was built in eighteen eighty? It seemed the Gaines family had told me when they hired me that the house I was working on was dated back to that time period, as well.

I waved the bartender over. "Can you turn up the tube? I want to watch that."

She looked up at the screen and then looked over her shoulder at me. "Not turning it up. It'll taint the ambience in here. Plus, I don't like that news guy."

"I wouldn't know. I haven't lived here long enough to know him," I replied back.

She stared back at the television in deep thought. "Yup, that man's a tricky one. He has four sides to him."

The other vet in the room, Larry, snickered beside me. "Alexis, don't start with all that human psyche stuff."

She rolled her eyes at him and continued, "Most people have two or three sides. Of course, they only show their best side to the world. The other sides they keep hidden and they juggle all of them to try to figure out who they really are. Nothing wrong with two or three sides that make up a person, but four different sides is not good."

"Okay," I flippantly responded. I was trying not to laugh. "Can I have a water, though?" I asked. My first reaction was to write her off as a loon, but after going to war, you tend to see things differently. Maybe that's why Larry gave her grace, too.

Alexis let out a loud sigh. "All I'm saying is there is more truth to the adage, *'Don't judge a book by its cover'* than we know. It's really about people. Trust me," she suggested and turned around.

Larry shrugged. "There's some truth to that, Trey." Then, he smiled over at me. "So, what's your full name?"

"Excuse me?" I asked.

"I told you mine, remember? So, what is yours? Trey, what?"

"Trey Reynolds, sir."

Larry's expression changed slightly. I couldn't make it out. Bewilderment crossed his wide face for a moment, but then it left almost as quickly as it came. He went back to smiling. "Nice to formally meet you now, Trey Reynolds."

We shook hands a second time and he added, "Again, welcome to Texas. If you haven't learned it yet, everything is bigger in Texas."

Alexis handed me a tall glass of iced water and looked at Larry. "Including egos," she inserted into our conversation with a touch of humor obviously meant only for him.

I lifted the glass to drink but a nudge from my other side made me almost spill it. I set the water back down and turned towards the new stranger. "Watch it!" I warned as my blood pressure began to rise.

I took a breath to control my rage. My therapist had given me some strategies that worked from time to time, just not enough sometimes. I remembered him saying that the anger was from my time in combat and it was to be expected. In return, I had said to my therapist, "Anger? I'm not angry." I honestly never knew I was blowing up on people. The reaction just came naturally.

I sat up taller and took in the man that almost ruined my afternoon. He was just a simple grunge dude about my age smoking a cigarette and wearing dark clothing with a few visible tattoos. Nothing threatening, except that he was clearly too excited to be among us. He smiled big and inquired, "Are you serious? Is your name really Trey Reynolds?"

I shot back, "Last I saw on my birth certificate serious, why?"

"Were you named after the famous Army Colonel, Trey Reynolds, from here in Galveston?" he asked with a raspy voice. I hadn't noticed it immediately, but by observing his posture and giddy questioning, I started to think that he was actually a lot younger than me. Maybe the age confusion was because he was a heavy smoker. His yellowed teeth gave that away.

Hesitating for a second, I began to feel even more annoyed. "No, dude, not that I'm aware of. My family wouldn't know him. We're not from around here, remember?"

"Hmm. Yeah, Pittsburgh. That's right. It would have been neat, though."

I looked back up at the television and nodded. "Maybe." I began to tune him out and watch the news again. Even squinting my eyes, I had trouble seeing the date under the picture of the house that was still showing on the screen. I shook my head. It was one of those times I could have used my glasses. But I hated wearing glasses. I had perfect eyes before I shipped out overseas, but not anymore.

My thoughts were interrupted again by the smoker next to me. I turned to see him light his second Marlboro Red and blow out his match. Smoker Boy then added, "You know they have a plaque for him by the docks?"

I leaned back a little. I hated cigarette smoke. "Sorry, him who?"

He pleaded, "Come on. You know, Colonel Reynolds? Your namesake. He was born in Galveston and ended up winning all kinds of medals in World War 1 saving other soldiers."

"Nice," I simply replied, realizing he wasn't going to let it go yet.

"Nice? He's a local hero. Did you know he was an orphan?"

I took another sip of my drink. "Nope."

Larry chimed into the conversation. "He don't care, Sammie. Not from here, remember?"

Sammie shrugged.

Larry sat back and crossed his arms. "But…"

I frowned at Larry. "But what?"

"Well, the Colonel was found by nuns from the Sisters of Charity orphanage. Trey Reynolds wasn't a popular name in the late eighteen-hundreds. That's part of the neat history behind the Colonel." Larry slowly turned his drink glass on the counter while in deep thought.

His bottom lip began to twitch as he studied his glass. After a few seconds, he continued, "I didn't think much of it when you told me your name. Or maybe I did." Larry's pointer finger began tapping on the side of his glass. "I don't know. Anyway, Sammy is right. It is an honorable name."

"Why?"

"He was one of the reasons why I enlisted, especially into the Army."

I just nodded.

Larry's slate blue eyes looked over at me. "Anyway, the Colonel couldn't remember his name when he was found as a child, too much trauma, so the nun gave him that name."

I swallowed harder this time. The unknown spice in my drink seemed to thicken in my throat suddenly. I moved my eyes from Larry, to the tube, and then back to Larry again. "Wait. So, you're telling me, this nun just randomly gave an orphan the name Trey Reynolds?" I asked.

"Yup. The Colonel had said that Sister Margaret told him he reminded her of someone she had just met because the boy was always fighting with the other boys and at war with himself. She thought that one day he'd be a soldier, too."

The other vet continued to talk about that nun, but I lowered my lids and drifted away in thought. I was trying to remember the previous night through an elixir of blurry vision and an extremely sore knee cap. Tuning out everything around me, I asked silently to myself, "What was the name of that orphanage in the old diary? Sisters of Charity?" I continued to wonder.

Larry leaned in closer to me. "Get this, the new friend she made, where she got the boy's name from, was a Marine like you."

"Oh?"

The bigger guy began to chuckle making his ice jiggle in his glass. "A Yankee Marine down here in good 'ole Texas now." Larry and Smoker Dude both laughed.

I couldn't help it; the tone of my reply was a bit sarcastic. "And you're a huge Texan drinking a girlie drink."

Larry started laughing harder. "Touché," he said and then he tilted his head. His laughing stopped. "It is just a little strange that we meet around the one-hundred-year anniversary of that hurricane."

My mind drifted off again for a moment, but then I finally asked, "What was the name of the nun and orphanage?"

"Sister Margaret of the Sisters of Charity Orphanage."

"Oh." His response was hard to take in. I set my drink down. "You don't say." I waved over to Alexis. "Can I get the check please?"

Larry frowned. "Leaving so soon? Figured we'd play a round of pool, light weight."

I looked over at Big Red and Glasses as they appeared to begin laying their entire bodies onto the pool table. They were drunk out of their minds. "Nah, I got work to do."

Alexis handed me my check. "Yeah, what's the rush? Larry didn't tell you the rest of Colonel Reynold's history." She lifted her brows at Larry.

I handed her cash and shrugged.

She continued anyway, "Colonel Reynolds and three other boys from that orphanage were the only ones to-."

I shook my head and interrupted her. "Gotta go."

A girl walked by in a mini skirt and winked at me. I was distracted for a brief second. When I snapped back and finished paying for my tab, Larry turned towards me. "Yeah, sad stuff, I tell ya."

He paused, held up one hand, and waited. When he saw Alexis turn away from us, he leaned in closer to me. With a hint of hazelnut laced on his breath, he said, "Look, buddy. When I said I had been there before, I meant it. And then I went on this expedition thing years back with fellow soldiers. We spent time together; did a bonfire together. It really helped."

"I don't need any help," I adamantly replied.

Larry just nodded slowly and picked back up his glass, dropping the subject.

Alexis turned back to face us. She looked from Larry to me before resting her forearms on the bar. "Trey, you really should check out Galveston's history now that you live here. The library is off of McDougal, if you want to."

Was it her lowcut top or the two of them hassling me that made me actually grin? But they were persistent. "Nope, that's not for me."

Larry lifted his drink again but this time with an unsteady hand. He chuckled and said, "Yeah, don't waste your breath, Alexis. You should know you won't ever find a crayon eater in a library."

I froze. Oh, was he really going there? Well, I could play, too. It had been awhile since I talked smack with other military guys. I tilted my head and added, "Ha. Ha. Funny, Army man. You of all people should know what Army stands for?" I paused for effect and then added, "Ain't ready for Marines yet."

Larry started laughing harder. His dog jumped to her feet. Larry smiled and exclaimed, "I like this guy! Come back anytime, local hero."

"I may. I'm renovating an old house for cash on Alamo Lane."

Alexis seemed pleased and gave me a thumbs up. "Good. And when you come back, we'll tell you more about our history now that you are a Texan."

"Nah, this place is only good for the off-shore fishing."

As I stood up, Larry added, "No, not just that. Alexis is right. Our history is important. And those nuns… they were special."

I nodded while in deep thought about that diary. And then Larry grabbed my right forearm and drew his brows together. His voice became serious. "You see, everyone, like those nuns, are all called to do something special with their life no matter how…" he raised his hands in exaggeration…

"*crazy* it may seem. Everyone has a purpose. But only some have the courage to actually do it."

I wasn't ignoring him, but I just couldn't focus after everything they had told me. I passively said, "Noted. It was nice to meet you, brother."

"You too," he replied and patted my back.

I headed towards the door feeling a little uncoordinated. Yet behind me, in pure Alexis form, I heard her blurt out, "Yeah, I can see how it would be hard to *learn* about that hurricane." She laughed while she spoke. "But have a good day."

****

I arrived back at my current residence still wondering about the conversation at the bar. It felt good to walk back into the old house. The place calmed me. I didn't know why it did that for me, especially because the night before, I remembered that I had begun hating the house. But why? Then, I realized why as I eyed its stairs. I sighed and told myself, "You got this, Trey."

I was able to make it to the first landing of the staircase more easily than the night before. However, I had to stop for a breath or two. Once there, I set my helmet on top of the first primary post and allowed my fingertips to trace the ornately carved wood of the banister and handrail. I loved that kind of thing.

A few spindles were missing from below the handrail. I knew that in order to keep the same look as the Gaines wanted, I would have to find a talented craftsman to spin carve me a few new ones to match. That would be a thought for another day when my mind was clearer. Something was eating at me. Something I couldn't explain. I only hoped I wasn't losing it.

I picked back up my helmet but continued to stand there. I let myself admire the intricate design on the post where my helmet had just been. It was circular with a flower cut into each of the four sides of the heart pine wood. The color of the stain on it was also consistent with all the baseboards in the house. Although it was darker than usual, the brown burgundy color was eye appealing and regal.

Each part of the post, spindles, and handrail had been impeccably measured. People did not build homes with this quality of craftsmanship anymore. The funny thing was that the only tools used back then were a hammer, saw, and a T square. I began to realize why the Gaines had given me a list of things that were not to be demolished, including the staircase. Most of the features inside the house were priceless. There really was something about the place.

I shook my head and decided to leave my helmet on top of the post to make it easier to walk up the rest of the stairs.

When I got to my bedroom, I sat on the bed. From that vantage point, I could see the buckled wood plank on the floor where I thought I remembered an old book was hidden.

Without wasting any more time, I let my curiosity guide me down to the floor. I lifted the wood plank easily. Sure enough, there *was* an old diary down there. I took a deep breath still trying to remember the previous night. I said aloud, "Okay, so, I did find a diary." However, I knew good and well there was no way my name was any part of what us drunks at the bar were just talking about an hour before.

Handling the old book with care, I flipped through it while talking, "Where was it? Where did she say it?" After a few pages, I saw it. Written in pretty handwriting were the words, "*God, am I even worthy enough anymore to be called, Sister Margaret?*".

Her name *was* Sister Margaret and the name of the orphanage *was* Sisters of Charity.

"What the-?" I spit out forcefully and dropped the book.

Okay, so I found a diary written by the actual nun they were talking about at the bar. That's cool. No biggie, right? It's just got to be by some strange coincidence that she always liked the name Trey Reynolds or knew someone with that name. Yeah, that's all it was.

I picked the diary back up and rubbed the cover thinking to myself that maybe I should bring the book to the Galveston museum. They would appreciate it.

But first, I decided to see if I really did write in it like I imagined. I continued to think to myself and debate my options. So, what if I did write in it? Wouldn't have mattered, right? Wouldn't have changed anything in history. Either way, the museum curator could take the page out where I wrote my drunk thoughts down. Problem solved.

I turned the pages to see if, in fact, I had added something to the diary. As I scanned through, my hands began to shake. I dropped the book again and said aloud, "Oh God."

When my heart finally stopped racing, I gazed down at the old diary opened wide next to me on the pine floor. Not only did I find that I *did* write in that book and I *did* tell her my name, but there was also writing on the next page after mine. Staring up at me from the floor on that next page was her pretty handwriting. *And* it was addressed to me.

To my surprise, written to me from Miss Nun Lady, were the words…

Dear Mr. Reynolds.

CHAPTER 3
July 1900
Sister Margaret

My hands froze after I saw that someone else had written in my diary. I took a deep breath and read the name aloud, *"Trey Reynolds"*. That name was unconventional, wasn't it? And he wrote strangely. Was it Mr. Lawson's doing? Did he get a hold of my diary? I thought I hid it well in this room. I slammed my diary shut immediately and placed it on the chair.

I had been traveling from the beach weekly to the town's hospital for the last few months to retrieve supplies and provisions for the orphanage. During my trips, I always stopped to visit Georgy here at Mr. Lawson's tenant's house. No one had ever tampered with my diary here before. Either way, someone had found it and wrote in it.

I got up from the seashell chair that Mrs. Davenport loved. I paced the room. When I finally sat down on a small settee by the window, I smiled. The crepe myrtles outside tapped against the window's glass ever so softly. Beautiful. I had always had an affinity for flowers. Back in Europe, when the sun finally made an appearance, those floral delights spread all over the countryside, at least the lands of my mother's home in Scotland. The only things my father's homeland in England offered were dirty streets and fog so thick that nothing of beauty could grow.

I focused for a moment on the movement outside the window to help slow my breathing.

Once my chest loosened up, I closed my eyes to pray. "Gracious God, I beseech You. Give me wisdom and acceptance to handle what is to come. My carelessness has allowed me to put into written words my doubts of Your care towards me and my place here. Almighty Father, should I read what has been written by another's hand or should I simply burn both my and Mr. Reynold's words immediately? I ask for your guidance. If I am to burn it, please speak it now. In Jesus' name I pray. Amen."

The plants outside stilled. I sat in silence for a few minutes in waiting. My tenuous state teetering on a simple response, that after a few minutes, never came. Again, as it had been for the last year or so, I could not hear anything from God.

It wasn't long after I arrived in Galveston that His voice was no longer heard. In fact, it was the first day here. I arrived at Union Passenger Station and immediately felt out of sorts. The heat was more than I expected. I had lived mostly in Scotland than in England. I knew it would take a while to become acclimated to Galveston's climate. As I looked around at the other women exiting the train covered in heavy cotton dresses that were almost completely soaked through with sweat, I wondered how on Earth I'd ever get used to it here.

A woman in a deep burgundy dress cinched tightly at the waist stopped short and turned around towards me. She had a no-nonsense swing in her hips when she spun around. The lady proceeded to frown down at me before saying with a heavy accent, "This place is not what you think, Sister. Stay close to your church for safety and drink as much water as you can. It gets incredibly hot that people drop dead. And the lawlessness-" She stopped talking and grinned mischievously. Then she continued, "In some parts, this is still considered the Wild West."

I gasped. I didn't know how to respond. The Wild West, still? I had only read that in books. Did people still pull out guns and shoot you on the spot?

When she walked back off, I lowered my head to pray hoping to find the courage to remove myself from the train. As I sat there watching the last of the passengers exit, not one sense of security came over me. That was when I first realized my prayers may have been ignored. I sat there shaking as I reconciled to the fact that God was not responding back.

My mind drifted back to present day. The crepe myrtles outside the window of the tenant's house begin to shake. A bird brightly painted in blue and perched on a nearby branch peered down at me. I watched him for a moment. Something was pulling on my heart and mind.

When I looked over at my diary, it seemed to beckon me. I thought about how wrong that strange lady was from that day on the train. Galveston *was* a safe place. The only thing she was correct about was the need to stay hydrated.

I stood up and fetched my diary before sitting back on the seashell chair. Without a second thought, I opened it to the last used page. Squinting, I tried to read the unknown man's poor penmanship. It had to be that he lacked the fine motor skills needed to produce formal manuscript. Mabel, the youngest orphan in my class, struggled with it, too.

I patiently read his writing until I finished the page. Poor technique aside, I could still ascertain a little of what Mr. Reynolds was trying to communicate. He was hurting.

I read over it again and then stopped to think about his words. He seemed a dreary lot. I felt incredibly sorry for him. His sweet heart was shattered. It was obvious that the mystery man wasn't from around here. And there was no way that those words could have been written by someone as heartless as Mr. Lawson.

No way. And there was something different about Trey Reynolds. And then to add to all of that, he said it was the year two thousand. No, it couldn't be. That would be one hundred years from now.

Or could it? Was this God's way of helping me with my loneliness that I had prayed so much for? Someone to write to and they write back? Someone who wasn't from here or this time so they wouldn't give my secrets away? I stared out the window and prayed again for a moment. When I felt strong enough again, I opened my eyes. A seagull flew over and landed on the tree a few feet from the house.

I smiled and with a little more courage, I dipped my quill and began to write back.

Dear Mr. Reynolds,

Whoever you are, you have a unique name. You remind me a lot of the little boy I just found and brought back to the orphanage. He lost his parents to the fever. He can't even remember his name because of the trauma he has endured. I am glad you wrote to me, even though it was in my diary. But I believe God has His ways, so I am going to trust in Him.

I am sorry to hear about your struggles and loss of faith. If you would like to share, I would like to know why you are struggling with your faith. Please know, no matter our thoughts on God, though, He has a plan. Knowing and trusting in that is how I keep going. I can perfectly recollect the first time I heard His voice a few years ago and in that miraculous moment, I knew what I needed to do. That night, I had been at my lowest point. I am … I … I don't know how long I can bear His absence.

I know you must have read that I am longing for Him to speak to me again. I feel He will. I am of a supple mind that He always knows what is best for us.

If you find my diary again, I hope you write back. I would like to know more about you and more of what happened to you in Somalia. I have never had the pleasure of traveling there. Tell me more about it.

When you wrote the year of two thousand, were you referring to something other than your date? Please don't have the misplaced distinction that I am not of sound mind, but I am writing from the date of July 1900.

Good day, Mr. Reynolds, and God bless.

Sister Margaret

I closed the diary and looked around before lowering myself onto the floor. I pulled up one side of the room's rug and felt the loose plank that I had only discovered a few months before while kneeling to pray for Mrs. Davenport. I lifted the plank, hid my diary back in its place, and replaced the rug. Before getting back up, I said a prayer asking for guidance again. As usual, God didn't respond.

I opened the door to the lady of the house - Georgy. She was holding a plate of cookies. Oh, how I loved her smile. At one point, she had told me that her full name was Georgianna Pierce. But ever since Mrs. Davenport found her on that horrible plantation in Mississippi where her parents had been slaves, she had asked to be called Georgy. It was her father's nickname for her.

"Sister Margaret, you leavin' so soon?" she asked.

I admired her spiral curled hair and how it seemed to bounce with the movement of her head when she spoke.

I smiled timidly. "Georgy, I have to get back."

Georgy stared off towards the bed where Mrs. Davenport took her last breath. "My missus loved these cookies."

"I know."

She perked back up. "Please take a cookie." Her apron was wrinkled and full of flour from her time in the kitchen baking the sweet concoctions. "Feeding you well when you come visit is the least that I can do. I cannot thank you enough for standing by me, Sister Margaret."

I smiled and decided to take a cookie anyway. A few crumbles fell to the plate. The indulgent creations were a well-made batch of sugar delight topped off with cinnamon sprinkles. "Georgy, surely you understand that I did not really intervene."

"He was gonna throw me out, Sister. Even though Mrs. Davenport paid him for another year of boarding."

"I feel he was just not adept at expressing himself. All I did was remind him of his promise to Mrs. Davenport."

"You did more than that. No one ever worries about people like me," she said with a petulance tone. She put her hands on her larger hips and gave them a shake.

I promised, "God does. And so did Mrs. Davenport."

Her voice softened. "Thank you. You know you will always be welcome in Mrs. Davenport's old room. You travel too much in the heat for that convent. Mrs. Davenport knew it and so does I."

I had to stop myself from correcting her speech. I was accustomed to doing that daily with the children. A habit that would offend an adult.

I took another bite of the cookie. For a chocolate chip concoction, the buttery flavor was the spotlight. It was no wonder that the local diner hired her part time for cooking and baking. Georgy didn't have to work since Mrs. Davenport left her plenty of money. However, that was not how Georgy was. She stubbornly wanted to carry her own weight now that she was no longer caring for Mrs. Davenport.

Plus, she was proud of the recipes that had been handed down to her from her ancestors from the plantation. Galveston's favorite was Georgy's recipe for an amazing pecan pie. Every now and again, she would send me back to the orphanage with a few of her famous pecan pies. The children loved those nights after dinner when they could sink their teeth into that gooey treat.

Talking about Mr. Lawson made me wonder again. "Georgy, has anyone been in here since last I came?"

"No ma'am. Just you. And I don't hardly like to come in here myself, except when I have to dust it or check on my coin. It makes me sad. I miss her." She drew her brows together. "But are you worried someone came in here? There really is no way possible. Last I heard the old shrewd was in Fort Worth. So, it can't be Mr. Lawson."

"No, I imagine not."

Still, Georgy frowned. She set the cookie tray down and moved towards Mrs. Davenport's old night stand. She swiped her hand under the lip of the nightstand and a secret compartment opened up. "Mrs. Davenport showed me this compartment." She pulled a small object out.

"What is that?"

"Between you and me, it is where I hide this." She lifted her hand and showed me a silver coin. "It was the first ever payment I made from selling my pecan pies at the diner. I keep it here for safe keeping. It is my special coin."

She hid it back in its spot and closed the hidden door. "I'll keep this coin with me until I die. It is my reminder that I am capable of earning my own money."

Georgy padded back over to me. "Oh, one more thing. I am having Teddy take some pieces of furniture to the local auction. I won't touch anything in this room, especially the nightstand, unless there is something you want moved."

I looked at the oversized seashell chair for a second.

Her grin got bigger. "It is unsightly, isn't it?"

"Yes." I laughed. "But it gives the room character. Thank you for everything, Georgy, and God be with you," I said and headed down the stairs to leave.

The taste of that cookie lingered on my tongue as I stepped out onto the busy Galveston street. The breeze was welcoming as more sweat poured down my back. Georgy kept that house under watchful eyes. I couldn't imagine that Mr. Lawson or anyone else could have gone into that room and messed with my diary without her knowing.

So, who was he? I knew it couldn't be from anyone around here. This Trey Reynolds was different. His ways were different. And something in the way his true heart presented itself in his words, intrigued me. It had to be God's answers to my prayers. Although it was strange, I knew that God worked in mysterious ways. However, I knew I had to confess my transgression to Father O'Brien. It was my agreement with God. I would do it sooner than later. I did not want to carry that on my heart for too long.

I smiled as I passed a little boy and girl holding hands and giggling. I stopped walking. Did I just genuinely smile? I did! Was it because I found a friend in the strange Mr. Reynolds? Someone to talk to. Someone that opened up to me, too, so I felt I could do the same with him. God was not speaking with me anymore anyway. Was this His way to show He was still with me?

I turned onto the next street as a carriage rushed by. The brick streets were lively before noon. After all, Galveston had surpassed New Orleans to becoming the top cotton port in the nation. It was no wonder that people were flocking to the island.

I kept walking while in deep thought. Trey Reynolds? Hmm. I decided I would follow this odd communication and see what happened. But will this stranger ever write back again?

It was still early in the day and I had time to spare, so I decided to head down to visit Mary Beth. A friend I made after helping her family through the trauma experienced when her nephew came back from the war with the Spaniards.

I walked by the two-story opera house and minded my steps as I passed two poor souls cowering down on the street in a sickly state. I gave the man and woman a small smile and said a silent prayer for them. Above them, a sign on the building mentioned that Buffalo Bill and Edwin Booth would both be making a return to the city for entertainment.

A few more blocks and the sweet oleander's fragrance was all around me. The street had tall palm trees surrounding a few of the buildings. An island city was a treat for someone who spent the later part of her childhood on the city streets of London. I remembered when my dad moved us to London from Scotland, I resented his decision to leave my mother's home. Not just because we were pulled away from the beauty of nature, but also because we would no longer be able to attend mass with my grandparents.

My father cared not. When I finally found a Catholic church not far from our residence and the scrutiny of the Protestants in London, my father did not attend service with us. Yet another reminder of the new life I didn't ask for.

I stared up at the roof line of the next building. Galveston had come a long way. Even though it had been devastated by a fire that spread through the whole city in eighteen eighty-five, Galvestonians didn't give up. They rebuilt, this time with all slate roofs. They were resilient.

Yellow Fever had taken many, but more kept coming. Maybe it was the excitement of innovation that the island offered. From electric lights to phones that allowed communication between locals and people far off, these were interesting times for Americans. Or maybe it was the entertainment. The beautiful beaches or the three concert halls, attractions that not all cities could hope to have anytime soon. I was happy to be a part of it all. To see all the hard work the Galveston people did to bring back their town.

After another few minutes of walking, I was one block from Mary Beth's home and was alerted by a passing street car. I stopped to let it pass. A child sat by one of the windows and had obvious heat-flushed cheeks. Still, he seemed happy as he waved at me and gave me the prettiest wide smile. I waved back.

I turned next to a building with an ornate cast-iron storefront and a sign that read, "May's Imported Jewels". An older man came out of the store with an item wrapped like a gift. He nodded while saying, "Good day, Sister." Everyone here was so kind.

Mary Beth Lee's house was at the end of the street separated from the businesses by fig and magnolia trees. I began to walk up a few stairs behind lattice work draped with vines. Some movement to my right stopped my climb. A grey-haired woman with a large straw hat was on her knees in the dirt. I frowned. "Mrs. Lee? It's over ninety degrees today. Why are you out here working?" I asked her.

"Hello, Sister Margaret." Mary Beth stood up and brushed off her skirt. She always held herself well, even when she was covered in dirt and sweat after what looked like hours of tending to her roses. "Many things to do, Sister. Galveston does not wait for unkept residences. We have our huge parade on Labor Day."

Her squinty eyes drifted across the street at her neighbor's house. A hint of petulance came into her voice as she said, "For some, it will be a wild fit of folly, I gather."

I sighed.

She smiled back at me. "For others, a celebration. You must come to the parade."

"The parade? No, I will be missing that event."

"You keep to the beach for the safety of the children. I do not begrudge you." She set her gardening shears off to the side. "Glad tidings when this heat lets up. I read an article in the Western World Magazine. The writer specifically referenced our fine city. You know what he said, Sister?"

"I do not partake in that kind of reading often."

She eyed me. "Yes, I understand. But he wrote, and I quote, 'The summer of nineteen hundred will be long remembered as one of the most remarkable for sustained high temperature that has been experienced for almost a generation'. I ask you sweet Sister, is that a blessing to our city for cotton season or does God have other plans?"

"I do not hazard to guess what God's intentions are with the weather."

She giggled and picked up her sheers again. The dull edges needed to be sharpened after so much use on such resilient roses. Mrs. Lee was very much like her strong roses. Her family had come to Galveston a few years back after leaving their plantation and lands nestled along the Louisiana bayous. Their hope was to thrive in Galveston like everyone else here with the famous port so close that routinely shipped out their southern cotton and brought in almost everything you could think of from Europe- including me.

Mrs. Lee's son had become a doctor. The hospital was where her and I met. The topic of her son came up as she clipped a vine that was intruding on her window. We talked for a bit about the updated number of sick patients, her concern about her son being among the sick daily, and about the spread becoming worse as new immigrants arrived at the port.

After a few minutes, Mary Beth leaned back against the wall of her home to get some shade under the awning. I moved in closer to do the same.

She smiled. "You should come in. I'll make tea."

"No, this was to be a quick visit. I have much to do."

She frowned at me. "Sister, you seem out of sorts today. What is troubling you?"

I was not about to tell her about the mysterious man, Trey Reynolds. But yes, my mind was not in my conversation with Mary Beth at the moment. "I am sorry I am not adding much to the conversation. We have many new orphans. My work has had me busy these days."

"Sister, I am sorry to hear that. I pray this sickness passes before there are too many more orphaned children." She pushed off of the wall. "I am keeping you. My apologies. Let me get you the batch of flowers I prepped for the weekend services. You should get back soon and out of this heat. Give me a moment." And with that, she disappeared into her home.

CHAPTER 4
Rise Up

I returned to the orphanage right as the sun was setting. The huge structure, that had been the former estate of Captain Farnifalia Green, was bigger than anything I had ever expected for the island. A random onlooker could easily mistake the wondrous vision as a central train station planted directly on the beach. Their attention would be drawn up high to the six roof lines atop two-stories of a massive rectangular building with wide porches secured from one side to the other.

On top of that, the architect brilliantly showcased the entire design with several prominent dormers, too. It was amazing to look at, especially since it was the only structure on the beach for miles. That made the sight of it seem even more enormous.

I pulled around to the back side and got out of the carriage. Sighing with relief to be back after the long trip, I smiled at the two doors festooned with seashell garland that the children had just made the day before.

Mother Gabriela came towards me with a wave. She began helping me unload the supplies. As we worked, she told me about the conversation she heard between Father O'Brien and one of the traveling priests that she did not recognize. She said he seemed upset.

I frowned. "Upset? Why?" I asked while putting away the last of the bandages.

"Nothing. Come, let's set these beautiful flowers up before they wilt."

I followed her into the chapel. "How is Georgy these days?" she asked.

"She's doing good."

"I'm looking forward to another batch of those pecan pies," Mother Gabriela said and winked at me.

I smiled. "Me too. She's been busy at the diner."

"I understand. Work is good, and God has given her a very special talent."

"Yes, He has."

As we set up the last of the roses in the vase beneath the altar, we continued to talk about how the people were holding up. Then, we shifted the conversation to the Labor Day Parade that was coming up. "They will spread the fever more so," Mother Gabriela promised.

"Is that what the traveling priest said that has you worried?"

She kneeled down to place the last white rose. "He said something about the prolonged heat having warmed the waters of the Gulf to the temperature of a bath."

"I figured that was normal for summers on this island, am I right? Why would that be a concern?" I inquired.

She paused and tilted her head. "These are preferred conditions for the thousands of new immigrants from Europe coming into our port. They are calling our city the Western Ellis Island. Many are even camped on the beach near the Army's new gun emplacements."

"Are they heading north?"

"Yes, they are getting themselves ready for the journey to open land and the riches promised to them by the railroads intent on populating America."

"Mother Gabriela, finding a new home away from England's rule is not always unfavorable. Or is it?"

The older nun shook her head at me. "You always seem to end your thoughts with a question instead of certainty. Why is that?"

I paused. "I never thought of it."

"Maybe something in your past has tainted your confidence. God gives you everything you need."

"Yes, He does."

She wiped a bead of sweat from her brow. "Anyway, I was saying that about the newcomers because they will bring more sickness."

"Oh." I thought about how Mrs. Lee made that same assumption earlier. "I see."

She continued to walk and talk. "You make too many trips into town. Let another person here help. The heat is furious and your children ask about you when you are gone."

"I understand, but I enjoy the trip."

She frowned. "Are you certain that is all it is?"

Just then, little Trey came running in. He grabbed at my sleeve. "Sister Margaret!"

I leaned over and embraced him. "Have you finished your chores, Trey?"

"Yes, Sister."

"Good. I have something for you."

His blue eyes lit up. "You do?"

I handed him a small horse carved out of oak. "Take good care of him."

Excitement radiated from him. "I will! Thank you. Thank you so much!"

"You are welcome. Now go wash up for dinner."

He ran so fast by Mother Gabriela I thought her habit would have been ripped.

I gasped. "Slow down, Trey!"

She placed her hand on her stomach. "Do not fret, Sister. He runs like the wind. I hazard to guess he will grow up to be a strong young man with a big heart." She smiled at me. "Thanks to you."

I sighed. "We do our best. I will see you at dinner."

"Yes, Sister."

                                  ****

     When I got back to my room, I quickly pulled off my
wimple so I could get some relief from the heat. My head was
full of perspiration. I pulled out a small mirror that I had
brought with me from England. My image had changed much
from when I was a young girl. Reflecting back at me now was
a woman with fine lines and spots I had never seen before
across my cheeks. Sister Mary called them freckles. "The sun
brings them out," she had said.
     My hair, although soaked in sweat, wasn't as honey
blonde as it had been either. Dark roots had begun to show as
it grew out. I no longer looked like my mother. Funny how a
change of climate can change so much. I put my mirror up
and finished my nighttime routine before heading to bed with
thoughts of a Mr. Trey Reynolds on my mind.

CHAPTER 5
Tumultuous Motion
July 2000

A rainbow? Why did that writer have to go there? What a way to cheesy up what had started out as some well-researched history and seamless writing. I closed the magazine and sighed audibly.

At first, I had been interested in reading it, but when the writer added the part about the sightings of a rainbow crossing the sky on that ominous day after the hell of a night the survivors must have had, I lost interest in the author's writing.

Maybe it was a personal vendetta for me. But seriously, rainbows are just a kind of weather anomaly that we stupidly marvel over for no reason. Mother nature nor God does anything special like that for us.

And when people said the climate was disrupted because of us. I ignored that also. Never had I bothered with those theories either. I was always too busy surviving. Who had time to worry about Earth when they had lived a life that started out of tremendous loss? Next, throw in a few thousand bullets shot at you on someone else's soil. And then, icing on the cake, getting betrayed by the person you loved most in the world. Yeah, I couldn't care less about weather events. I had always been too focused on surviving. Every… single… day.

I plopped that magazine back down on the table in front of me. The light smack on the glass top from the magazine disturbed the snoring old man next to me. He shifted in his uncomfortable waiting room chair and then went back to sleep.

I guessed I needed something to get my mind off that nun. That was too crazy to entertain. Heck, I didn't know how to explain it. And when there were things I couldn't explain, my best policy was to avoid them. So, that was what I was doing; I was avoiding Sister Margaret and her old diary with its strange ink producing quill.

I squeezed the arm rest on my chair letting out some familiar indignation thinking about the writer of the article I just read instead and his love of rainbows. I mean, come on. Pretty pathetic how we view things. God brought the rainbow as a message? Seriously? Here's the thing, we usually see rainbows in between storms. Right when the sun peeks through the clouds giving you a slight glimpse of hope only to take it all away again. And that's God's plan?

I took my last picture of a rainbow when I was twelve. I didn't care if I ever saw another one of those things again.

I shifted in my chair. I was obsessing over things again. Letting my anger and personal problems fuel a rage that wasn't needed was always my problem after the war. "It is just another symptom of PTSD", my therapist had told me.

So, I decided to watch TV instead. On the hospital's television above another row of waiting patients, Jordynn Wallace, the Houston news reporter, popped into view with his bright veneered smile. He excitedly began his story over a ghost sighting at the Hotel Flores in Galveston. Something about dead kids haunting the halls.

I watched for a few more minutes. The reporter was enjoying the sound of his voice as images in black and white flashed on the screen. Still, I wanted more details but got distracted when I heard a feminine voice say, "We're ready for you."

"Huh?" I asked.

"You like to make women wait?" Standing above me and shifting from one foot to another was a fairly pretty lady with an olive complexion and wispy bangs accentuating her large eyes.

I added, "Nah. Women never wait on me. It's always the other way around." I tilted my head taking her in. "Sorry. I never heard you call my name, though."

"You are Sgt. Reynolds, right?" she asked. Her skin looked as soft as cashmere.

I smiled up. "Yes. That's me."

"It's your turn."

"Okay…" I drew out the last vowel. "By the way, VA staff doesn't usually call us by our rank, miss".

"We're not a typical VA hospital. Now, stop questioning and follow me, please."

I stood up slowly being careful not to let my prosthetic pinch my hamstring. "Give me a sec, sweetie." I had always hated these appointments. The long drive into their centralized locations. It wasn't like there was a VA hospital in every town. We couldn't be that lucky. This hospital in Houston served veterans from central Texas and all the way to Louisiana, pretty much a sixty-mile radius.

Her brown eyes warmed as they lowered down to my right appendage. "Having trouble with it?"

Even though my own eyes were brown, I still admired that color on women.

"Yeah, a little. I may ask the doc about it." I took a step forward. "Let's get this over with."

She turned and walked ahead of me. Her tiny form barely filled out the pink scrubs she was wearing. Too bad.

She took a left turn down a wider hall. A handful of other veterans walked by us headed out to the lobby. The first two geezers nodded at me while continuing their conversation back and forth. Both had on black Army caps with a huge red symbol in the middle. Behind them, a frail veteran rolled by in a wheelchair wearing several bright yellow Air Force pins. As we got closer to the end of the hall, another vet rounded the corner with a jersey styled shirt sporting the saying, "Marine for Life" across the front. I nodded at him.

Maybe it was an age thing, but as a thirty-year-old, I didn't feel the need to wear apparel at the VA hospital to identify my branch. Not saying that I wasn't proud to be a Marine; it wasn't that at all. My time in the Marine Corps was the best of my life. Sure, I lost a leg in the poverty-stricken, dirt covered streets of Somalia, but I gained a family I never had. A close and understanding family.

The nurse escorted me into a small triage room. She asked me the usual medical questions along with handing me some suicide organization packets. "Down here in Texas, you're lucky. We have plenty of these support groups, if you need them."

I blinked rapidly at her. "What you saying, Nurse? You think I'm suicidal?" I asked bluntly. Marines never sugar coated their responses.

"Common practice." Her eyes trailed off. "And I know for a fact that when troops get back from combat, they are not completely aware of the help that is available to them."

I nodded. She was correct. I frowned down at my boots. I didn't mean to come off too harsh. I hadn't always been like that. Before I enlisted in the corps, I was a goofy, insecure teen with pictures on my bedroom walls of Milla Jovovich, Winona Ryder, and Sea Ray fishing boats. No cares in the world. That all changed when I turned eighteen.

I enlisted in the Marine Corps in July of 1989. Boot camp was twelve weeks long, and it was insane. However, nothing was quite like the feeling of knowing you were no longer a weakling. The drill sergeants pushed us to limits we never knew we were capable of, and not every man survived it. But the ones that did, wow, we felt elite. And we were.

I could still remember a cold and wet morning in that tenth week of training when our DI had us up at four in the morning. We were assembled in front of the barracks, wearing only our sweat shirts and pants. He called it "attitude training". Our DI felt we might be getting a bit cocky because we had won all the boot camp testing banners. Like all the other recruits in my platoon, I stood there motionless, unabating, and ready for anything. We were freezing, though. Rainy mornings at Parris Island got that way sometimes. It didn't matter. We were ready.

The DI walked around surveying his men. He was dead set on tripping us up. He was going to give us everything he had to try to break us one last time. I was still ready, and I would continue to hold back a grin or any kind of expression of pride on my face. I knew we were, or at least back then we were, bullet proof - impervious to anything he could muster up. Nothing could shake us at that point. We knew it, and he knew it. That's what a Marine becomes - a fearless warrior. But that's what it meant to be a Marine. The Corps knew how to get that job done. They had been doing it for over two hundred years. So why did that façade begin to crack and fall away not long after I began my first tour at war? It felt like powdered sugar through a sifter only to leave behind lumps. And those lumps were suffocating. But was that the point? Was it a way to make us solid? Because anything sweet can't last without consequences, I guessed.

My nurse removed the blood pressure cuff and sighed. "Marines. All the same."

"Semper Fi," I added and lifted up my chin.

She smiled slowly and put her hand on her hip. "Pittsburgh?"

"Huh?" I asked.

"Before the Marines. You lived in Pittsburgh?"

Fixing my gaze on her almond shaped, caring eyes, I asked, "How did you know?"

"The accent is obvious. I have two uncles that live up there. Why did you not go back there?"

When I rubbed my chin with the back of my hand, I felt it hard to respond. "Life as I knew it back in Pittsburgh was over. I needed a new start. Always liked fishing and the ocean, so figured this would do it."

She lifted one perfect brow. "How long have you been here? I see this is your first appointment at this VA hospital."

"Just a few weeks."

"You're already getting some sun." She winked. "Dark, sexy brown eyes and dirty blonde hair, the girls will be crazy for ya here."

"Flirting?"

She laughed. "Nah, I'm engaged. Just telling you that you'll like it here." She typed in a few things on her laptop before acknowledging me again. "And I see you're staying in Galveston."

I cleared my throat. "Yes. I visited once as a kid. Always remembered the experience."

"You will definitely enjoy Galveston. Any part of Texas for that matter. However, Texas can be a humid, ridiculously hot state in the summer, as you've probably already noticed. But Galveston is surrounded by a nice ocean breeze that helps a little at different parts of the day. You'll like it. I hope you stay."

"We'll see," I replied and this time avoided eye contact. The common formality of the conversation wasn't what I was used to. Maybe she made me feel uneasy. Or maybe I was just in a hurry to hear my news from the doctor.

"Okay, then," she finally added. "Doctor Walters will be in soon. It was good to meet you, Sergeant Reynolds." Then, she turned to leave.

"Thanks," I added as I watched her slowly shut the door leaving me in that sterile room awaiting my test results. I needed to know what I wanted to know and the doctor was going to tell me it today. As I sat there studying the anatomy poster on the wall, I began to fidget with the bed cover. I was never a patient person.

The next morning, I was up early thinking about what the doctor told me. After about an hour of letting myself get worked up again, I decided to let it go.

I started debating on which project to start first on the old historic home. Keeping busy would be for the best. I was not in a good mood and I knew it wouldn't get any better just stewing on it.

I began my morning hygiene routines along with stretching my hamstrings and a few pushups before I headed downstairs. In the tiny kitchen, I made some coffee with the small electric pot I found at Wal-Mart.

As the coffee was brewing, I stepped into the formal sitting room and looked at the old fireplace set back in the corner of the room. It was also an original with the house. The mantle needed some sprucing up, but not much. The red brick inlay with its messy mortar job was a debacle. I knew chipping away at the excess mortar would take a special tool. I could start that today after another run to the hardware store.

I touched the dusty mantle and unwillingly noticed my mind wander back to yesterday. I felt all the motivation to get started on the house drain completely from my body. But I needed the money. I needed to complete the renovation. I remembered one of the officers telling us that when we start back into civilian life that we need to take one task at a time. Other than that, no other advice was given to us. The nurse at the VA was right. It sucked.

I looked down at the fireplace. Maybe if I just did this part first, I thought. Then, I started to think about how that nun had probably spent many nights being warmed by this same exact fireplace I was now about to fix up. That nun? Was I seriously still thinking about her?

I shook my head. "Oh heck." I went back into the kitchen and poured my black coffee into one of the Christmas cups I had found on clearance at the VA Hospital. Then, I headed back upstairs to my room because I couldn't shake her from my thoughts.

Once I was upstairs, I set my cup down before slowly kneeling onto the floor with my good knee. I sighed. "This is stupid. You know that, Trey? And so is she. Her, questioning my faith? She'd never been through even a minute of what I've been through." Still, I continued to mess with the plank of the floor until it was lifted enough for me to lower my right hand down. I slowly pulled the book back out and stood up.

After a minute or so of flipping through it, I realized that she had written something new in it. I closed the diary. This is crazy, I thought. The new drugs the VA gave me were messing with my mind or… was this whole place haunted?

I laughed that off. "Come on, Trey," I spoke aloud. "Now you sound like a kid. Obsessed with ridiculous fantasy."

I looked down at the diary and thought to myself, But what if? What if she was from the 1900s? And if so, what would I say? I mean, some nun wanted to know why *I* gave up on my faith. Why would I tell *her*? Ghost or not. What was really going on here anyway? I'm writing to a dead nun?

A sharp pain traveled up my back. I popped a few pain pills and adjusted the way I was sitting. There were many moments when I first got back to the states that I questioned more than my faith. I questioned life itself.

It was harder in the beginning when I first came back home. Seeing the drug abuse in my buddies, the suicides…

How would I ever explain myself to a nun from over a hundred years ago? Did people even commit suicide back then? I shuddered and sat down on the floor while thinking about Sgt. Harris.

I met Sgt. Harris on our first day in the field. He had already been overseas and came back to a family of three. We both worked in urban warfare training. He talked about how much he hated being deployed and away from his family. His daughter was ten and his son was eight. When he got back, both were teenagers and all three of his family took off not long after his return. He talked about everything he missed while he was gone and blamed himself for the divorce.

Sgt. Harris came from a typical middle-class family as I did. However, where I grew up in the city, he grew up on a farm in Oklahoma. He learned how to shoot when he was just five years old. I didn't fire my first weapon until bootcamp. Where I was struggling to be a better aim, Sgt. Harris' seasoned skills made him his platoon's best sniper.

He lived in the barracks a few doors down from me since he no longer had a family for the military to allow separate housing. He didn't complain, maybe because he spent more time drinking when we were off duty.

Our favorite weekend hot spots were Tijuana and Lake Tahoe. After another bar fight in Tijuana, I realized that my friend could have a problem. Something that I was ill-equipped to help him with. I tried talking to him a few times, but it just made him angrier.

After I deployed, I learned that he didn't come with us. He was found dead in his bed on a Wednesday after attending some party close by. I learned later what I didn't have the ability to recognize, he was also into drugs. The word on the street was that the VA doctors failed him by continuing to refill prescriptions for hydrocodone – generic for the narcotic painkiller Vicodin. It went on for twenty months without them once requiring him to come in for a face-to-face meeting.

Sgt. Harris wasn't the only Marine brother I lost from suicide. He was just the first.

I shook my head and shoved the diary into my backpack. I needed fresh air. I knew I was losing it.

****

I took my motorcycle a few blocks away and down to the docks of Galveston Bay. Boats of all sizes were anchored all around. I parked my bike before walking a few feet to get closer to the water. I sat down on someone's dock and stared off at the still Galveston Bay. I went back and forth wondering about that nun and whether or not it was a good idea to come down to Texas. Nothing was making me feel better. I still saw images pop up in my mind from that terrible day in combat. And the anger rose quickly even with the comforting exposure to my favorite thing - salt water.

I leaned over and reached into my backpack. The cold steel of my Glock brushed against my fingertips and then to my palm as I grabbed it and pulled it out. Staring down at the weapon, my breathing sped up and warm tears rushed down my cheeks. But then I heard a familiar voice yell over at me.

"Hey! The Yankee Marine, right?"

I quickly shoved my gun back into my backpack so Larry couldn't see it. I wiped my eyes just as he got closer to me. His trusty pup was at his side.

I cleared my throat and responded with, "Oh, hey, man. You following me?" His dog stepped closer and licked my face.

Larry laughed and motioned to his dog. "No. But apparently Stella is."

My shoulders relaxed with the humor. "Is that right?"

"Nah, I'm just meeting my buddy here. Gonna do some fishing. What ya up to today?

I gazed over towards the water. "I really don't know anymore."

Larry sat down on the dock next to me. I could tell from my peripheral vision that he was studying me. When he looked forward, he asked, "Can I tell you something crazy?"

"Sure."

Larry began, "After I got home from overseas… and after the second wife left me, I fell into some bad depression.

Let me tell you." He paused. "But finally, I said screw it!" He looked back over at me.

I petted Stella and prompted him to continue. "And?"

"I went out, met some new friends, and began joining them in stealing Cadillac converters!"

I couldn't help it, I broke out laughing. "What? Really?"

"Yup. Did a few years' time for it."

"You stole Cadillac converters? You lie."

"Why? You think my big ole Texan-self can't climb under cars, too?"

We both laughed for a few seconds. Then, Larry eyed me seriously. "But I learned something. With God, anything is possible. Took me too long to realize that. I've made some huge mistakes when I ran away from pain." He paused. "But those priests."

Larry gestured with his hand to his neck. "You know the ones that do sermons at the prisons wearing those collars and everything?"

I nodded.

"Well, one came every week to my prison. He held mass for us in a tiny room off detention block D. Things he said… Or heck, maybe it was just the fact that he tried. Something about it spoke to me. It got me back on track. And then, he gave me a brochure for this organization that helps soldiers with PTSD. So, after my release, I went to meet them. The other veterans I met there…" He debated his words. "It became like a second brotherhood. I wouldn't be where I am now, back on my feet, if not for God and them." He smiled while reminiscing.

"So, you're a Catholic?"

He laughed. "Catholic? No. I'm not any denomination. I just pray and talk to God wherever and whenever. He hears me all the same."

"I had a good friend when I first joined the Marines. His name was Sgt. Paul Harris. He had been overseas not long before me. We both worked together on the base. He hated being away from his family during his first deployment. I lost a lot of buddies during war, but to lose them at home…" I shook the chill off me. "He's just on my mind a lot this morning."

Larry's green eyes followed mine out to the water. "I understand."

I continued, "He hated killing during war. But do you know what the odd thing is?"

"What?"

"It turns out his last kill was…" I stopped talking and shook my head. I was done sharing. I just looked up at the sky.

Larry sighed. "So, is that what's haunting you? You know, it's hurting a lot of us and families. American military veterans have a suicide rate of about twenty-two per day, all ages and all over our country. So, is it that?"

I looked over at him. "Not all of it. But you know? I'm not you. I didn't turn to theft."

Larry smirked and simply said, "Let me shoot straight with you. We all have our problems and ways to cope. But what I see before me is a man who is simply shutting down. What you need, as I did, is a healthier way to cope."

He scooted over closer to me and pointed at one of his fingers. "It's like a thorn. Your mamma tells you when you're a kid that it's not gonna hurt for her to take the thorn out. But if you wait… the pain will get excruciating and it may even get infected. Even though, that woman shoving those tweezers into your finger further than you were expecting hurt pretty darn bad, she still got it out. Pain over. My point is that it hurts to talk about our pain, regrets… sins. But left unchecked, that stuff will fester and hurt way worse over time."

My neck started to burn. "What is the deal with people in Texas?"

"Pardon?"

"Unsolicited advice." I moved over a bit. "And, you know what else? I was just asked yesterday by someone about why I lost my faith. It wasn't just Sgt. Harris' suicide that led to the loss of my faith… nor my leg… nor my other brothers I lost overseas. It was a lot of things. Things that this *woman*…" I shook my head thinking of the nun. "… she would never understand."

"Maybe… maybe not. You don't know what someone would truly understand if you don't give them a chance."

I sat up straight. "Let me ask you something, hypothetical. If you could write to someone that has already died… and let's say they write back, would you think you were losing it… like losing your mind?"

Larry bluntly asked, "You writing to this dead Sgt. Harris guy?"

I wanted to smile or even laugh. Larry had that kind of personality. But my cheeks were still taking orders from my heart, so I just looked at him with a deadpan expression and said, "No, not… it's not that. It's a woman…" I paused when a Hispanic guy came up on the dock and waved over at Larry. Stella stood up and ran over to the other man.

I continued, "Um, never mind. It's crazy. You go ahead and go, Larry. It's fishing time. Hope you catch something."

Larry waved back at his friend and then looked back at me while pulling his long hippie hair in a low ponytail. "You hadn't figured it out yet, have you?" He laughed then and patted my back. "We all crazy, brother," he said with a small grin. Then, he stood up blocking the sun off my face. "Trey, you're going to be okay."

I studied him for a second. His honest face and the sureness of his voice. I lowered my gaze and said, "Thanks, Larry. Let me know what's biting. I may go out tomorrow."

I looked back up to watch Larry, his friend, and his dog leave before I pulled the gun back out of my backpack. I unloaded it and slid it into a separate pocket. Then, I reached back in to pull out the old diary. I opened it, took a breath, and began to write.

Dear Ms. Nun,

I'm not sure why I'm writing you. Heck, I hadn't written letters back and forth to someone since Emily.

I stopped for a second and wiped the sweat off my face with my hand. The sun had risen enough that it was giving me a full dose of its heat.

I stared back down at the one sentence I had written. Then, I sighed and continued to write.

Let's just say that didn't turn out well. I enjoy writing, but to be honest, I don't fully believe I'm talking to a nun from over ninety years ago. But why not? If you are from when you say you are, I've been hearing all about a place called Sampson's Manor. I'm told it is haunted by a family that possibly lived there during the early 1900s by the same name. Whether its them as the ghosts or not, tell me something about them that I can't find in history books. Then I'll believe you.

I closed the diary and put it back into my backpack before heading back to the house.

CHAPTER 6
Without Pause or Rest

I tilted my head while I read his words. I could understand Mr. Reynolds not believing that I was who I said I was. I didn't know that I fully believed he was either. Still, I trusted in God's plan. And more than that, I never backed down from a challenge, or did I? And then I thought of Mother Gabriela's words about my confidence.

I slammed the diary shut. I knew of the Sampsons and I had time to go by there before my day was over.

I ran down the stairs into the foyer. Georgy noticed and tried to quickly pull herself up off a chair next to a painting she was studying. Her wide hips barely squeezed out from under the arm rests. I didn't give her time to fully stand up. I waved bye and said I'd be back tomorrow.

Outside, I rushed to my carriage hoping I wouldn't change my mind about where I was going. The Sampsons didn't live too far away. Still, I rode as fast as the foot traffic on the streets would allow.

As I headed there, I began to wonder what on earth I would say to them as to why I was going to visit today. I bowed my head and prayed. God would give me the words.

It was ten blocks towards the west and another five or so south until I arrived at the Sampson home.

I exited the carriage and was immediately greeted by a nicely dressed man. His grey jacket had to have been made of the finest silk. The clothes reminded me of Henry's, but thankfully the man's looks did not. He was handsome.

The tall, dark haired man smiled down at me. "Sister, are you hear at my wife's request?" he asked with blue sparkling eyes.

"Your wife? Oh no, I am just coming to…" I paused. I had no idea of what to say. God didn't tell me anything to say yet.

"Well, that is just silly. She requested for a nun from the orphanage. Of course, you came quicker than we expected, but she'll be glad you are here."

I hesitantly smiled back. "God has His ways."

"Yes, he does. I am Walter Sampson," he said sweetly.

I smiled again. I still had no idea what I was doing. How could I just rush over here on a whim? What was I thinking? This wasn't me at all.

Mr. Sampson then lifted a brow at me. I began feeling uneasy again. From what I knew about Walter Sampson, he was a very important figure in Galveston. A smart man who made a living off of reading people and situations.

I clasped my hands in front of me. "Something wrong, Mr. Sampson?"

"Your name, Sister. You haven't given it yet."

Relief pulsed through my veins just in time before the sweat under my tunic would surely wash me away. "Sister Margaret."

"Ah! Hello, Sister Margaret. Now, don't let me hold you out here in this ridiculous heat any longer. Come."

I took a deep breath and followed him over to his tall Victorian-style home. A beautiful work of architecture filled my vision. It was built similar to the smaller manors from back home. It had the same French-like aesthetics as Mr. Lawson's tenant house, but was more captivating with its elaborate transoms over Italian-styled doors and excessive wings drawing your eye to the two octagonal towers with a steep roof around them.

The houses back home were usually painted in one color and the color of choice was either white or beige on the exterior. In Galveston, the homes had more vibrant colors like Mr. Sampson's home where the contractor toyed with a brighter earth tone of brownish yellow. It was nice. Serene in a sense. The colors on the island were growing on me.

Mr. Sampson nodded over at me. I dropped my gaze and allowed him to escort me up the entry steps and through the front door.

Once inside, two children in the parlor were stacking blocks as tall as them. Both children were in deep thought and collaborating well together to finish their work.

I was escorted into the library first where I sat to wait for the lady of the house. My eyes continued to wander around. Was I missing that part of my life? The extravagance? Or was I simply gawking at the useless waste of money when our orphans still needed more pencils instead of the slate boards they had to rely upon to prove their math calculations.

I shrugged off the useless agitation and wondered over the high ceiling of the expansive room I found myself in. The colors of the space were all part of an oceanic palette. Blues and pale golds accented a solid black fireplace. Perfect for the ongoing theme of island life. It was beautiful.

The ceiling, however, was covered in a dull white color with shamrock carved molding rendering the inhabitants of the space a little less business of which to relax their eyes on. The part that beguiled me the most, after seeing so much of the Sampson home, was not the Victorian enhanced architecture - it was the cracks in the paint. They were more pronounced above each entryway and around the fireplace. A perfectly beautiful home, yet it missed a smidgen of maintenance where it was needed the most. Why did that bother me?

Mr. Sampson came back into the room. "Here she comes. Follow me."

I walked back out into the main entry. Coming down the wood carved rotunda staircase was a woman about my age with ash brown hair pulled up in a perfectly stable bun. She smiled at me. Mr. Sampson gestured towards me. "Dearest, this is Sister Margaret from the orphanage."

The comely woman reached out her elegant hand. "Sister, I am Rebecca Sampson. It is so nice to meet you. I hear wonderful things about your orphanage."

I nodded and smiled back. "It is very nice to meet you, as well."

Mrs. Sampson had a small chip on her front tooth that made me question how someone as lovely as her could have succumbed to anything that would have tainted her perfection. She continued to hold my hand as she began to tug me towards the stairs. "Please come. I understand that you are a very busy woman, so please accept my apology for not having these ready."

I let that statement set in. "Busy woman," she had said. "She obviously respected me, but still treated me like one of her own - a woman. Not a servant of God, but a woman that she admired. "That is quite alright, Mrs. Sampson. I have time."

I followed her up one flight of stairs where there was a grand piano being played by a little girl with golden blonde hair. Behind her, a little boy frowned at his violin before smiling over at us.

"No, it is not. You were called from the orphanage for me. Yet here I am not ready," she apologized again.

I motioned to the children. "They play beautifully." I could tell they were being raised in the strictest fashion.

"Thank you, Sister. Of all my nine children, only Clara and Mark have musical talent."

We started up another flight of stairs until we reached the third floor. I was escorted into what Mrs. Sampson called her art studio. There were a few unfinished sculptures lining the far wall. It was hard to imagine the way they would turn out. They seemed to be of animals larger than us.

I watched as Rebecca headed to the opposite side of the room. The bodice of her exquisite dress was tight around the waist and billowed out softly as it draped to the floor. It had scallops of pink lace around the bottom hem. She must have loved the color pink because when I looked over at the sitting area in the middle of the room, there were dozens of blush colored roses in glass vases on the tables and all the fine china was accented in subtle mauve designs.

Rebecca slid out a crate from under one of the side tables and removed the box's lid. I walked over. Inside the container were dresses of bluish greys and soft purples. "Will these do?" she hoped.

"Of course. They are beautiful."

Her face showed a flicker of relief. "I am so glad. I'll have Fred bring them down and load them in your carriage."

"Thank you for your kindness. God bless you."

Mrs. Sampson shook her head. "Thank you for what you do for God's children, Sister Margaret. You are a quite an agreeable soul."

"I do what is right, Mrs. Sampson." I looked around at the artwork. Could I use that for Trey? Something about the art? How was I to know what they knew about the Sampsons in the future?

"Call me Rebecca."

I wasn't sure how to respond to that. "If you wish."

Rebecca smiled then. "You adore my new work?"

"Um, I have never seen anything like it."

She sighed and rubbed her neck, almost like my response had made her tense. It was the first time I saw a woman of her station not sit up perfectly. "And no one else ever will," she said solemnly.

"Why?"

She clasped her hands together and appeared out of sorts suddenly.

"Are you well, Mrs. Sampson?"

Her face stiffened. "Excuse me?"

I lowered my head. "I regress. I'm sorry to give you even the slightest provocation, Mrs. Sampson."

"Oh no, not all. It was me." She leaned forward. "But please, can you just call me Rebecca?"

My heart slowed back down. "Yes."

"I am doing that style of art as a way to… how do I say it? Escape."

"Oh? May I ask from what?"

"It's…" She paused. "You care for so many children without a worry in the world. I only have nine and yet I…" She stopped talking again and took a breath.

I reached over and took her hands in mine. They were trembling. "Don't. Motherhood is not for the weak, Rebecca."

"But the art is not fully about that." Her eyes dropped to the floor. "Escape from everything. Finding life after death."

I didn't say anything. I just nodded.

Glossy eyes returned and took in mine. "That's what they mean to me," she promised.

After a few quiet moments, she motioned me to the sitting area where we had a bit of tea and moved the conversation to spice imports and then on to a few references in the scripture that Rebecca had been curious about.

Before I said my goodbyes, I wished them all well and promised to return because Rebecca kept asking that of me.

I left the Sampson home with only a few hours to spare. I wanted some time with my diary before I needed to be back at the orphanage.

****

When I arrived at the orphanage, I took a moment remembering how I had first judged St. Mary's Orphan

Asylum when I arrived on its steps a year ago. To me, it seemed too incredibly fancy for an orphanage.

The building's large two-story dormitories were right on the beach. I remember thinking that it was more of a beautiful vacation property than anything.

I had been asked to travel to Galveston by Bishop Henry Williams back in England. He had told me of the need across the seas. His words were solid as he said, "It is a new world, Sister. Many in need of our help. Bishop Claude Dubois had begun this endeavor years ago. Now we must do our part. There are children that need guidance and care because they lost their parents to Yellow Fever."

In between my daily prayers and work at the orphanage, I explored. There were moments when I would stand on the tall sand dunes and wonder about the salt cedar trees that supported those dunes. I was told they were good protectors from rising tides.

I shrugged off the year's memories and walked inside just as the sun was setting off to my left.

Once inside, I noticed that the halls of the orphanage were lively with little feet heading to their beds. I smiled at Trey as he waved me goodnight.

Two more boys ran furiously through the hall. "Boys! That's enough! We must always act with some decorum."

"Yes, Sister," they stopped and said. Then, I felt a hand on my shoulder.

I turned around. "Father O'Brien?" I asked and lowered my head in greeting.

The priest wore his same black clergy cassock he had on from the day before. It was wrinkled at the top. I presumed he had grasped it throughout the day in an act of fanning himself.

"Sister Margaret," he returned. "Can I have a word?"

I followed him into the study between the kitchen and the collection rooms. He waved for me to sit. "Sister

Margaret, I am told that you spend many hours fetching supplies for the orphanage. We have some concerns."

"Father O'Brien, it is my pleasure."

He shook his head. "How have your prayers been? Do you find peace and solace as you used to?"

I frowned down at his pontifical sandals. His smaller feet didn't match his stature. Leave it to me to notice such tedious details. "Yes, of course."

I wondered on who told him of my recent concerns. I only shared them with the traveling priest, Father Miller, in my last confession. And even then, I didn't say much. "My prayers are of thanksgiving at my ability to care for God's special and most needed."

"Yes, my dear, but if we are not vessels of our Father's goodness, we are merely just doctors or acquaintances."

"But the work we do, not many people would take on. To care for another's child as our own. I don't understand your questions and concerns."

"You are not supposed to be like other people, Sister Margaret. You are tasked with the vocation of not only caring for their physical and mental well-being but also their spiritual welfare. And in the case of the children, their upbringing."

I lowered my head again. "Yes, Father, I understand."

Father O'Brien sighed. "I know it is all tiresome, the suffering, the heat here. However, I was told that of the recent nuns to arrive from Europe, you were one of a rebel sort."

I looked up with what couldn't have been anything less than an astonished look. "Father?"

He shook his head and stood. "No worries, dear child. God's plan is not to be questioned, and you are here for a reason, so I will trust in that. But don't think my visits here will be fraught with ignorance. These children and all the residents of Galveston are my responsibility. Clear your heart and leave it open only for God's works and words."

I wanted to yell out, "I'm trying! But He won't talk to me anymore!" Instead, I nodded and thanked Father O'Brien for his guidance.

****

A few mornings later, I made my way back to the hospital for new supplies. I was hoping to find time in my day to go by the tenant's house. My diary was not far from my thoughts lately. I was excited to tell Mr. Reynolds that I met the Sampsons. Of course, I would not betray Rebecca's confidence. What if I was wrong and Mr. Reynolds was not from the future but of our time? If so, what Rebecca told me about her doubts as a mother would be devastating if it got out. She trusted me as a woman of the cloth.

But if Mr. Reynolds was of the future, almost one hundred years from now, it wouldn't matter. I wanted to believe it and trust him with what I was told, so he would believe me. But no matter how much I believed my talking to him was God's plan, my faith had not been as strong as it used to be, especially after Father O'Brien's concerns. Therefore, I decided to do what was right by Rebecca. I would not tell Mr. Reynolds everything. Would it mean I would lose him as a friend? If so, then it wasn't God's plan for us to correspond with each other after all.

Mr. Reynolds,

I hope my words find you well. I went to visit the Sampson family. They are such a lovely family. Their children are bursting with talent in the arts. I hope you understand that I cannot succumb to your bidding in regards to speaking of anything private in regards to this sweet family. However, I still traveled to that part of the island to meet them. As it turns out, I was

I closed the diary and thought about Mrs. Sampson. There was something in her voice when I met her that I just couldn't shake. As a person who should be committed to the care of others, I ignored my original gut feeling when I first met her. After I wrote Mr. Reynolds about her, I headed back to the orphanage with a plan to pray the rosary for Rebecca. For whatever was ailing her.

CHAPTER 7
Round us Gather

Dear Ms. Nun,

I can see that. I can see how it would be wrong, but how do I know that isn't just an excuse?

Either way, I'll tell you of my hell. I'll tell you of war. Want to know of my nightmares? If so, tell me one thing, why did you become a nun of all things?

To tell you about myself and where I'm coming from, I think I'll start with my time in the VA hospital when I first came back home injured...

As I wrote, I also remembered it like it was yesterday. I had been laying in that hospital bed staring at the ceiling for hours. Originally paralyzed from the waist down, I didn't have much to live for. My brother, Jed, visited me several times. His optimistic presence infuriated me. His wife, Ginger, placed a vase of white roses next to my bed before she grimaced at the machines I was attached to. "They could do better for our heroes," she remarked.

Jed placed his hand on her shoulder, "Not right now, hun. Not the time nor place."

She brushed him off. "Sorry that I'm a realist and I married an idealist. But you know I'm right."

Ginger was a nurse at one of the biggest hospitals in Pittsburgh. Corporate money versus government allocated money was all she talked about. Funny how that wasn't enough to push her to leave her big paycheck to work at a shoddy hospital like the VA.

Jed rubbed his eyes. They had just flown in that morning to come see me. "These hospitals have come a long way since our guys came back from Vietnam to rat infested hospital rooms back then."

"I hate hospitals, period," I replied. Adjusting my prone position, I grimaced at the tightness in my chest.

"The VA still hasn't come far enough," she added and then smiled down at me. "We love you, Trey. I'm sorry for being so negative. You're like a kid brother to me. It's important that I know they are taking good care of you."

I didn't reply. Ginger really was the best, but the thought of her pity made my chest tighten up more. In an effort to mask how uncomfortable I was, I rubbed at my temples.

"Headache?" she asked.

"Yup," I lied.

She walked over to my chart hanging from the foot of my bed and flipped through it. "Prognosis is good. Paralysis won't last long. He has you set for a good round of physical therapy three times a week."

"That's not what the doctors say," I smarted off. "Dang, I need to get out of here. Having to wear a johnny all the time, and you know what that means? I get up and there's a breeze up my you know what."

Jed sucked his lips in. "Trey, you know medical science is not an exact science, right? If you believe you can come out of this soon, you will."

Make me sick now. "Jed, you have no idea what this feels like. Don't even start with all the motivational speeches because you and I know they are coming. Make yourself useful, Brother, and go to the packie. I need some beer."

Jed's typical worry lines seemed to deepen to annoying caverns above his sharp hazel eyes. "There you go again. We came here to check on you and you start acting like that." He shoved the applesauce on my tray closer to me. "Consume better food and then maybe you won't be so cranky."

"Cranky? You're not the one stuck in a hospital bed missing a leg! Or carrying the pain of a fiancé that left you right before it happened!"

"I'm sorry about Emily, but when you get out, which you will soon, I have friends that are state troopers. I can help you get on there."

"Paralyzed and missing a leg?"

Jed paused and looked out the small window of my room. I remembered when we were just kids and I followed him and his friends around wanting to ride a skateboard, too. In an attempt to ride my Tony Hawk skateboard down a half-pipe to get acceptance, I lost control and rolled onto the unforgiving cement. Jed had rushed over and checked me all over. I felt something different that day. It wasn't appreciation for a brother's care. It was aggravation that he could do something better than me and pity me when I realized that I couldn't. I looked up at Jed. "Don't look like that. I'd rather you not be here than to see that… pathetic looking…" I wave my hand. "Just stop."

His eyes drifted back to mine. "Ginger said you won't be paralyzed for long with physical therapy."

"And what about the missing leg, chowderhead?"

"You'll have a prosthetic. Think positive."

Ginger grabbed her husband's forearm. The sleeve of his white dress shirt crumbled under the squeeze of her hand. "Jed, just stop. He needs time."

Jed took a breath and sat down on the couch by the window. "Sorry, Trey. I'm just trying to help."

"It's not helping. Plus, I'm not gonna be no statie. Sit in a car all day bagging idiots? Come on, now." Truthfully, I didn't want his help. I didn't join the Marines because he said I should. I joined because it was what I felt I needed to do to make a living. After the fall out of the steel industry in Pittsburgh, I saw the effects of our city's recession had on my parents. The armed forces was my best option for a good and stable income in order to marry Emily and make her happy. It was the one decision that was all mine. Little did I know the bump in pay was still not good enough for Emily. And now, my body wasn't anymore either.

A few nights before, my doctor came in with his reports and bad news. Dr. Roberts checked a few of my vitals, reviewed his notes, and then gave me one of those placating smiles. "You're improving," he had told me.

"Good. How much will I improve and how soon?" I asked.

"Time? I don't know. I needed to tell you something that may be hard to hear."

"I'm a Marine, Doc. Shoot straight," I replied adamantly.

He dropped his eyes to my legs. No words were said just yet.

"Yeah, I know, it'll be awhile until I walk, right?" I added for him.

His eyes met mine. "I really don't know, but I'm most concerned about your reproductive health. I saw on your check-in information that you do not have children."

"That's correct, but those are some big words you are dishing out right now." I semi-smiled to hide my embarrassment. But it was still difficult to fully understand what he was getting at, even though I already knew. "Get to the point."

"You will not ever be able to have children."

My body went stiff. I simply turned my face towards the television and flipped the channel to a re-run of Beavis and Butt-Head.

Dr. Roberts took that as his cue and patted my shoulder. "We'll talk more later. I'll let you rest." Then, he left the room. I watched Butt-Head and cringed at his annoying laugh. "Yeah, go ahead Butt-Head, laugh at me. Doesn't matter. Emily is gone anyway. Life sucks. Joy, joy."

In front of me now was my brother scowling at me. "So, you just gonna give up? Do nothing the rest of your life? You're a Reynolds'. You'll get past this." He was a few years older than me and still treated me like I was that hurt boy that busted it on the half-pipe.

After a few moments of ignoring him and feeling my sister-in-law rub my shoulder, I added proudly. "I may get back to writing."

Jed grimaced. "Writing? That crazy dream you had as a kid?"

I responded with, "Ha, and your plan to promote to partner at that firm ran by that rich family isn't a delusion? It's a *family run* firm, Jed! They only promote their own."

Jed's wife stepped in between of us. "Okay, boys. Let's take this down a notch." Then she grabbed my only cookie off the tray before addressing me. "Trey, we are concerned about you," she said while chomping on my cookie.

"Because I'm paralyzed and can't walk? Because my fiancé left me the way my mom left my dad? Yeah, I guess you can be concerned."

"No, I mean your attitude. Your brother loves you," she retorted and pointed at my applesauce, too.

I rolled my eyes. "Like he loved me so much when I sat at our dad's apartment telling him that dad was in tears only to hear him hang up the phone on me." I pushed the applesauce to her. "And I don't want this dang applesauce, mommy. You eat it. You seem to want all my hospital food anyway. You know, I really wanted that cookie."

She swallowed her last bite. "Sorry." She smiled. "It was really good, though."

Jed stepped back and ran his hand through his hair while shaking his head at us. Where I had dirty blonde hair like mom, Jed had the same dark and wavy hair as dad. But Jed's hair was always perfect. Mine had always been unruly with a jagged hairline that gave me no options for a cool hairstyle… ever. It was the reason I didn't get upset with the new recruit induction we all went through at bootcamp. I remembered standing up from the chair without a care in the world after I watched the other guys sit there in shock rubbing their newly bald head.

Finally, I noticed that my brother was still there when he said, "It wasn't like that with Dad."

"It wasn't like that, how?" I asked.

"You never wanted to know the whole story. You were Dad's favorite. The star athlete. He adored you. There was never a chance that you would care to hear Mom's side. Dad fixed that with his narcissistic behavior."

"That's enough." Then, I nodded over to Ginger. "Good to see you, Ginger. Thank you for coming by." I turned back to Jed. "Now it's time to go, Jed. Get out!"

"Fine!" he said and stormed out, almost running into the nurse coming into my room.

Ginger remained. "Oh, the Reynolds' boys. Your family sure knows how to talk to each other. I'm sorry for both of you that this visit didn't go well."

I let out a breath and finally felt my chest loosen up. "It's not your fault."

"You know he did come here to check on you. He really loves you."

"Funny way of showing it."

She turned and walked back to her purse as my nurse gave me my afternoon meds. When Ginger came back over to me, she handed me a box wrapped in light blue birthday paper.

"What's that?" I frowned.

"Jed told me once that you and your whole family went down to Galveston, Texas for a short trip. A getaway of some sort. He said that trip was when you discovered your love of the ocean and fishing."

"True," I said and swallowed my last pill with my water from the little plastic cup the nurse had handed me.

"He also told me your dad bought you both a seashell."

"A conch. I could hold it up to my ear and hear the ocean. Did he also tell you that he broke mine a few years later?" I asked while holding the blue wrapped gift.

She slowly nodded. "I'm going to let you rest." Ginger tilted her head while staring at the gift in my hands. "He was going to give that to you himself. I hope in some way it helps."

After she walked out, I ripped the wrapping. I lifted out of the box a large conch and studied it. It was light pink with spots of grey. I held it up to the side of my face and a gentle sound whispered into my ear. Suddenly, everything came back to me. The happiness of that day on the beach with my family began to flood my senses. I grimaced and dropped the conch back into the box.

"Whatever," I said aloud. Then, I rolled over and tried to go back to sleep. But it didn't work. I squeezed my eyes shut harder, yet my mind was still thinking back. Flashes of images continued to engross my thoughts. All of them were surprisingly of Galveston, Texas.

CHAPTER 8
Thy art our Mother

When I opened my diary, there it was. Mr. Reynolds had written back. His words had poured out from deep inside him. My heart hurt for him. The exchanges between him and his brother were unusual for me to see. I imagined, since he was from a time almost a hundred years after me, that things had changed. But I still couldn't see how brothers would be so harsh with each other.

I never felt that way with a sibling. My sister and I relied on each other, as most siblings did. But from what I gathered about Mr. Reynolds and siblings during his time was that mediocre problems were entertained more so than survival. How nice would it be to live during such times.

The soft amber glow of the setting sun began to spill into the room. I didn't have much daylight left to wonder over Mr. Reynolds and the ways of people in that time. I wanted to respond back quickly and get back to the beach.

Mr. Reynolds,

Thank you for sharing so much with me. I feel it wasn't an easy feat opening up to someone else.

You asked why I became a nun. That, in itself, is a long story. If given the time, I will explain more in later correspondences. For now, I will tell you of my position here and what brought me to the island of Galveston.

I am part of what is called the Sisters of Charity of Saint Vincent de Paul. I began my calling back in England after my husband unexpectedly passed away. The Sisters of Charity is a Roman Catholic order of nuns devoted to carrying out Jesus' call to mercy and kindness to the less fortunate. It is among the many Catholic orders devoted to the care of the poor and sick. At the time, God spoke to me and revealed that there was a need in America. When the local diocese put out requests for volunteers, I took note. It was honorable what they were trying to do in America. The Bishop at the time in Texas, Bishop Dubuis, was originally from France. He had reached out to Mother Angelique Hiver in Lyons, France, to get help starting a charity hospital. It was to be the first Catholic hospital in Texas and it was being built in Galveston.

I am assuming that you found my diary and are in Galveston, so you know where that hospital is. And you may also know that Galveston is a huge port for America. The need was great, so I offered my assistance. I left England and traveled across the vast ocean to America. You see, I made a commitment to the greater good. In time, the need changed from helping at the hospital to caring for the children that lost their parents to Yellow Fever. I have seen great loss during my short time here. As you probably already have read on the previous pages of my diary, I have also been having my share of doubts lately.
I still carry out my duties well, and no one can say that I do not love the children. In fact, the boy I took in that I named after you, is now thriving. It was not easy, I dare say. Many nights I spent rocking him to calm him back down. Glory to God, he has now started opening up and playing with the other boys.

I would like to know more about Emily when you are ready to share. I remember what it was like to love another only to lose them. Granted, my story may not be similar to yours. Either way, my loss cut me deeply, too. In a way, I partly joined the convent for the wrong reasons, and I question that reasoning

I closed the diary and put it back in its place with the quill. The creaking sound on the floors outside the room caught my attention. Georgy was pacing the floor waiting to talk to me.

I wasn't ready to leave just yet. I loved it here. The room I was in had been outfitted well. The Victorian bamboo finishes were a nice touch under a beautiful chandelier crafted with four layers of crystals instead of the usual two that fine bedrooms were outfitted with. Georgy had told me that the chandelier was moved on purpose from the parlor into the bedroom by her missus' request when her health began to fail.

I stared up at the chandelier and then back around the room. Everything was truly elegant, except for the odd small touches of a beach theme. I pondered if that was Mr. Lawson's doing to make visitors feel more like they were on a tropical island. The porcelain boat anchors hanging above the dresser were nice, but I still did not see the reasoning for that old folk-art chair made with seashells clinging to its legs.

When I finally walked out of the room, Georgy smiled at me and took my hands. "Sister, you must tell me about Mrs. Sampson. I hear good and bad. I also heard she a lady."

"I don't know that she has the title of a lady, but she is a very warm person."

"I heard differently. I heard she is royalty. Her husband, too. At one point, that family had over fifty slaves even after Lincoln declared our freedom."

"Slavery was abolished everywhere in the states in 1863 because of your president, President Lincoln."

"Not fully, Sister. It took that General of the Union army to come down here and read federal orders right in the middle of the city to ensure that we be free. The Texans held out longer. Stubborn people. But if those Texans didn't avenge that Alamo incident then where would we be? Would there have even been a Lincoln to free us?"

"That is a lot of what ifs, but I admire these Texans in a way, too."

Georgy tilted her head. "And now we are Texans."

I laughed. "I guess you are correct, my dear. But you are the finest of all these Texans."

She seemed uncomfortable with that statement. "How you figure?" she smarted back.

I replied, "You came from the hardest of situations and rose above it. Excelled at your craft, taught yourself how to read, and became one of the most precious friends I have ever had. I am thankful that God orchestrated our friendship."

She shook her head. "And you, as well."

CHAPTER 9
Thy Little Child

Dear Ms. Nun,

You are a very special woman to care for other people's kids like you do. It is nice to hear about your selflessness when so many women are not like you anymore. Yellow Fever? That was eradicated generations ago. Here in the year 2000, most we see is the flu and chickenpox.

So more about me. I was originally from Pittsburgh, Pennsylvania. I moved here to Galveston after my post deployment work in Pittsburgh dried up.

If you want to know about what happened between me and my fiancé, I'll tell you. However, I should probably tell you about Webster first. So, here it is. It was an unusually hot afternoon in Somalia when I first met a little Somalian boy. He was about twelve. He had been following me around in his oversized and torn clothes. I was so full of sweat from all my gear that I couldn't wait to get back to the compound to strip down and get clean, so I brushed him off and finished my patrol quickly.

There were so many kids out there without parents since the latest civil war claimed most of them. A few more patrols later, the kid was still trying to follow behind me and mimic my steps. I turned around to stop him, but his big eyes and adorable dimpled smile made me hesitate.

The next few patrols, he'd be there again and again following me with that huge smile. Among all the sadness and devastation, it floored me at how happy he was. Always so happy. He had told me his name, but I couldn't pronounce it, so I just called him Webster.

At the time when I first met Webster, he could only speak broken English as Somali was their native language. The longer I spent with him the better he got. It wasn't long after that, I started sneaking him into the compound with me so I could teach him how to read. Later, we moved from books to letters that were sent to me by my family and friends. I especially enjoyed giving him some of the gifts in the care packages that my mom sent because I couldn't stand my mother anyway.

The first time I let him read a letter from my fiancé, Emily, it was the 8th letter she wrote me while I was deployed. I scanned through it first to make sure there was nothing inappropriate in it, of course. Then, I handed it to him and helped him pronounce the words. It took almost an hour, but he could finally read a one-page letter fluently. I remember his excitement…

"I did it, then?" Webster asked. His stutter trailing on the last word.

"Yes sir. You did great!"

Webster sat down cross legged on the floor and clasped his hands in front of his chest. "Are there any more letters?"

"Not yet."

He looked over at the letter from Emily that laid next to me on my bunk. "Trey?"

"What?" I always smiled when he used my first name. In the beginning, the kids we met called us 'Americans'. After they got to know us, they began saying things like 'Marine' or 'Black Boots'. It was touching how we'd walk through the town and hear little voices holler out, "Black Boots, Black Boots!"

Webster stood back up in front of me. "Why did she say she may not be able to write you as much now?"

I grimaced and grabbed the letter off the bed to put it away. "Don't worry about that. Women. They can get cranky sometimes."

"Cranky?"

"It means angry."

"Did you do something to make her angry?" he asked.

I stashed the letter in my bag with the other seven. I wondered what Emily meant by that too, but I wouldn't let it bother me just yet. "Time to go, Webster."

The deflated adolescent followed behind me. "Okay. But next time, will you tell me more about that MTV? And that funny show you always watch. I want to know more about these funny cartoon characters that say stupid things."

I laughed and began to walk him towards the gate. When we got to the exit, I tapped his little head. "See you later alligator."

"Okay crocodile," Webster returned. It was cute how we bantered back and forth after he picked up on certain sayings. I even wondered about what it would be like for him to see a Ren and Stimpy show for the first time. Geez, it would probably ruin the poor boy to see a sociopathic dog torment a good-natured cat. Still, it was a funny show. I laughed at the thought.

After I returned to my cot that night, I laid there with my stomach starting to knot up. I tried not to, but I couldn't help thinking about what Emily had said. What do I say to that? How long would it be until she wrote me back? I lived for those letters from her. It was the only thing that kept me going.

I would be lying if I didn't say it was strange timing. Just a few weeks before that letter, Paul, my best friend from back home, had sent me a letter saying he thought he saw Emily at the bowling alley with Carlton, the mayor's son.

As a few other Marines came into the compound and made their way to their cots, I heard them steadily griping about their patrol. Lance Corporal Boudreaux, my next cot over buddy, who had come from somewhere in the southern regions of Louisiana, plopped down next to me. "It's so hot."

I gave him a blank look. "You're from the South. You're used to this."

"You never get used to the heat, bro."

The constant sun exposure in Somalia had his Cajun skin almost as dark as the Somalians.

Boudreaux drummed his hands on my bed. "Reynolds! You bastard! You got some stash in that last package?"

"Why does everyone assume I got the booze?"

He scratched at his chest. "Because everyone knows that Pittsburgh people are big drinkers and are proud of it!"

"Yeah, but who says we share, chucklehead?"

The other Marines laughed. "Ah, that no fair, bro."

I rolled over and placed my pillow over my head. "Get over it. I'm going to bed."

Boudreaux laughed. "You know what I got?"

I removed the pillow. "What?"

Out of his duffle bag, he pulled out a new cassette tape with a funky looking angel on the cover. "Look!"

I sat up. "Is that Nirvana's newest album?"

"Hell, yeah! It's called In Utero."

"I can read, you stupid Jarhead." I smacked his shoulder and took the cassette out of its plastic shell. "This is brand new. Just released. How did you get it?"

"My brother. He knows people."

"This is neat. You close to your brother?"

Boudreaux shrugged. "He's my big brother. You got one, too."

"Yeah, but we're not close."

"Why not?"

I looked at him squarely in the eye and then around the room. "Doesn't matter. You boys are my true brothers. You get me. I don't need anyone else."

"Hell, yeah."

The others hollered, "Oh yeah!!! Marines!!!"

Corporal Jones set down his cards on the box between him and Private Michaels. He lit a cigarette and smiled big with his pearly whites. How he kept white teeth with all the smoking he did was beyond me. He tapped his chest. "Thank God for Marines, right?"

Whooping and hollering filled the space. Private Michaels added, "Yeah, you know what Eleanor Roosevelt said about us?"

"What book nerd?" Boudreaux asked while grinning.

Private Michaels replied in his best formal female accent, "She said, '"The Marines I have seen around the world have the cleanest bodies, the filthiest minds, the highest morale, and…'" He paused to stand up with his hands now behind his head. He circled his hips provocatively while the others laughed. He continued, "'And the lowest morals of any group of animals I have ever seen.'"

"Hoorah!!!!!!" everyone shouted! And then in perfect unison, they yelled, "Thank God for the United States Marine Corps!"

Everyone, whether tired from their patrol or not, all began clapping and hollering. But Boudreaux let his smile fade as he looked down at me. "You okay, Reynolds?"

I gave him back his Nirvana. "Affirmative. Now I gotta sleep, bud. Early patrol."

The tall Marine eyed me for a second. "Alright, buddy. We'll listen to it tomorrow. Get your beauty rest."

I laughed and laid back down as he hid his cassette back in his duffle bag. As the laughter began to fade and everyone settled in, I reflected on how I felt about them. I meant it when I said these guys were my brothers, especially now. They were the only ones that could relate to me. We leaned on each other, not on our families. No one could understand what we've been going through, nor could anyone know what life was like being away from those you loved while your life was threatened. People in the States… their lives went on. Their MTV and movies on Friday nights kinda life all went on like usual. But us… we were out here alone, missing home, and only getting breadcrumbs of what our families and girlfriends easily got without waiting weeks for.

I pulled my blanket up over my face to block the cigarette smoke that began to drift over towards me from my bunk neighbor. I needed to go to sleep before my mind raced too much. But I knew sleep would not come easy that night. Something about Emily was worrying me. My stomach continued to be in knots. God help me, I couldn't lose her. Not like this. She was the only thing keeping me alive out here.

So, there is my story.

I'm going to bed.

Goodnight, Ms. Nun,

Trey

I placed the quill down on top of the nun's diary. It hurt even to this day to remember all that from back in Somalia. I sat there for a moment thinking of how much I hoped this nun appreciated me sharing so much.

CHAPTER 10
All Merciful

Dear Mr. Reynolds,

I apologize for my delay in writing back. My duties at the orphanage had me indisposed for a short while and kept me from my travels here into town. Your correspondence has become somewhat of a delight for me. Thank you for continuing to write me. You question this exchange between us as do I, but I have decided I will not let it keep me from continuing. I believe that there are reasons for everything. Many we have yet to understand or never will.

What I have found is that your life is not much different than mine, but yet it is in so many ways. For that is the mystery of life, no matter our age or time we live in, we are all the same and bound together under God.

Your relationship with the boy you called Webster, warmed my heart. I hope you see what a blessing you are to him and that you one day return to check on him. I do have to ask, what is MTV? It seems to me that you all valued this entertainment more than anything. Please elaborate.

One day, I may return to England or even Scotland. Those are my homes. I miss them dearly. America does fascinate me. However informal the people here seem, there is a common thread here among them that is undeniable. It is a sense of hope and merry that I didn't encounter back home. Even though the virus is devastating many on this island, the people are resilient like I had never seen before.

You say you are from Pittsburgh. When I first arrived in America, I was sent to Fort Worth, Texas to help with the sick there. Fort Worth was a horrible place. Texans love their guns and take matters into their own hands without a second thought. I was terrified there. However, I did meet a family there that immigrated from Ireland and were headed up to the Pennsylvania and Massachusetts areas. They spoke of it being a place that most of their family and other Irish folk settled at after the Great Irish Famine. Are you of Irish descent?

On an earlier entry, I told you I was called to this place by God. I wanted to explain further. I had been married before I chose the cloth. I was young then, though. It was an interesting time in my life. I was an eighteen-year-old running a manor of over twenty servants. I seemed to do well at it until the night it all ended. I want to share this with you now.

I had been asleep for a few hours when I heard shouting coming from the library. My husband, Henry, wasn't due back until the next day, so I was surprised to see him in there. He was arguing with Marvin, our butler. When I saw Henry throw his glass at Marvin, I rushed in. It was not my place to get involved in such affairs, but Henry had taken to the drink so many times before and hurt many of our servants that I couldn't bear another incident.

The rest was a blur. All I remembered after that was walking in the cold night air with no shoes and no destination. The fire from our home still burned in the distance. I was shaken up and unaware of my surroundings. I made my way into the nearby church. Walking through the door felt like a warm blanket taking me in. I sat in the last pew and lowered my head to pray. After a while of sitting there, my limbs and eyelids felt so heavy that all I could do was lie down to sleep. So, I did just that. In my sleep, I dreamed of an ocean. Waves crashing in on the sun kissed sand and large white birds dancing here and there above the surf.

All around me on the beach were children laughing and playing. Many ran up to me and grabbed my hands. We spun around and enjoyed the warm sun until dark clouds covered the skies. The wind picked up and rain began to drench us. We tried to run but our bodies couldn't move. Then a large wave rose above us and the poor children, they screamed and grabbed onto my skirts.

I woke up to the sound of the parish priest calling my name. I sat up and saw him walking down the aisle asking if I was well. I did not have to tell him of the fire at my home or the passing of my husband. He already knew. He sat down next to me trying to comfort me, but all I could think about was that dream.

For the next few months as I settled the end of my former life, I visited my church almost daily and prayed constantly until I finally decided that there was more to that dream than just a fluke nightmare brought on by a traumatic event. God was showing me something. It was a gift that he was giving me. An invitation to something better. The scripture that spoke to me the most and guided me into such a big decision was Isaiah 6:1-10. Do you know this one?

I know it word for word. It reads, 'In the year of King Uzziah's death I saw the <u>Lord</u> seated on a high and lofty throne; his train filled the sanctuary. Above him stood seraphs, each one with six wings: two to cover its face, two to cover its feet and two for flying; and they were shouting these words to each other: Holy, holy, holy is <u>Yahweh</u> Sabaoth. His <u>glory</u> fills the whole earth.
The door-posts shook at the sound of their shouting, and the <u>Temple</u> was full of smoke. Then I said: 'Woe is me! I am

lost, for I am a <u>man</u> of unclean lips and I live among a people of unclean lips, and my eyes have seen the King, <u>Yahweh</u> Sabaoth. 'Then one of the seraphs flew to me, holding in its hand a live coal which it had taken from the altar with a pair of tongs. With this it touched my mouth and said: 'Look, this has touched your lips, your guilt has been removed and your <u>sin</u> forgiven. 'I then heard the voice of the <u>Lord</u> saying: 'Whom shall I send? Who <u>will</u> go for us?' And I said, 'Here am I, send me. 'He said: 'Go, and say to this people, "Listen and listen, but never understand! Look and look, but never perceive!'

'Make this people's heart coarse, make their ears dull, shut their eyes tight, or they <u>will</u> use their eyes to see, use their ears to hear, use their heart to understand, and change their ways and be healed.
'I then said, 'Until when, Lord?' He replied, 'Until towns are in ruins and deserted, houses untenanted and a great desolation reigns in the land, and <u>Yahweh</u> has driven the people away and the country is totally abandoned. And suppose one-tenth of them are left in it, that <u>will</u> be stripped again, like the terebinth, like the oak, cut back to the stock; their stock is a holy seed.'"

Mr. Reynolds, this bible verse spoke to me on so many levels. Although, the last three lines remain a mystery to me still to this day. For some reason, God wanted me to carry those lines with me, too. And so, I did.

The next year, I joined the convent.

CHAPTER 11
God of the Sea

I set the nun's diary down and laid back onto my bed. I noticed a notification light on my answering machine from across the room. It wasn't my doctor's office at the VA anymore leaving me messages like before. I had already been given my news. So, who would leave me a message? Family? Friends? The idea was to find a way off the grid away from my former life. I decided not to pay attention to the message yet. Instead, I picked the diary back up and wrote back to the nun.

Dear Ms. Nun,

I am sorry to hear about your husband and the loss of your home. I know that could not have been easy. Thank you for sharing that with me. There was a time when I believed in God like you do. I used to pray a lot. Like I said before, so much has happened that I question everything now. The sad thing is I am not sure how much I care to even be here anymore.

I paused and set down the quill before rubbing my face. The anger I felt when the doctor at the VA Hospital reported the results of my scans crossed my mind again. I shook it away and picked up the quill again. I thought about telling her about our forms of entertainment, including MTV, but I figured it would only confuse her. Or was it that? Here I was, this foul-mouthed Marine talking to a perfect and sweetest of souls' nun. Nah, there would be some things I would leave out. But she really wanted to know about Emily.

And for once, I really wanted to tell someone. As I began to think of what to write, my mom crossed my mind again.

Ms. Nun, when I talk about Emily, I want you to know that she was not always horrible. The betrayal was. She betrayed me the same way my mom betrayed my father. I guess I carry that distrust for all women with me. But I trust you for some reason. Maybe because I still question how real you are. In my world, good women are few and far between.

My mom kept writing me while I was deployed, by the way. The sad thing was, I didn't care. I would hand the letters over to Webster to read and give him the teddy bears and chocolate my mom sent. Webster always loved the days when my mom's packages came in...

"Trey, why do you not care for your mom?" Webster asked as he stuffed the rest of the Snickers bar into his mouth. "I wish my mom was still with me." His round face lowered and emphasized the puckering of his bottom lip.

Webster's comment was sobering. "I'm sorry, Webster. I know that's hard. I should appreciate my mom more."

"Then why don't you?"

"I have my reasons. Reasons that a kid won't understand."

Webster swallowed the rest of the chocolate and stared down at the box from my mom. "Next time, I will bring some of this good food to my friends."

I leaned over and rested my elbows on my knees. "What happened to that kid that was with you yesterday?"

"He back at home."

"No, I mean his…" I thought for a second. I didn't know how to ask it. "… his hands? He's missing both hands."

Webster didn't seem surprised that I asked. "Oh that. He was bringing those little bombs home. One day, they went off."

I grimaced and sat back thinking about all the grenades that were left after the last Somali civil war. "That's horrible. You know not to touch those things, right?"

"Yeah, we learning."

"You better. No more little bombs, okay?"

"Okay."

I rubbed his head and handed him a Hershey's bar. "Here, bring this to your friend. It's time to go."

His big eyes lit up. "Yes, thank you, thank you."

After he left, I tore up the letter from my mom as I did all of her letters.

CHAPTER 12
Tempest Wild

Dear Mr. Reynolds,

I better understand your sadness. The poor children there. I am not sure what you referred to when you said the children carried home little bombs, but from the horrible disfigurement this caused, I can only imagine that the brutality of these bombs was hard to witness. I am sorry you had to see that.

I do not judge you for your doubts on life after everything you have been through. I will pray for you and ask our Father to give you strength as you continue to heal. Please know that God loves you unconditionally and when you are ready, He will be there. He never leaves us.

I stopped writing to the sound of a horse carriage pulling up to the house. Georgy went out and greeted them as I sat in Mrs. Davenport's former room thinking about how I told Mrs. Davenport the same thing a few hours before she passed.

I went back to writing…

Mr. Reynolds, I am sorry about your distrust of women and the broken relationship with your mother. I barely knew my mother. I hope you at least continue to try to mend that. Do you visit your father?

After the fire at the manor, I left everyone to come here to Galveston. I didn't look back. I felt it was better for everyone.

There were a few taps on the door. I closed my diary and set it back in its hiding spot before opening the door to a familiar face. "Mrs. Sampson? What brings you here?"

Georgy was right behind her with a big grin. "She has news!"

I tightened my veil and waved for Rebecca to have a seat. "It is so good to see you. Come. Sit. Did you get to formally meet Georgy?"

"Of course. She had me try her delicious cookies." The hem on Rebecca's ivory skirt brushed the baseboards as she sat on the farthest chair in the room. "Please forgive my forwardness in coming. I originally came to bring you more clothes for the orphans. I was told by a doctor, a Mr. Lee I think his name was. He told me that you rest here before you travel back."

"Yes, I do." I sat on a chair in front of her. "Your generosity is greatly appreciated."

Georgy worked quickly to pick up an empty tray on the table and a few scattered books. "I'll leave you two to talk."

Rebecca held up her hand. "No, please. This involves you, Georgy."

"Me?"

"Yes. You and Sister Margaret."

Georgy sat down while keeping her grin shining towards Rebecca. "It do?"

"Are you familiar with the town's huge Labor Day Parade?"

I shook my head. "Not really, but Georgy has been here longer than me."

Rebecca pulled out a napkin and wiped a few droplets of sweat off her forehead. "Well, they decided to still hold the parade. But it's for a good cause. My husband is on the committee, you see, and he says that since Galveston has more experience with the fever, we want to send supplies and people to help in Fort Worth and even as far as Tennessee."

"How can I be of help?" I asked.

Rebecca continued, "The diocese hasn't written back yet, so I thought I'd ask you, Sister Margaret."

"What can I do?"

"Is it a Mother Gabriela in charge of the orphanage?" she asked rhetorically.

"Yes."

"Could you be so kind and inquire about locations that have the greatest need?"

"The hospital here could tell you more than we can," I answered.

She splayed her hand over her stomach. "Sister, the hospitals will tell us to deliver all the supplies to other hospitals. The committee is in need of a list of places with the greatest need, families or even other orphanages. I am told that Mother Gabriela keeps in touch with the priests in the northern counties."

I nodded. "I will do what I can."

"Thank you," her smile grew. "And Miss Georgy, I would love it if you could make a few batches of your cookies. I will pay for the ingredients and your time, of course. But my plan is to auction them off at the banquet after the parade and use the proceeds to help fund some of this."

Georgy's face lit up. She almost dropped the tray. "You don't have to pay me a cent. I make my cookies out of love and am just thankful that you enjoy them."

"I can't possibly not pay," Rebecca countered.

"Then, I won't bake them Mrs. Sampson," Georgy adamantly replied.

Rebecca crossed her hands on her lap. "Well, then. At least let me help you."

"Now, Mrs. Sampson, you have your hands full with those children and I can't possibly ask something like that of you."

"You're not. I'm insisting. I need some time away from my motherly duties anyway," Rebecca said and stared down solemnly at the floor. It was that same stare that I had noticed back when I first met her in her home.

I stood up. "Then, it is settled. And you two must count me in. If there are three of us and under Georgy's guidance, we can make triple the amount."

Rebecca looked up at me and smiled. "I would love that."

Georgy frowned. "Wait. I don't know. Are you women going to ruin my cookies?"

Rebecca and I both laughed. "God willing," Rebecca said with a giggle and put her hands on her narrow hips as she stood back up.

The friendly exchange had all three of us laughing. In that one moment, we weren't known as a former slave, a nun, and a well-off lawyer's wife. We were a very unlikely friendship of women just wanting the fellowship of other women.

After Rebecca left, I was about to leave too when Georgy followed me to the door and skirted around me. "That Ms. Rebecca is a rare white woman."

"What do you mean?"

Georgy pondered her next statement before saying it. "I mean, including me in all this."

"She is a good soul."

"I reckon, but for someone of her stature to be so kind to those beneath her, it makes one wonder."

"Wonder what?" I asked. I knew what Georgy was getting at. Georgy spent most of her life being looked down on. It was normal for someone who had gone through so much to question people's intentions.

Georgy tilted her head. "No, I think you're right. But it's not just that. There is something sad in her eyes. You can't not see that, too, Sister Margaret?"

I pondered Georgy's words. I had seen something, but I added, "Whatever it is, I plan to wait until she reaches out to me. As a servant of God, it is not my duty to pry but to be one of patience and strength for when I am needed."

Georgy scowled at me. "Oh, hush that nonsense, Sister. If you sit around and continue to wait when you know there is something wrong, you will surely regret the support that could stop the torment of another woman. Do you want to be that kind of friend?"

When Georgy said *friend* out loud, something fluttered inside me. Yes, I see Rebecca as a friend, but that can't be the way it should be. I am supposed to be a spiritual advisor, nothing else. But I couldn't deny that my heart strained and twisted every time I saw the torment in Rebecca's eyes. As if the depredation of life's affliction would eventually pull that tender heart out. "No. It is not," I told Georgy.

"Good. Now I will pray that it is not what I think it is but that your inquiry will be fruitful. However, patience was never my strong suit, Sister," she spit out. And then added her cute, "Hm, hm," with a twist of her mouth.

I frowned at the comment. "I can see that, so what you are really telling me is that you could never be a card shark."

"Pardon?" she asked bemused.

I laughed. "You show your thoughts all over your pretty face, that's all."

Georgy giggled. A small snort trailed the end of her laughter as she replied, "Oh, Sister Margaret, a transplant of England's serenity. Remember, you a Texan now too, silly woman."

CHAPTER 13
Exceeding Danger

The leftovers from Poppy's weren't as appetizing as before. Fried shrimp warmed back up was just not the same. In fact, anything fried heated back up was disgusting. Even still, I was hungry. I dipped the soggy battered shrimp into the tartar sauce to make it more edible.

The light on my answering machine still blinked. I threw my food away and slammed on the button. The message was distorted at first, but then I heard my mom's voice. "Hey, Trey, I've been trying to get a hold of you. Call me back. It's about your dad. He's not feeling good. He tried to call you but when he couldn't reach you, he called me. I hope you call back soon."

I was going to pick up the phone and then Jed's message came on. "Trey, Dad's not that sick. I checked on him. He does want to see you, but don't let it get you upset. He's known to blow things out of proportion. Just being honest and thought you should know."

The next message came through with my dad saying, "Son, I am fine. Just having some issues with my chest. I miss you. I hope you are okay down there in Texas. I would like to see you. Call me."

And then another message. This time it was from my childhood friend, Paul. "Boy, where have you been? I know you said something about coastal living. I would like a heads up on how you're doing, though. Hey, did you hear your dad got sick? My dad said he had been sick for a while. Something about persistent indigestion. But then your brother came into the store saying your dad was perfectly fine." He paused and then sighed. "I guess I shouldn't leave all this on your machine. Call me."

I picked up the phone and called the long-distance number to Pittsburgh. A few rings and then Paul's raspy voice came on the line. "Hello."

"Hey, Paul. It's Trey."

There was movement on the other end of the line. "Hey, man. Give me a second to put out this cig."

A few beats later, he came back to the phone. "You still there?"

"Yup," I returned.

"How are you?" he asked and I heard Sally in the background asking who it was. "It's Trey, hun."

"Tell him I said hello. I'm going on to bed," she added with a yawn.

"Sally says hello. So, fill me in. You okay?"

"I'm fine."

"Been fishing yet?" he asked.

I started moving around the room, stretching the phone cord out to its full length. "No, been busy finishing the work on this house." I lied. Nothing had been finished on the remodel yet.

"Oh yeah, gotcha."

"How's work?" I asked. Paul was the smart one. Him and my brother both went to college on academic scholarships while I waited around on a football scholarship that never panned out. Still, it was Paul that supported me the most in joining the Marines. He even wore a goofy shirt saying, *"My best friend is no one you wanna mess with!"* to my graduation ceremony. After the ceremony, he actually made me sign the dang thing while Emily, Jeb, Ginger, and my mom stood off to the side laughing. My dad wouldn't come around my mom, but I remembered him being there in the front row smiling up at me.

Over the line, I heard Paul pour himself a drink. "It's good now that the whole Y2K stuff is over. Thank goodness

Clinton took the threat seriously. However, Sally and the other techs are still fixing a few problems for their clients at some of the nuclear power plants that didn't change their coding. But anyway, our head broker wants us pushing tech stocks now. Silicon Valley is working on something big. Sally is even thinking of taking a job over there. Can you believe? We may actually leave Pitts."

"Yeah, fresh starts are always good. So, what was this about my brother again?"

"Ah, well, you know your brother. He is concerned about you. You know what he told me?"

"Enlighten me."

"He said that your dad is just doing that because your mom is getting married again and your dad wants you there to help him through it. It's crazy, you two. I know I've been friends with you and Jed for many years, but I don't know about your family stuff. Still, you need to talk to your brother more."

I ignored the last statement and dwelled on one new bit of information. Mom was getting remarried? Pathetic. My ridiculous family.

Paul continued, "It's some guy from her work. Have you met him yet?"

I didn't reply to Paul but only acted like I already knew the news. "No, but I imagine that would be hard on Dad. Hey, I'm going to head out. Got some things to pick up."

"This late? It's after nine."

"Not here, remember? Different time zone. It's only twenty-two hundred here. It was good hearing from you, though."

"You too. Don't be a stranger, okay?"

"I won't. Bye, Paul."

"Will do. Bye, Trey."

After I hung up the phone, I thought about my mom's news. I picked up the handset again and stared at the yellow lit up numbers. Maybe I should return her call. Then, I thought of my dad. Truth be told, I didn't have the emotional stability to call my dad right now either. I figured he was in a bad way. But I knew I wasn't in the right mind to deal with that. The dial tone changed to that annoying loud racket it does when you leave the phone off the hook too long. I slammed the phone back down and returned to my bed. I picked up the diary and a strange feeling came over me. Was it peace? It was fleeting, but it felt good. Yeah, it did. I guess I enjoyed escaping into my little fantasy world with a dead nun. One of whom, I could talk to about everything. Finally, someone who would listen without bias or judgement. Someone who would have no choice but to read everything I wrote without having a chance to shut me down with their take on things.

Dear Ms. Nun,

Yeah, the bombs were everywhere in Somalia. They are called grenades. They are bombs people throw, and they cause a big enough of a blast that it can tear apart a body in seconds. But that wasn't what made me the way I am. So much more. I'll tell you of another part of my past.

It was a typical day in Somalia. The kids would lead us around the town showing us things. They were really cute and surprisingly happy given their predicament. Most were orphans wore nothing but torn pants and oversized shirts. They went to school in an old building that was missing half its roof. I was led in there one day alone. This big Marine with two weapons strapped to my body that I stuck out like a sore thumb. I wasn't worried about it. I always had eyes on me from my guys, so I went willingly to see what they wanted to show me. I had a soft spot for the kids. When I got in the room, they all yelled in English, "Surprise!" On the broken chalkboard behind them were the words, "Sergeant Reynolds, the Mayor of Good Hearts."

It was a special moment seeing them smile and do something so sweet for me. I went back to our compound and told the rest of the guys. We were cleaning our weapons and talking about the rest of our shift when the news came in. Private Lopez, my best friend who was on patrol the shift after me, didn't come back in. His team reported that he had been taken while helping a widow lift a piece of furniture into her room. It had been in that same building where the school was. Hours later, we heard of the pictures and what happened to Private Lopez. I never knew anger like the anger I felt that raged through me that day. He had been ambushed by a hostile faction, the same radical tribe that tormented the innocent people of Somalia by cutting them off from their food supply. He was then later dragged naked in the streets. They were sending a message to us, the Marines. They wanted us to stop helping the innocent and poor Somalians.

So, you ask me why I gave up on my faith? Where was God when my best friend was killed and his body humiliated like that just for helping people? Poor people. For that matter, where was anyone for me either? All while I'm trying to help orphans in another country, my fiancé moves on to another man. She left me. I had no one left when I came home, but a foolish brother and a broken family of my own. They say join the military and help your country. All the while they send us to help people in another country who didn't care if we lived or died. Just wait; your kindness will bite you in the … um, just trust me. Everyone lets you down.

CHAPTER 14
Thy Seven Griefs

Dear Mr. Reynolds,

Once again, I am horrified at what you have seen and been through. I have no words to console you, but I will continue to pray that you can calm the storms brought on by such vile human indecency. Your friend, Mr. Lopez, was a special soul that was taken from this life in a horrible way. As you probably remember, the apostles Peter and Paul both died in brutal ways, too. Martyred in Rome under Emperor Nero. Paul was beheaded and Peter was crucified upside down. The rest of the apostles suffered similar fates.

This may not be a consolation to you and your suffering, but from what you have told me about the good acts of the Marines in Somalia, rejoice in yours and Mr. Lopez's good deeds. You both were a blessing to the poor and sick.

I cannot say the same for myself in my early years. I can't continue to let you talk so highly of me if you don't know the whole truth of who I was. You see, I loved someone as you loved your fiancé, but I hurt him deeply. It was not the other way around. His name was Myers. This was before my husband. Myers was a baker's son with curly brown hair and a sweet smile. We were young then. Young and in love thinking the world would revolve around our love, similar to how it was for you and Emily.

"Good day, Myers. How is your father?" I asked him with my hands clutched in front of me.

His smile faded slightly. "He is well. What troubles you? Just a few days ago, you were smiling. We had a plan to help you and Cecilia. I thought it was a good plan."

"It was a good plan, Myers."

"Then what is it?" he asked.

"It just isn't enough," I told him. I stepped back and followed a passing carriage with my tear-soaked eyes. Myers was someone who would never give up. He would find a way, even if it killed him. I couldn't bear to be a burden to him. He was young still, as was I. But he could still find a young woman without the added stress of a sick sister-in-law. In my heart, I felt it was the right thing for both of us.

"What do you mean?" he asked. His furrowed brows showed what his mind was already realizing.

My eyes met his. "I do not love you. My father was right. It was just a phase. I am to marry Henry Bartholomew this spring. I know you will not understand right now, but in time you will."

He began shaking his head. "No, no, this is not you. These are not your words. They are your father's. Your father is not here anymore. You can choose now. Choose us."

I began to cry. "I am sorry. I must go."

He reached for me, but I ran away as fast as I could while hearing his broken heart yell out my name behind me until I could no longer hear his voice.

CHAPTER 15
Pity Lady Save

I slammed the diary shut on the nun's final words. The sun was making its way up to its mid-morning position. I needed a drink. Hopefully that bar was open. As I got my prosthetic back on and my shoes, I cursed myself for feeling good for a moment. What was I thinking last night? Hoping the nun was different. All women are heartless.

I jumped on my bike and headed a few blocks before parking by the stone back wall of Anchors Aweigh.

When I walked into the bar, Alexis was there. Her eyes were tired and her posture more slouched. "I need a vodka," I demanded before I even sat down.

She eyed me. "This early?"

"Your bar is open, isn't it?"

"Yes," she replied. She wore the usual black cropped shirt revealing a lot of her midriff. You'd never have been able to tell she had a grown daughter. Even her long reddish, brown hair had not a smidgen of grey in it, just a few dyed in blonde tips below her shoulders.

"Then what is the problem?" I asked impatiently.

"Okie dokie, one vodka on the rocks coming up."

She walked off and I nodded at Steve from behind the bar. He gave me an open fingered salute that left his eyebrow with a twist of his wrist.

I smiled and shook my head as I watched him go back to chopping his onions.

Alexis brought me the drink. I downed it.

"Wow, what is your deal today?" she asked.

I shrugged. "Why do women always think it's society that makes their life hard? Women have it good. Smile, look pretty, and the world is your oyster. Women are running companies now. More educated than most us men. My best friend's wife is even getting promoted to some great job in California where she'll make more money than him. So, what's the problem with your sex?"

Alexis slammed the vodka bottle on the bar. "Seriously? Is that what you're here to talk about today? Today of all days?"

A man sat down next to me. "Miss, I'll take a Manhattan."

"Coming right up." She pulled out a tall glass and began pouring the liquor into his glass from a smoked bottle. "There you go."

I leaned over the bar on my forearms. "What is your deal today?"

"Why? Are you the only one that can have bad days."

I shrugged. "No, but I was just curious."

"It's nothing."

"What is it?" I pressed.

"None of your business." She moved away but stopped walking. Then, she slowly turned back around. "Trey, I like you. But you are still a man."

"What does that mean?"

"Remember I told you how people have several sides to them?"

"Um no," I smarted back.

"The night at the bar when you were watching that reporter about hauntings around Galveston. I told you I didn't like him."

"Remind me why."

"He has too many hidden sides."

"Are you talking multiple personalities?" I asked.

"No. A person with multiple personalities is not only rare but when one personality takes over, the others have no control over the body anymore. I'm talking about the majority of us that have many different sides to them. That's human nature."

"Like a devil on one shoulder and an angel on another?"

She rolled her eyes and pulled back her fluffy curls into a low ponytail. "It's not that simple. I'm not talking just good and bad. I'm saying the masks that people wear and the baggage they hold within them that they hide from everyone, especially their family. Some hold hurt, shame, or they simply think they can handle their problems on their own."

Alexis always seemed a little eccentric, with all her incense candles around the bar. I sighed. "Okay. What about it?"

"Just my point is to not judge a book by its cover. Including yourself, war hero."

My body warmed. "I'm not a war hero."

She leaned over in front of me and rested her chin on her palm. "Maybe in the beginning you wanted to be a war hero and maybe you trusted everyone to be the same when you came back. Or better yet, you hoped they'd be in awe of you. Whatever you wanted, you're dealing with different sides of who you are too," she said and handed me a fresh drink.

"I didn't bring that up about women for therapy," I said before sipping it.

"It's bothering you, though."

I swallowed my drink and raised my hands by my sides. "I just don't understand why women always choose the option that includes money."

"Not necessarily money."

"What do you mean?" I asked.

She smirked and leaned over on the bar. "History lesson."

I threw up my hands. "Fine. Shoot."

She began with, "Who voted first in America after the white man changed the law, a white woman or a black man?"

I thought back over my history lessons, but that was not something that stuck out in my mind. "A white woman, of course. Blacks were still treated horribly back then."

"Wrong!" she said and raised up to her full petite height.

"What?" I asked somewhat in shock. Now, I knew I hadn't been taught that in school. I would have remembered it.

"The powers that be gave that honor to the black man first, because why?"

I shrugged.

She continued, "Because they were *men*. Now, you say that women can run companies and do just as well as men, right?"

"Yes."

"I beg to differ. I told you about my daughter getting that huge promotion, right?"

"Yes."

"Just a few days ago, she told me how she got it. She wanted to come clean. The guilt was killing her."

I shook my head. "I don't understand."

"What did you say women do best, 'smile and look pretty'? Well, what good is that if the man can't have her?"

"What are you saying?" I asked and noticed Larry come into the bar. Walking close to him was his pretty black and brown German Shephard.

"Hey, Jarhead," he said and I just smiled back. He sat down next to me. The dog sniffed my prosthetic. "What's wrong with y'all?"

Alexis frowned. "Aww nothing. I'm just filling in the war hero here."

I nodded at him and then turned to Alexis asking, "Then tell me. What was it?"

She paused and then continued, "She slept with her boss. That's how she moved up so she could get out of her college debt and pay rent. Even though she hated herself, I saw it for what it was. She was surviving, so she didn't have to call on me for help. I'm upside down on attorney bills from my divorce, Trey. My daughter was trying to carry the burden all on her own and then come back to pay off all my bills."

I lifted my brows. "So? She could have found another job."

"Another job? It would be more of the same. Actually, it could be worse."

"How?" I asked.

Alexis poured Larry only a coke. "Her boss could have been a woman that would see her as a threat and not hire her at all."

"What kind of threat?"

"That's how some women are, Trey. They are brutally competitive because if another woman looks or performs better than her, then the…" Alexis lifted her fingers making air quotes. "*The Man* would notice the other woman over the boss woman. No matter how much progress we women have made, Trey. Men still run this world. Women have just found a way to maneuver through it in order to survive."

"Wow. That's a lot of information."

"There's a lot to people like that, Trey. A lot. And everyone has a story hiding among those many sides of themselves. Everyone."

I heard Larry laugh next to me. "Agreed. Hey, Alexis, is Steve making some of those fried crawfish po'boys for the lunch special today?" he asked her before turning to me. "Ever tried them? Lunch is on me. Let me treat you."

Alexis rolled her eyes at him, having realized what he was doing it. Then, she sighed and walked to the back.

I addressed Larry, "Oh no, I'm good. Thanks, though. You do come in here a lot, don't you?"

"My favorite bar. And that Steve can really cook."

I nodded. "Yeah, he can."

"So, what's all the back and forth about this early?" Larry asked while dropping a pretzel down to Stella from the bar snack bowl.

"Nothing. Just about women in general. So where did you find your dog?"

Larry looked down at her. "She's a service dog. But she's not a full-breed."

"She's not?"

"Nope. Her owner found her at an animal shelter. Turns out that the lady, Mrs. Sutter, wanted a dog she could get trained to help her once she started losing her sight. But she couldn't afford a full-breed."

I looked down at Stella, who had already finished off the pretzel. Her tall ears were perked up, but she wasn't begging her owner for another pretzel. She had a lot of self-control that I admired. "How did you get her?"

"I inherited her, I guess you'd say. Mrs. Sutter didn't live long after she went completely blind, so Stella went back to the animal shelter. I was at a low point, so the guys I fish with said maybe a dog would help. I was in the same boat as Mrs. Sutter. I couldn't afford a service animal. The VA had brochures of organizations that were supplying well-trained dogs, but their waiting list was too long. One day, Alexis told me about how her friend at the animal shelter talked about this great dog. Two Christmases ago, Alexis surprised me with her."

Stella dropped her head onto her paws and let only her eyes look up at me. I leaned down to pet her.

Larry smiled. "You didn't cross any line with Alexis that she doesn't deserve. She's got a foul temperament. But she does have a point about women. As you know, I've lost two wives that told me they couldn't be military wives. I felt that same resentment towards women, but there are good ones out there." He looked down at Stella and dropped another pretzel. "Not just females that are dogs."

"Yeah, I know."

"The thing is, most women are really good. Sometimes it just comes down to finding them at the right time in their life."

Right at that moment, Stella gave out a loud bark. Larry and I both laughed.

CHAPTER 16
Think of the Babe

The entire time, Rebecca, myself, and Georgy were mixing the batter for the cookies, Rebecca and I were distracted. It had been awhile since I heard from Trey. And there was something he said in the last entry he made. Something about my kindness would bite me in the… something. He did not elaborate. I guessed I knew what he meant, though.

Georgy slapped a bag of flour on the countertop in front of me. "Sister, you and Rebecca are not with it today," she said and widened her eyes as she looked over to Rebecca.

Rebecca nodded.

I wiped my hands on the apron Rebecca had provided us. The fabrics were matching with pink and green peony flower designs all over.

Georgy lifted one brow at me and pushed harder into the flour and water mixture. Rebecca continued to keep an oblivious expression on her face. I cleared my throat. "I just have many things on my mind."

"The orphans? Is everything well with them?" Rebecca asked. Her eyes gave away a flash of true concern.

"No, no, not just them. I worry about everyone."

Georgy wiped her hands on her apron. "Oh look at that, ladies. We will need more cinnamon."

Rebecca tilted her head. "Cinnamon? I thought we measured that out correctly."

Georgy waved her question away. "Nope. I tasted the last batch. It is not enough. Let me check the larder room for more."

"Larder? I thought you were looking for more spices. We definitely do not need more oil." Rebecca pointed at the jar referring to Georgy's mistake.

Georgy laughed. "Oh, right, but that's where I keep certain spices. I will be right back," she said and disappeared out of the room.

My jaw was slack. This was not the correct way to handle such situations. I knew Georgy came from a harsher upbringing, but surely she would have known better than to make it so obvious what we were up to.

I turned away towards the window to hide my face. It was an embarrassing moment for me. There was not a chance that I would bring up anything fragile. I lowered my eyes thinking of something to say that would lighten the mood.

Before I could come up with anything, I was relieved of my worry. Rebecca sighed behind me. "Sister?"

I turned and saw blue eyes that had turned almost grey and lost. "Yes?"

"I had been wanting to ask you something."

"Ask."

She swallowed hard. "How far is a husband allowed to go before he violates his vows?"

I was taken aback. "How far?"

"I mean…" she took a deep breath and tears ran down her cheek. "When you arrived into my life, I realized that there could actually be someone that I could talk to. I had thought about going to Father O'Brien, but I knew what the reply would be."

"And what would that be?"

"That a Catholic wife bears even the worst of her husband's sins."

I walked slowly up to her and grabbed her cold, tiny hands. "I am here if you want to talk. I can't tell you that I would offer any consolations that differ from a priest, but you should know that I am here."

"He has had several mistresses," she blurted out just as I thought the conversation was over for today and that we could revisit it at a different time when she was ready. Apparently, the sadness was brimming so much at the top of her being that she couldn't hold it in anymore.

"I'm sorry," I said.

She looked down the hall making sure that Georgy wasn't returning just yet. "And he's obvious with it. My heart is broken, but yet I must take care of our children and keep a smile on my face and continue to play the charade of a perfect marriage in public and I just…."

I didn't think first, I pulled her in for a hug. I knew the act of hugging others was not something nuns were allowed to do. But as her breathing continued unsteadily and the weight of her tears made her shoulders droop beneath me, I didn't care about rules.

I held her while she cried thinking of what to say. I said a silent prayer to God asking for guidance and words from Him but again, no reply. As Rebecca wept without hearing a comforting word from me, I grew angry. Was it at God? Was it because her situation reminded me partly of my own marriage back in England?

She pulled away and her face was splotchy and red. I studied her embarrassed expression and shook my head. "Marriage is sacred in God's eyes. But the success of the sacrament of marriage should not rely on the wife alone. As it says in the Bible, a husband should love their wives as their own bodies. All men love themselves and wouldn't do that to themselves, right? Then it sounds like your husband is not at peace with himself. A wife's responsibility is to help him and respect him when he fails, but never was it written that you should continue to be mistreated." As I was telling Rebecca those words, I thought back to my marriage. I had doubted my choices, but realized right then that there was no changing my former husband.

I stepped away and let go of her hands. "Pray and seek guidance from our Father on how to help your husband. If no change comes, your decisions ahead need to be decided with God's guidance. I cannot tell you what to do."

She wiped her eyes. "No, I know, Sister. I am sorry to burden you with this."

"No, you don't understand what I am saying. As a woman, I know your pain. But almost too well. And that is the problem. You need someone unbiased to guide you now."

"I see. Yes, I understand. I can't believe I blubbered out all that," she said visibly shaken.

I shook my head. "No, don't do that. It took courage to tell me this. And you were not wrong seeking guidance from the church. I'm just saying that I don't want to tell you wrong because of what I have been through."

Her eyes squinted. "Are you saying a man has done this to you?"

I opened my mouth and then closed it again before giving a slight nod.

"I am so sorry, Sister," she said. And even though it was frowned upon, she pulled me into a tight hug. "We were meant to meet. I believe it now. You give me strength to handle what I am going through. Now, I know that God is with me. Thank you so much."

She pulled away and smiled. "I will do as you advised. I will try to help my husband. I will not give up on him. Then, I will seek God's continued guidance if it becomes too much for me alone."

As Georgy slowly came back into the kitchen, I added, "God is already with you. He will give you your strength to handle whatever comes."

A few hours later, I went into Mrs. Davenport's room, closed the door, and took a moment to think over everything. After a few minutes, I pulled out my diary to write.

Dear Mr. Reynolds,

I did not see you write back. I hope I did not discourage our friendship by my telling you what all I said. I write again in hopes that you will read on anyway. I wanted to tell you what happened today. Paul, one of our youngest orphans, started walking today. I had lifted him up on his feet and barely let my fingers slip from his and then he leaned forward. His first step was towards me. He went for a second step and turned a little towards Trey. Trey waved at him to keep going, and he did. He took a few more steps and fell into Trey. We all clapped.

You may not ever write to me again. I sit here and think that maybe I am writing into the void of nothingness now. That is fine. I still want to get my thoughts out, whether you ever read this or not.

My story goes back further than the moment I broke my true love's heart. It goes back to the day I broke my father's heart.

My mother died when I was twelve. The birth of my sister, Cecilia, was too much on her body. After that, my father wouldn't hold my sister. Her tiny body was placed in my hands, in my care. From then on, Cecilia was my world. However, that little baby suffered too. She was born with many infantile defects that the doctors couldn't remedy. I knew from a young age that I would always be the one to take care of her, to watch over her, and to be her guide even into her adulthood.

As I continued writing, I saw Cecilia's cherub face looking up at me. In the background, my father was arguing with the doctor...

"I will not listen to this. I lose my wife and now my second daughter is deformed."

The doctor's voice came back so low that I could barely hear him say, "Sir, please."

"Don't go there. Get out!" my father yelled back.

The front door slammed and after a few minutes, in walked my father. His face was no longer stern but weathered with several new lines around his mouth and eyes. At the time, I thought he was very selfish.

He sat down next to me. "Amelia, your mother was the strong one. I can't…"

I placed my free hand on his shoulder. "Father, stop. God will help us through this."

"Your mother believed as you. I'm just not as faithful, my dear."

I lowered my head in an attempt to calm my nerves. "You can't mean that. Faith is what you need now most of all."

"Don't lecture me on what I need, Amelia."

I couldn't hold my feelings in no matter how hard I tried. "You lost your wife, Father. I lost my mother. And this is how you act? I never thought I would see the day that my father could become a self-righteous coward."

His blood shot eyes pierced mine, sending a surge of regret throughout my body. But he didn't say anything back. He lowered his head, stood up, and walked out as I held the baby that he would never look at again.

CHAPTER 17
Within the Manger

Margaret,

I needed time to think. If we're being honest here, then I will say that at first, I didn't want to ever talk to you again. But I'm back. I had to talk to you.

By the way, you called yourself Amelia in that last entry about your father. Is that your real name?

So anyway, I gotta say that I now realize that after all these years, it wasn't something I did that made Emily quit on me. She may have just needed the money and security. You see, both of us grew up in a town that was devastated by the closing of factories. We both came from divorced families. Actually, it was why we related so well.

I just want to say that a lot happened to Emily when she was young, too. I always felt that it was why she was always searching for something better. When she opened a bottle of wine, she would say it was to make her feel better than who she really was. "Rich people drink wine. We should too," she would always say. I went off to war because it was my only option to support her. We tried to make it work, but a few months into it, she started hanging out a lot with the Mayor's son, Carlton. Deep down, back then, I knew why she did that, but I didn't want to admit it to myself. I knew she wanted a life of wine and fancy. I started to realize that Carlton was her ticket to that life. It became more obvious on her 10th letter...

Webster's big eyes were taking me in. "Trey, what is it? Can I read the letter now?" Webster asked as he then began shifting from one foot to the other.

"No."

Private Jones walked in behind Webster. "Kid in here, Sergeant? You know they'll tan your hide for that?"

"Don't you have somewhere to be, Private?"

Jones set down his pack. "I was just saying…"

"Go away."

Webster looked back and forth between us.

The younger Marine shrugged. "Sure sir. Guess I caught you at a bad time."

"Bye, Private."

Webster watched the other Marine walk out. "I'm sorry to be a bother. I will go now too."

I shook my head. "No, it's not you. But yeah, it's getting late."

I clutched the letter in my hand as Webster snuck out. I couldn't believe it. How could this be?

Emily was pregnant.

CHAPTER 18
Help us Now

Dear Mr. Reynolds,

I am thankful to hear from you again. I am sorry to hear about Emily and the pregnancy. I am assuming that it was with another man. Please give her grace as it will do you better than her. I know that doesn't make sense now, but it is true.

You see, perspective is a word that not everyone fully grasps the meaning of. In human nature, perspective is everything. For me, I did what I did because women had no choice during my time. I do not know how it is where you are, but from what I am hearing about your Emily, maybe nothing has changed. I am so sad to hear that. I'm not sure what happened with her, but I hope you can one day find peace with it.

I will confess, I do not fully agree with the church. How much of the Catholic faith do you know about? It is not the church that I fully follow, Mr. Reynolds. It is the faith.

Do you know of Mary Magdalene? If not, I'll tell you. Mary was the one who committed adultery and then Jesus saved her from getting stoned. He took her in, even though his apostles disagreed because of what all Mary had done. The church speaks of her a little, but I believe she had a bigger place with Jesus. I believe that God found her just as special as the apostles. But like you said, as the years passed, some things changed. But one thing that was left and written for us to read in the scriptures was about how it was Mary who Jesus first revealed himself to after he rose from the dead. Why her? Why this woman? A former sinner? You see, Trey, the church is no different from the way society is because it is run by man. But the faith, the core of the Catholic faith, is different. And that is why I stay. I stay for Jesus. I stay to do the work that Jesus needs me to do. I sinned greatly when I was younger. It was how I, as a woman, was able to survive. If your time is still like mine, there is much you need to understand about a woman and her options.

And yes, my birth and baptismal name is Amelia. Nuns change their names when they take their vows.

God bless and safe keeping,

Sister Margaret

CHAPTER 19
Lady of the Wave

Sister Margaret,

I'm not sure about the grace thing, but I understand what you are saying about Mary Magdalene. What you have told me about your past and what Emily has done to me is really hard for me to understand. I don't see myself as a particularly forgiving person, I guess. After all, I've never really been easy on myself either. I was never really happy with who I was. Not until the Marine Corps.

The proudest I ever felt about myself was the day they pinned that anchor on me at my Marine Corps graduation. I had become part of something that meant something. It wasn't easy. The bootcamp alone almost killed me. Not every candidate passes. The United States Marine Corps only takes the best. Or at least back then, I thought I was one of the best. When we first landed in Somalia and heard the bullets firing at us, things started to change. That's when the cocky young eighteen to twenty something year-olds begin to see themselves differently.

Marines are usually always the first to touch down and secure an area. We had a rough go at it for a few weeks until we finally got a secure site. We felt at that time that we could breathe a sigh of relief, especially because the letters and packages began coming in from our families from back in the States.

I stopped writing for a moment and lowered my eyes to my hand that had begun trembling. I hadn't talked about what all happened with Emily to anyone, nor had I cared to think about those events since it happened. But there I was, sitting on a dusty old mattress listening to the wind blow outside bringing rain in from off the Gulf of Mexico.

I picked up the pen to write again.

Sister Margaret,

I'm feeling odd, almost scared, but I want to write through this…

As I wrote the breeze picked up outside and suddenly I found my mind drifting off and back into Somalia. The sounds changed from a soft howl to loud helicopter rotors.

My hand was no longer shaking, and I was not alone. Sitting in front of me with some pretty white teeth behind a big ole grin, was Webster, the little Somalian boy I took under my wing a few weeks into my tour. I continued to write in the diary and thought about how proud Webster always was to come into the compound with us.

In front of me, I saw Webster lift his hand and say, "Come on!"

I shook my head at him. While I wrote in the diary, my mind was back in Somalia with my little friend.

Webster continued pleading as he held up an unopened letter in front of me. "Why don't you just open it?"

I smiled at how well Webster's English had gotten. "Because it's the twelfth letter and I haven't read the eleventh yet."

I pointed at the right corner of the envelope. "See? We have our friends and family number them, so we know."

"But why?"

"It's what deployed military people do, Webster. We read the letters from our families in order. No exceptions. We all do it."

"That's a stupid rule."

"Maybe, but we miss our family so much that reading the letters in order makes us feel like we are there with them living in the present with them. Make sense?"

"I still think you should read it now."

"Nope," I said and put the letter in my chest pocket. If I were to be honest, I was too scared to read it. I knew it was coming. The stupid girl was pregnant with another man's baby. So why did I still hang on with any sense of hope? What was I thinking?

Then there was screaming. I grabbed my rifle and rushed out to the sound of bombs.

"Sergeant Reynolds, left gate," another Marine called out.

"Yes sir."

I ran without a second thought as another explosion ripped through the air. In front of me about twenty feet was a car on fire. I ran up to the Marine on duty, Private First-Class Roberts. "What's going on?"

Squinty blue eyes looked back at me. "They were shooting. We took them out, sir."

The warmth of the flames carried over across the checkpoint. Then there were more shots. We both dropped down to assess the direction of the attack.

The sun's rays had just appeared from behind a cloud making the light off the opponent's barrels easier to see. I pointed to the building a hundred yards from us. "There! On the roof!"

"Got it." The younger Marine lifted his weapon with me. A few shots and the threat was neutralized.

"Good work, Roberts."

He shook his head. "I may have gotten one."

I saw a slither of blood run out of his sleeve. I pulled up the fabric. Thankfully, it just grazed him. "Go get that checked out. I'll keep watch."

"Yes sir."

As he retreated, two sets of boots came running up behind me. "Sergeant Reynolds?"

"Yes."

"Did you have a kid in here? That Webster boy again?"

I kept my eyes on the building ahead intensely assessing the situation to make sure there wasn't another threat. I didn't pay much attention to the tone in my Captain's voice.

"He comes in sometimes for supplies, sir. I know it's not allowed. I'll tell him."

Captain Simmons kneeled down beside me and that's when I saw the look in his eyes. "You better come see. I'm sorry. It's not good."…

My mind came back to the old house making me realize that I was no longer in that horrible place overseas. Before me was the vision of a red bird tapping the window with his beak. My hands were shaking uncontrollably making me almost drop the diary. The flashback had been tough. Everything about that was hard to share. I closed Sister Margaret's diary and noticed that the storm must have blown over since the bird had stopped by.

There was also a stillness in the room that was extremely unnerving. I reached for the vodka that I had left on my nightstand. A few swigs and I was calm enough to lay down. I grabbed the diary and opened it back up to the page I had been on. I couldn't believe it, I really did write all of that down about Webster.

CHAPTER 20
Up to the Shrine

A tear fell down my cheek for Mr. Reynolds as I took a shallow breath and grasped the ivory quill Mrs. Davenport had given me it as a gift when I nursed her through one of the toughest nights of her sickness. She kept saying how I should be back at the orphanage with the children. How unimportant an old widower was. I ignored the self-pity and continued praying.

She coughed and coughed before handing me the pearly quill. She said it had been in her family for generations as a rosary before the ivory was molded into a casing for the quill. She had said, "My father found more use of it as a writing tool than a prayer necklace. It is fitting that you take it."

I wanted to deny the generosity, but it would only serve to hurt her more.

After she passed away, Georgy insisted that I take a few hours rest in Ms. Davenport's room before I headed back to the orphanage on the beach. Sitting there one day, praying and hoping for a reply from God that never came, was when I decided I needed a way to express my feelings without scrutiny from the church.

Sitting here and reading over Mr. Reynold's words, even with prayers, I didn't know how to respond or comfort him anymore. I could now see why he suffered so. Instead of offering more words of comfort, I decided to tell him everything about me. He had shared so much with me. I felt I needed to do the same with him.

I heard Henry holler out, "Frederick! I told you to inform me when she leaves!" Henry's voice was so loud that I could hear it clearly up the stairs and down the hall.

I rushed out of my room in hopes that I could calm Henry down before he beat another servant. After all, it had been my fault. I left the night before to meet up with Myers. He had been my refuge since Henry started hitting me. It was the only way I could survive. The night before, I had told Myers that I thought Henry knew of our relationship. Myers had begged me to leave Henry, but I couldn't. Now, I had put the servants in more danger for my selfishness.

As I ran down to the library, I cursed myself for being like my father. The same words I used that broke my father's heart, I yelled to myself just as I was rushing into the library.

Henry had thrown another glass at Frederick and then turned with eyes of fury toward me.

I froze and stepped back. "Henry, please don't punish Frederick for what I have done. Please."

He hissed at me. "Ungrateful woman."

Before I could duck, he threw a glass that hit me square in the face. The pain was so overwhelming, I collapsed to the floor.

"Sir, please!" I heard Frederick holler out.

As I tried to stand, fists slammed into my chest and sharp pains stabbed into my stomach as Henry kicked me violently. "Everything I did for you, Amelia. You and that idiot sister of yours. You have embarrassed me for the last time."

I could tell by the anger in his words that these were the last breaths I would take.

I remembered Frederick running out to get help, but the kicks and punches continued. Between beatings, I managed to stand in hopes of escaping out the door. But Henry was too strong. He pushed me into the wall next to the fireplace. I grabbed at the table next to me hoping to find something to help. I managed to get a grasp of the iron poker for the fireplace and stabbed it right into Henry's chest.

He stood there in shock, as did I. Then, he grabbed me and threw me into the mantle of the fireplace. My vision got blurry. All I remembered after that was the candle on the mantle falling into the curtains and the fire starting. Darkness claimed me as I passed out. When I woke, I saw Frederick's face above me. He had lifted me into his arms and was carrying me out of the house.

There was darkness again. When I woke up the next time, the entire house was in flames. I could barely talk, but my eyes searched the grounds for Cecilia. "Cecilia! Frederick, where is Cecilia?"

"I'm sorry. Miss Amelia, her room was right above the library. The fire spread so quickly. I am so sorry."

Mr. Reynolds. I did it. It was all my fault. God had been with me for many years now. But Mr. Reynolds, you have probably seen in my diary that God has stopped talking to me this last year. I don't know why. Sometimes I worry that it is because of what I've done. That was part of the reason why I started the diary. Just a way to think things out. I never knew why He stopped talking to me. Do you think it is because of what I've been hiding? Not to others, but to myself?

CHAPTER 21
See the Glimmer

Dear Margaret,

Do not blame yourself. You were the victim. The man beat you and yet still you write that it was all your fault.

I stopped writing and stood up on uneasy legs. I picked up the candy bar wrappers I had thrown on the floor while thinking about what Margaret just told me. And I thought I was messed up. Life sucks.

I sat down again and looked around at the four tall windows on both the north and south walls. I let myself imagine Sister Margaret walking in and smiling over at me.

She was paranoid about someone at the orphanage finding her diary and that was why she hid it in the house with Georgy. It made sense. The things she confessed in that little book were really intense. Really tough stuff for a nun. But then again, I wondered if many nuns carried with them sad stories. Such pure hearts tormented with so much baggage. Or did they? Isn't that what becoming a nun is good for? God washes away their sins when they commit to Him? But something was holding her hostage. It was keeping her from accepting God's help. Dang, was that my problem too?

I pictured Margaret sitting by one of these windows. Maybe the one on the north side since it faced the Galveston Bay. I could tell she enjoyed transferring her thoughts onto paper. Her diary wasn't just to decompress. She wrote because she enjoyed the process of thinking things out thoroughly. I used to enjoy writing. For both of us, writing to each other had to have been helping us.

I sat back down and opened the diary to write again.

Margaret,

I wasn't expecting to read about all that. I had to step away and take a breather, because I'm angry that he hit you. I hate him and yet I've never met him. You're an amazing woman. I can't imagine what you've been through either. Thank you for sharing back.

I can tell you also enjoy writing. Did you ever write a story for others to read? I used to write stories. Lots of them. You'll laugh but they were about pirates come back as ghosts. Anyway, I was on track for a scholarship in English Literature, but I lost the drive somewhere along the way. I haven't wanted to write since I was sixteen. Meeting you and putting my thoughts down for someone else to read has been nice. I hope you feel the same.

I think you are just as courageous for doing the same by writing to me. You say you are embarrassed by all this. You shouldn't be. We are human, Margaret. We make mistakes and have doubts. Don't let that get you down. But I understand. I do it too.

Anyway, you said you never go out into the water. You just walk on the beach while the kids play. What a waste. The reason I moved down here was because of the ocean. I love to walk in the surf. Feel the warm water surge around my feet. I challenge you to be more courageous. And then tell me all about it. I can't wait to hear.

Also, while you are out there, find a conch. You really can hear the ocean when you put it up to your ear. I guess receiving that conch from my brother and sister-in-law from back at the VA

I closed up the diary and placed it in its hiding place as the blinking from my answering machine got my attention. More messages? I stood up and clicked on the button. This one was from my mom.

Her shaky voice said, "Trey, please call me back. Something has happened. Call me right away, please."

I stood there looking at the machine. I did not want to talk to my mom, but something told me by the sound of her voice, that it was something bad.

Picking up the phone, I called before thinking twice. She answered immediately. "Hello?"

"Mom, it's me."

A deep breath came across the line. "Oh, thank God. Trey, I have news."

"What is it? I know you are getting remarried and I don't care."

"No honey, it's your dad."

I squeezed the phone tighter. "What about my dad?"

"There were complications."

My palms started to sweat. "What complications? Last I heard, he was suffering from indigestion."

She paused and took another deep breath. "It turns out, he had been having heart problems, not stomach issues. Baby, he passed away last night."

The room started to spin. "What the hell do you mean?"

My mother cleared her throat and then said, "He had a heart attack. He had been having the precursors of a heart attack a few days before but thought it was just indigestion. I'm sorry, baby. He's gone."

I dropped the phone.

CHAPTER 22
Down on us Afar

I put on my rosary and headed out of my room to the carriage before anyone else was awake. Mornings came earlier for those living in a coastal area. I didn't know if it was because the sun seemed brighter or the seagulls were louder than typical land birds.

I got to the hospital and noticed that there were more sick people lined up along the walls. The outbreak seemed to be getting worse. I waved at the nurses and headed over to the supply room to retrieve the week's supplies for the orphanage. "Sister Margaret?"

I turned to see Dr. Lee coming towards me. "I would say that it probably isn't good for you to keep coming here with the recent surge in sicknesses, but I believe you are immune as I am. My mother, that is another matter. She really wants to be a part of that parade."

I clasped my hands in front of me. "If it makes her happy."

"She can be happy tending to her gardens. I really wish you could convince her to not get involved in this crazy petri dish along the streets of Galveston."

Dr. Lee had a very domineering personality. He was especially over protective of his aging mother. I lowered my head. "I hope you are not asking me to get involved in a family matter."

When I looked up, his wide eyes told me that he didn't realize what he was doing. "I'm sorry, Sister. I didn't mean to ask that of you."

I touched his hand that was holding the clipboard for his recent patient. "I knew you weren't. You are just tired. You are working so much. You need to rest."

"I can't. It is my duty."

"Doctor Lee?" a nurse behind him pulled his worried eyes off of me.

"Yes?"

She pointed behind her. "Your patient in room three twenty won't wake up."

"Pulse?"

"Yes."

He nodded at her and then turned back to me. "I have to go. Please be careful, Sister."

"I will. I'm going to pick up a two week supply this time."

"Very well. I will see you again in two weeks."

****

A little later, I made it back to the tenant's house. Georgy was at work. I had just missed her. I went upstairs and took in the room. Georgy had the windows open to let in the breeze. It felt nice. I knelt down by my hiding spot and said a short prayer.

My fingers trembled slightly when I lifted the wood plank and pulled out my book. I had come accustomed to hearing from Mr. Reynolds. When I turned to the fifteenth page, I saw his usual sloppy handwriting. My heart lit up. He said, "We are just human." He was right. He wrote a something about playing on the beach. And then he wrote, "Be courageous."

I closed my diary and immediately headed back to the orphanage. I grabbed several girls from Sister Mary's group and told them we were going on an adventure. Hand in hand, we all walked down to the beach. I explained the usual rules to the children and then let them tarry off to play.

Staring at the waves, I got a slight chill from the breeze, even though the day was still very hot.

Immediately, I smiled. Mr. Reynolds loved the beach water. I was going to see why for myself.

I took off my shoes, one at a time and very slowly. Then my socks. The sand felt slippery. I lifted the skirts on my habit, looked all around, and when I saw that the children were not paying attention, I took my first few steps into the water. The first wave splashed at my lower calves. It almost tickled at first. It was a sensation I didn't expect, so the surprise was even more thrilling.

Another warm wave came in. My balance was thrown off-center so much that I took a step to the side to keep from falling. That was when it happened. Something I hadn't done in years; I laughed. I couldn't believe it. I continued to stand there feeling like a child myself as more waves broke against my legs. At first, I tried not to get my skirts wet, but then I dropped them and let them swirl around in the water. I raised my eyes to the sky and thanked God that he brought this strange man into my life, no matter how odd the circumstances were.

Sister Mary's voice came across the breeze as I turned to a sweet smile. "Well, Sister Margaret, what are you doing?"

I sunk inside myself. "I, um, thought I saw a jellyfish and wanted to keep the children away."

Sister Mary laughed. "Oh, is that right?" she said sarcastically and lifted her skirt to walk in with me. "I love the way this feels, too."

I was shocked. "You come out here like this?"

"Of course. I love the water. I grew up by the ocean back in Scotland. But not up in the highlands like you did as a child. Still, take my word for it, this water is warmer and not as pretty. But the ocean just makes you feel alive."

I nodded. "I'm not an ocean person, not yet. I do miss the highlands." I shrugged. "I still wish my father never took us to England. There was so much beauty in Scotland."

We both smiled and took in the moment. What a lovely day.

****

When I got back into town a few days later, I couldn't wait to tell Trey about our outing.

Dear Mr. Reynolds,

You are truly a blessing. I had never had as much fun as I did the other day. I went out into the water. It was so nice. I even let my habit get wet. The children and I danced in the surf until the sun started to set. Thank you for convincing me to take that risk. From a young age, I thought I had to give up on fun things and take care of my sister only. It conditioned me to miss out on life in general. Thank you for helping me see that.

I hope all is well with you. I would be dishonest if I didn't say that I wasn't concerned that I hadn't heard from you again. It has been a few days and there weren't any entries in my diary. I understand that it takes me a few days to write back, but usually I come back here to see several entries. My heart says that there is something wrong. Please write back when you can. I want to share more about my outing with the children.

Little Trey, as you call him, is doing well still. His abilities in math have improved so much that Sister Anna constantly talks about him. He has also made many friends. I hope to hear from you soon.

God bless and be well,

Sister Margaret

CHAPTER 23
Pittsburgh

Emily changed a little. Her hair was darker and her hips were wider. She also didn't exude the same amount of confidence that I used to admire about her. Or maybe it was because my confidence grew from my time in the Marines.

"Where is Carlton?" I asked her with a hint of disdain that I didn't care to hide.

She took a sip of the punch my uncle had made. "He's at work."

I looked around at all the black dresses and black suits that filled the living room of my uncle's house. "Emily, why did you come here?"

"To pay my respects."

"Okay. Thanks for coming," I said and turned away.

She grabbed my arm. "Wait. Can we talk?"

I turned back towards her. "About?"

"About why you never wrote me back."

Aggravation began to build. "What does that matter? You went on with your life. I went on with mine."

"See?" she snapped back. "I knew you would be like that."

"Like what?"

"Never mind," she blurted out and turned towards the kitchen.

I needed fresh air. I had to get out of that house with all those people and away from *her*. What did she expect? Either way, Emily was dead to me. They didn't make women like Margaret anymore. It was a sad thought, but I learned that truth just after a few letter exchanges between myself and a possible ghost. I didn't care if I'd never ever get to see Margaret. Just the little time I got to spend with her was all I needed.

When I walked out into the yard, I saw Jed standing there silently. I put my hands in my pockets and just stared at him.

"I need to talk to you," he said.

"I don't care to talk to you."

"I see Emily came," he mentioned while looking up at our uncle's house.

"Did you tell her about this funeral? Invite her? Jed, she's married. What's the point?"

"I didn't tell her. She read it in the paper. Cut her some slack, Trey. She lost a baby not long after you got back from Somalia. She's been through a lot, too."

I sarcastically added, "I would say that she and Carlton deserved that, but I'm not that heartless."

He nodded. "No, you're not."

"So, what do you want?"

Walking by us were a few other family members dressed in those cold and dull black outfits that I saw inside the house. I hated seeing a lot of people dressed in black. The family and friends gave us a sad smile and nodded on their way in.

Jed sucked in his lips. "I'm sorry about Dad. I really thought it was a ploy for attention."

I shook my head. "You're pathetic. Had I not listened to you, I would have gotten to see Dad before he died, maybe even help him."

"I'm pathetic? You're the one that disappeared. Wanted nothing to do with us. You took off with your self-pity and never returned our calls. You gave up on this family."

"Family? What family? That ended years ago."

"Is this still about Emily? Your leg? Your stupid war?" He walked forward and shoved me.

"Don't touch me, big brother. I'll lay you out right here and you know I'm trained to do it. Don't tempt me."

He put his hands on his hips. "See? That was your problem all along. That stupid chip on your shoulder. No one will ever reach you, will they? You will always carry this anger. You had it before the war and now it's even worse. Many people have tried to reach you. Tried to help you, but you were always so hard-headed. You believe what you believe."

"What the hell do you know about me?"

Jed shook his head. "Dad had too much time with you. He corrupted you."

"Don't talk about Dad like that as he's lying under fresh dirt. Don't you dare!" I yelled. Two kids that were playing in the yard got up and ran inside.

"Emily tried to talk to you after."

"After? And what do you know about Emily, a whore that acted just like Mom?"

"There it is again. Dad said it, so you believed it. Did you ever question anything?"

"What was there to question?"

He ignored my reply. "Mom tried, Emily tried."

"Why do you keep bringing up Emily? She left me, remember??? She left me while I was fighting a war that took my leg!!!!"

"She reached out to you again and you never responded. You never give anyone a chance once you make up your mind."

"Go to hell!"

Jed put his hands up. "You know what, fine. My bad for loving you. Goodbye, little brother."

I rushed up and grabbed his arm. "Don't you dare say you love me. You tried to turn me against our dad."

"That was not it at all."

"Yes, it was. And why take Mom's side. Jed, she was the one that left!" I stepped back. "You know what, don't answer that. You'll spin it however you like. I know the truth."

"Yeah, bud, you know the truth. Go on back to Texas with that tainted truth. Have a good life."

I couldn't see clearly after he said that. I punched him directly in his snobby face. I heard the crack and saw him fall immediately onto the wet grass. "To hell with you, Trey!" he hollered up at me from the ground.

My breathing was erratic. "Have a good life? Is that what you said? You know how much I didn't want to live? Let me tell you what you don't know about me, you pathetic excuse of a brother."

I slammed my fist into my own chest. "I wanted to die."

Jed wiped blood from his nose. "What?"

Without hesitation, I answered, "When the doctor said my tumor wasn't cancerous, I was pissed. I wanted to die."

"You were mad because you didn't have cancer? Were you even going to tell anyone that you were being tested?"

"I figured you would learn all about it when my body got shipped back up here."

I turned to leave and heard Jed yell behind me, "You have problems, Trey."

"No, you do."

I wanted to go home after all that, but I had one more stop.

****

A few hours later and after my detour to the nearest bar, I finally made my way to my dad's house. When I exited the rental, I stared up at the old shutters that my dad never cared to replace. I wasn't surprised.

When I got to the front door, I moved to get a key out of my pocket before I heard, "It's unlocked. Come on in, Trey."

I walked in and saw a familiar man sitting on the couch. It was Tony, my dad's closest friend.

As usual, Tony was smoking a cigarette and watching reruns of M*A*S*H. "Sit, Trey."

He put his cigarette out just as I sat down next to him on the leather sofa. It was the one piece of furniture my dad splurged on. I still couldn't believe he was gone.

Tony put his hand on my shoulder. "How are you holding up?"

"Not good."

"Your dad was so proud of you."

I nodded and took in the absence of family pictures that used to hang from every wall. After Mom moved out, I guessed he couldn't take looking at them anymore. "He wouldn't be proud of me now."

"Why do you say that?"

"I'm so angry."

"You've been through a lot. Hell, anyone would be angry like that. You're a hero, Trey. Now, where is that Purple Heart that you sent your dad? I figured it would be hanging up somewhere. You got to take it back home with you now."

The walls and the tables were all void of any sign of me. "I don't care to take it."

Tony shook his head and sighed. "If I find it, I'll send it to you." Then, he turned and looked at me from the side. "I saw you and Jed fighting this morning."

"And?"

"Not my business. That's between you two."

"He thinks mom is some saint and not in the wrong."

Tony frowned. "You still holding a grudge with her about all that? After all this time?"

I sat up straight. "All what time? None of that matters. If she…" I stopped short. I didn't want to blow up on him.

He sat forward and put his elbows on his knees. "I think it's time for you to know something."

"What is that?"

"It wasn't easy on your mom. She tried to leave your dad many times before she finally did. He didn't let her."

I clutched my car keys so tightly that the tip of one key felt like it was already drawing blood from my palm. "No, they were happy right up until she left him."

"Not true. He was very domineering and she was too sweet to stand up to him."

I thought back over the times my mom stayed in bed. All the times she seemed so unhappy. "I don't believe all that."

"I know you don't. But I'll tell you, when she finally left him, he gave her even more hell."

"Not true."

"Yes, it is. I was there." I rubbed at my thigh above my prosthetic. "Sorry, sir. I just can't believe all that."

"I'm just saying what needs to be said. Your father was a good man. He just had some struggles. He consumed her in a way that was unhealthy. I'll leave it at that. Now is the time for your family to heal. Your dad wouldn't want you two fighting. No matter his problems with your mom, he loved you two boys."

CHAPTER 24
Light of Our Eyes

On Mr. Reynold's request, I decided to talk to someone here in my time. But no way was it going to be Father O'Brien. Luckily, the traveling priest, Father Michaels, was available that morning. I was told to find him in the chapel.

Where I thought I'd see Father Michaels, a different priest was sitting in the pews of the empty church. I sat down next to him and clasped my hands in my lap. "Hello, Father. I thought I was meeting with Father Michaels."

"No dear, I am Father Wyeth. How are you?" he asked. He had an accent that I couldn't yet place. I had heard it before but did not remember where.

"I am well."

"I am glad," he said with a smile. Father Wyeth must have been the newest traveling priest. His long grey hair was a little wild spiking up everywhere, but he didn't seem to care about his unruly appearance.

"You haven't been here long, have you, Father?"

"No, I haven't. The ocean is beautiful. I am in awe of the breeze off the Gulf of Mexico. It blows in differently than it does from the Atlantic, don't you think?" He said and smiled at me as I relaxed back into my seat.

"You really like the water."

"When I first got here, I was entranced. Water is the building block of all living things. I could spend all day marveling at its perfection."

"Did you come through the port, too?" I asked, still trying to place where I knew that accent.

"Yes, Sister. On the vessel Borkum. Nice ship. Many families on there that were eager to come to America."

He turned towards me again. "Sister Margaret, am I correct? I hear so much about your work with the children here. I am glad to finally meet you. What is it that troubles such a kind soul?"

"Thank you. It is nice to meet you too. We are thankful for your visit to our part of the island." I swallowed hard before continuing, "I have something I need to share with you if you have time."

"Yes?"

My mouth went dry and my jaw froze. I didn't reply. I just sat there.

Father Wyeth tapped on the wooden pew in front of us. "Did you know, Sister, that much of this church was built by a handful of Scottish immigrants passing through from that same Galveston port as us? Their craftsmanship is the best I've seen."

His content smile and green eyes took in the ceiling above us. "It is also said that those men were on the run from persecution from England."

"For what?"

"Their involvements in recent uprisings against the protestant king. It was said these Scotts murdered many Englishmen. Scotts like you and me."

"You're Scottish?"

He shrugged. "That and French. Actually, I've lived many places."

As I was thinking about how his accent made sense now because it sounded like my butler from back home in England who came from France, my thoughts jumped back to the word *murder*. "Murder? That is horrible."

"It is, but look what beauty that was erected here for God," he added.

"I'm not understanding and more so, how did you know I was of Scottish descent?"

Father Wyeth smiled over at me. "You are seeking my counsel because why?" he asked without answering my question.

"If I'm to be honest. I am not sure of my choices."

"Your choices?"

"I felt I was called for this. I used to hear God speak to me." I lowered my head. "But lately, He has abandoned me."

"Dear, He does not abandon anyone."

I thought to myself how I had just recently told Rebecca Sampson the exact same thing. Funny how we can give advice but not take it for ourselves. I continued to do just that when I said, "I have done things in my past that were not befitting a nun."

He interrupted me. "That is where you harm yourself."

"What do you mean?"

"You are too hard on yourself."

I sighed. "Maybe, but I also hide my feelings and I only talk about them to one person. A man not of the faith. Or at least not anymore."

"Good. As long as you get it out. Talking is therapeutic."

I frowned. "But it is not to God that I share this."

He leaned back into the pew. "And that is why you think you should no longer be a nun?"

"Yes."

"Because of rules set by the men of the Catholic church?"

"I am not following."

"The church was formed by Jesus himself. Jesus was not a man, per se. He was God. What you must understand about our church is that there are some that have changed it a bit but the faith itself remains the same," he said with a solid conviction in his voice.

"Changed it?"

"Humans. Over time, humans corrupt many things, churches are no different. There are many men throughout the church's life that have felt certain things should be a certain way. Not necessarily Jesus' way."

He looked at me and my expression was not one of understanding, so he continued, "Some members of the Jewish faith did the same. They became harsh in their interpretation of God's plan. Well, now we have many Catholics falling into the same rut. Many forget that the Christian faith was started with the greatest commandment of all… Love."

He smiled up to the front of the church. "Now, I am not saying that God wants you to sin and continue to sin. What I am saying is that God knows your heart. Your true heart. And He knows that it is a process to change. You have made great strides, Dear. God knows this."

I nodded in understanding while remembering that I told these same things to Trey.

Then he added, "You must know that God puts people in our lives at exactly the moment they are needed to help us. And no Catholic or Protestant or any person of faith is perfect. Only Jesus holds that honor. Don't forget that. And don't forget that God knows your true heart and that is all that matters."

"I understand," I said just as the bells began to ring outside alerting the children to transition to their next class.

"But do you understand what I am truly saying?"

"I feel I do, Father." I began to stand.

He added, "And maybe you are in someone else's life too for that same reason. God does not want to lose *any* of His children."

I nodded and felt a tingling sensation move through my shoulders. "I see. I do understand. Thank you so much for your time."

"You are welcome. So, no more worrying. You need your strength to continue to take care of the children." He looked out the window. "Even more so in the days to come."

I stopped moving and turned to ask, "What is to come?"

However, he didn't respond back. Instead, he lowered his head to pray. I assumed he meant more illnesses on the island and left it at that. I had to rush off to teach. Michael, one of my younger orphans, was to present his prayers in front of the class first. I wanted to get there early enough to give him some encouraging words before the rest of my students arrived.

I left the chapel and was met by Sister Anna. She was headed into the chapel for her daily prayers. She saw my teary eyes and took my hands. "What is troubling you, Sister?"

"It's not anything sad. I am happy."

"That is great! What brings this joy?" she asked.

I eyed the bells over her shoulder knowing I needed to hurry. "Just a talk with the traveling priest. Father O'Brien felt I needed it. A good talk. That's all."

"Oh, with Father Michaels?"

I frowned. "Oh no, the new one. Father Wyeth."

"Who?"

"Father Wyeth. I think he is from Scotland."

"How is that possible?" She tilted her head. Her hazel eyes had more specs of green in them than usual as they took in the rays of the sun.

"What do you mean?" I asked.

"You hadn't heard? Because of the weather reports from Cuba, the port has not had any new ships come in."

"Maybe he made it in before then."

Her brows drew together. "Maybe. Anyway, I am very glad to see you smiling. I'll see you in a little bit."

"Yes, I have a trip into the hospital after my last class today. I'll be back later in the day."

"God be with you on your travels."

"Thank you, Sister."

After she walked into the chapel, I stopped and turned around. A feeling crossed over me that I couldn't explain. I

wanted to simply peer back inside the chapel. When I did, I
didn't see Father Wyeth. He was no longer sitting in the pew I
left him in. I let my eyes scan the church. There was no sign
of him. A sweet realization hit me as I remembered that the
front door was the only way to exit the chapel.

****

Back at the tenant's house later that day, I read…

Dear Margaret,

*Sorry that I haven't written back sooner. I went to a funeral for
my father. I need some time to get my head right. Something
happened with my brother. It was a nice funeral, though.
Anyway, I hope you are doing okay?*

I clutched the diary close to my chest. My heart was
broken for him. I lowered my head and prayed to God for
healing for the Reynold's family. Then, I thought of how
there was something in his words that had me perplexed. He
talked a little of his brother and his anger towards him, but he
never said why.

I knew he was grieving and understood the short
response, but I wished he would be more forthcoming with
me now. I set my feelings aside and lowered my head again.
"God, please give me the words that will help Mr. Reynold's
suffering. Only if he fully opens up will he be able to heal.
Help me, help him."

I opened the diary again and closed my eyes. When I
opened them again, I couldn't believe how easily the words
flowed from inside me.

Dear Mr. Reynolds,

I am sorry to hear of your loss. I can tell from your previous writings that you were very close to your father. You and your family are in my prayers as you continue to heal. And heal you must. There is a special light inside of you that you have kept hidden for years. I have gathered that much in the little time I have known you. My only question is, why do you continue to hide it? It peeks through when you talk about your special relationship with Webster. It shines brightly when you give advice to help me. You alone have. You and your light are a blessing to me as I finally got the courage to talk to someone here about everything. Now, Mr. Reynolds, I am thankful because God is speaking to me again.

What He is speaking to me about now is all about you. He knows you better than I do and He won't reveal everything to me, but I want to know more about you. I want you to open up to me the way I have with you. Share with me. Tell me more about your family and the divorce of your parents. Tell me why you speak vaguely of the brother that seems to always be there for you, but you never say it like that. He's in a lot of what you talk about, but you never say that you appreciate that. You only say things about how foolish he is. I want to know more. Tell me what he did to you.

I wrote a few more things before finalizing my thoughts. It was getting late and I had to get back to the orphanage. I closed my diary and kissed the cover. I put it back in its resting place awaiting Trey's hands to lift it back up and his special words to grace its pages again.

CHAPTER 25
Ne'er Grow Dimmer

My next two trips to town were not what I had hoped. Trey hadn't replied back. Again, he was silent for longer than usual.

Dear Mr. Reynolds,

I hope this finds you well. I haven't heard back from you and I worry that it is because of what I asked of you. In my last entry, I told you of how God was speaking to me again. I firmly believe that it was with your help. Not just because you got me to smile again by challenging me to play in the water, but because after all these years, you were the one I could finally trust enough to write the truth. Speaking about things that are hard to do truly helps.

I feel that you are in the same position that I was in back in Europe after the fire. The priest there, Father Walters, once told me that the truth will set you free. At the time, I was not ready to speak it, not even to God. Mr. Reynolds, you must do as I have. You must learn to forgive. Forgive your mother. Forgive your ex fiancé, maybe even your brother. But most importantly, forgive yourself.

In meeting you, I finally could forgive myself.

You have told me so much up until now. Why stop?

I also wanted to add that little Trey continues to do well. He has had some slip ups. Still, he is trying. And that is all that

I left town and made it back out to the beach just before sunset. The tide had come in enough to warm the foliage that grew a few feet beyond the dune. It had been several days since Mr. Reynolds had written in my diary. Fear crept in. Was it because I upset him or was it that whatever miracle led us to meet may have now gone since I was hearing from God again?

Hearing God again was a good thing. But why was there still a longing in my heart?

I thought about little Trey. He was in so many ways, a younger version of Mr. Reynolds. If I never get to talk to Mr. Reynolds again, at least I can help little Trey. I vowed at that exact moment to always look out for little Trey. No matter my situation, I would make sure that little Trey's light can continue to shine.

I slipped off my shoes and socks. Lifting my skirt a few inches to protect the hem, I moved slowly into the surf. The breeze picked up and blew my headpiece off. I didn't reach out for it. I didn't care. Why didn't I care?

Then, Mr. Reynold's came back into my thoughts and his name graced my lips. "Trey," I said against the ocean's vastness. "Where are you?"

Ripe clouds rolled in, signaling rain. The humidity made the air so thick I could taste a hint of salt. I lowered my head and moved my hands up to my stomach. I felt, without truly feeling, his hands touch my shoulder. Full lips, I had never seen, smiled warmly down at me. "Trey," I whispered out into the void. "Come back to me."

I closed my eyes and imagined a man, I had never met, hugging me. His warmth pulled me into a world of sweet escape. His scent was a swarm of musk and a twist of something tropical. He continued to smile down at me as the last rays of the sun stole the stage.

I pulled away from my special friend. Immediately, the cool air rushed in. What was I doing? I shook my head and ran back up the dune to the orphanage. I was embarrassed. No, that wasn't it. I was ashamed of myself. Did I have feelings for him other than a close friendship?

CHAPTER 26
Till in the Sky

I held her diary and read the new entry. I was about to close it again and maybe even next time not even pick it back up from under the floor. I sat there for just a second thinking about what she said. Why would I need to forgive all these people? What had they done to deserve my forgiveness?

I couldn't shake the feeling that I missed talking to Margaret. It had been refreshing to be able to conversate with another flawed human being who was also expected to be perfect for others. She hid so much from everyone because she was supposed to be this perfect nun. The pressure of that had to be exhausting. She said she was like me. Was that true? It couldn't be. She never debated her own life. She never drank herself almost to death every night to numb the pain. Suicide probably never crossed her perfect, sweet mind.

I leaned back against the chipped headboard of the bed and stared up at the cracked ceiling I had yet to fix for the Gaines. I started to think back on what my brother had told me in the hospital when I first got back from Somalia. He had said that I was the perfect sport's boy. That dad was the proudest of me because of my time on the high school football team. Sure, I made some good passes and helped my team win a few games, but was that really who I was? I couldn't deny it, it was who my dad wanted me to be. No way I could be that anymore in this condition, physically and mentally. I became somber and even more lost debating it all.

All that time in school, I was an insecure and shy kid who dreamed of geeky things like pirates and living on a fishing boat. I never really thought about it until now about how much my father did not really know about me. No one did, but my mom. She was the one that would bring me to all the libraries hunting those books. She was the one that bought me the posters of fishing boats to go on my walls.

I laughed remembering back about how I would cover them when my football friends came over. After they left, my mom would come in for dirty clothes and frown at the sheets I pinned up on the walls over the posters she had gotten for me. She would always say, "Why hide what you really want to be?"

It wasn't long after that, my dad told me that her constant time in bed was because she was drinking too much. I took everything he said as the gospel truth. He said she was unable to handle reality so she hid behind bottles of wine. A few years later, she left him. She never talked bad about him. Only my brother did.

My brother had been older. He said he knew everything that went on. He had said she drank to numb the mental abuse. At the time, I didn't believe him. There was nothing abusive about my father! My mother was just a failure. The funny thing was, the last few times I visited her, she had not a single bottle of alcohol, nor had she been drunk the way she was when I was younger. She really seemed genuinely happy.

I rubbed my face and looked over at my bottle of vodka. Had I been doing the same thing my mom did when I was a kid? Running from my problems with alcohol? Did I carry the same gene of poor emotional regulation or did I get this way only after seeing my brothers killed in battle?

I didn't regret joining the military and helping those children in Somalia. But if I were being honest with myself, I did it to impress my father since I didn't get the huge football scholarship that he had hoped I would get to go to that prestigious college he kept bringing up every time he could.

And then I thought about what Tony had said. How he asked if I remembered my mom withdrawing. How he said my dad could be overbearing. I let that conversation with

Tony settle into the folds of my heart's armor. What had I missed all these years because it hurt too much to face it? And then I added war on top of it.

I squeezed my eyes shut. It hurt. The truth. Everything just plain hurt. Tears ran down my cheeks. "Oh God, please…" I hollered out and continued to cry. Is Margaret right in that the truth will set you free?

I reached over and picked up the diary. I planned to tell Margaret everything. Heck, I just wanted to talk to her period.

Dear Miss Margaret,

I hope my words find you well. There is so much I need to share with you as you've shared so much with me. I never thought about your secrets and how hard it was to keep them since you were a nun. I have a lot of pain inside. Things I never wanted to acknowledge. Hopelessness, loss, regrets… I'm just… Okay, where do I start from here? I'll tell you more…

I wrote a lot about my mom, but in a more positive light for a change.

For days and days after, Margaret and I continued to write back and forth. In between working on the remodel of the Gaines' house, I had her diary filled with my thoughts.

Before I knew it, more days had flown by and not once did I go down to Anchors Aweigh Bar to drink. No drinking at all. I just kept on working and writing. I told Margaret all about my love of pirates and ghosts. Of which, she replied…

Dear Mr. Reynolds,

I don't think it is odd that you have an interest in ghosts. Now, will I say they are real? Of that I am not sure. However, I will say that to not believe in a being not of flesh would be the same as saying that God doesn't exist, wouldn't it? Or angels? Or even our loved ones that have passed? You intrigue me with your thoughts. Please keep telling me all about the books you have read.

Dear Miss Margaret,

I've been watching the stories on television about it here. There are rumors and supposed sightings of ghosts in Galveston. The house of your friend, the Sampson Manor, is supposedly haunted…

Dear Mr. Reynolds,

Sampson's house is haunted? By whom? Have you seen such a thing? I have not. It was just recently built during my time. Where are these other hauntings you talk about? And what is a television? Is that a book that stores all the information about these apparitions?

How is the remodel going on this house? Has anyone said there are hauntings here? From what I understand, this house was built before the Sampson family home was built.

Dear Miss Margaret,

If you call a mysterious diary and pen that allows me to conversate with a woman from a hundred years before, haunted, then yes, I would think this house is haunted. Sorry, just making a joke.

The remodel is going well. I finished the kitchen cabinets and re-laid laminate on the floors. Tomorrow, I will tear down the fireplace mantle and casing to tile it and put a new cover over it.

A television is how we get our information now. It is a form of technology where we can see images and hear the person talking.

It is like a newspaper come to life. By the way, I'm putting a picture of me with Webster in your diary. I want you to see what I look like.

Dear Mr. Reynolds,

A newspaper comes to life? Yes, surely the island has become haunted. I have never heard of such a thing.

I don't see your picture. The exchange between us must not allow for other objects. I am sorry, but you'll have to tell me what you look like. I have blonde hair and now a few freckles from the sun exposure here.

Also, did you write that you were going to tear down the fireplace? You can't possibly. It is the most beautiful feature in this house. Its stone finish reminds me of the ornate fixtures from the manors in London. From what I understand, the materials on the fireplace were brought in from India. Is it in bad condition during your time? Are you sure you can't just restore it?

The back and forth writing continued between Margaret and me almost daily now. How she did it, I didn't know. It meant she traveled to the tenant's house every day from the orphanage. No matter, it was one of the most special times in my life. I held the diary next to my chest and smiled wondering about her. Blonde hair and freckles, she had said. But what did she smell like? What would it be like to hold her? I laughed. Hold her? What am I talking about? This was crazy. Not only was she a nun, but she had been gone for almost a hundred years.

I let my eyes drift around the room. If I had been there during the beginning of the century, would she have talked to me like she did now? Would I have made it hard for her to continue with her vows? Would she have even looked at me? A woman like that was special.

Oh heck, it blew my mind debating that stuff. I'd never get to see her. I would live in this fantasy world as her pen pal and that would be all I'd get out of it. But I knew deep in my heart that it wasn't enough. I loved her. There was no doubt. Although I could never be with her, I loved her. And I cherished every letter between us. It was like I was off at war and she was back at home waiting for me. Only this woman wouldn't leave me while I was gone. No, Margaret would never leave me. That thought was incredibly comforting. I had found someone that I could rely on. Someone that, until her passing of old age or mine, I would have.

I squeezed her diary tighter against my chest. I felt a warm blanket of emotions pass over me and I let myself be embraced within it. Could I be so lucky that she really was a ghost? If so, ghosts live forever, in a sense. I wanted her to haunt me. Lay with me and hold me like this every night. If not a ghost, I'll at least take the next fifty years or so.

I started running numbers in my head. I could buy the house. That's right. I had war pay from my time in Somalia that was pretty good. I sat up. That was it. Tomorrow I was going to go to the bank and work out what kind of offer I could make the Gaines for the house. The real estate market in Galveston was stagnant and the Gaines did say they were desperate to fix the house up in hopes for renters or vacationers to help rejuvenate their finances. Mrs. Gaines even went as far as saying that if interest in the property didn't pick up soon, they would be in a bind. Why else did they hire a disabled vet to do the renovation? Their money was tight.

That's it. I knew my direction. I shook lightly with excitement and actually smiled. I hadn't been this excited about my life's direction in years. Then, I began to hear singing.

I set the diary down on my bed and looked around. I walked over to the window and looked down. The music was coming from the East side of the house. Curious, I went down the stairs and out the door before turning onto tenth street. There on the corner was a young woman with an acoustic guitar. She was singing something so beautiful. I walked in closer. A few other people gathered and some even tipped her.

When she strummed the last chord, she looked up and smiled. "Thank you, everyone."

A man next to me dressed in cut off shorts and wearing a Los Angeles Chargers hat asked, "What song is that?"

She responded, "It's a French hymn. It is the song the nuns sang. It is called, Queen of the Waves."

He responded, "It's beautiful. They sing it at mass?"

"No, not really. It was the song they sang to calm the children when the hurricane hit back in September of 1900. You know… the big one. Its one-hundred-year anniversary is in a few days. It was horrible. It took out most of Galveston and took many lives, especially the nuns."

I stepped in closer to join the conversation. "Wait, wait, are you talking about the nuns at the orphanage? The Sisters of Charity nuns?" My heart was dropping as I asked.

"Yes. From St. Mary's Orphan Asylum. I can tell by your accent that you are not from here, but I'm guessing you have already learned about it, right?"

"Hold on. Tell me, how bad was this hurricane, really?"

She tilted her head. "Bad, bud. Many died," she said and then she frowned. "Maybe you haven't touched up on the history here. Then how do you know about the Sisters of Charity?"

I didn't reply. I ran back to the house and grabbed my bike.

****

I arrived at the library just before closing. The structure was like most of the buildings in Galveston; square and crammed close to the others.

Inside and at the front desk, a young elementary aged boy sat reading a book.

I waved to get his attention. He sat right up with innocent brown eyes. "Can I help you?"

"You running this place?" I asked.

"My mom works here. I'm just with her for the day. My babysitter canceled last minute." He looked behind me. "Hey, mom."

I turned to see a woman not much younger than me. She had the palest of skin that heavily contrasted against the boy's deep dark skin. Her blonde hair was braided into two sections with both braids laying over her shoulders. She gestured to the boy. "Up you go, Ralph. Go read by the window."

"Awe, mom!" he exclaimed and stood up to a size almost taller than her.

"You heard me," she replied and then the brightest blue eyes looked over at me. "Can I help you with something?"

I looked over at the kid as he walked away with his book clasped to his chest. "He loves to read. Cute kid. Is he really yours?"

She set a stack of books down on the desk. "Of course, why?"

"You're kinda young for a kid that tall. Is his dad a basketball player?"

She paid no mind and simply said, "Oh, technically, I adopted him. He's the best thing that ever happened to me. Now, how can I help you?" she asked.

I couldn't help but start to count the freckles across her small nose. A lot of people by the beach spent too much time in the sun. "I'm looking for books on the Hurricane of 1900."

She paused for a moment and looked over her shoulder at a sketch of a woman.

I waited a few seconds. "Something wrong, Mrs.?" I noticed the picture had a rosary hanging off the corner of it.

"Ms.," she replied and then tapped the screen of an older Xerox Alto on her desk. "Avery. Avery Weeks."

"Nice to meet you." I didn't give my name. No time for small talk. I was in a hurry.

"I had family that died in that storm you're asking about. One in particular." She lifted her chin towards the charcoal picture. "She's where our family's devout faith began." The young woman then wrinkled her nose at me. "I know, strange, but I'm not always odd like this. It's just the timing of someone coming in and asking for those books. On this day of all days."

"What do you mean?"

She spun around as if out of her daze. "Nothing. So, books on the hurricane, huh?"

"Yeah."

Avery shut off the computer. "You know it won't be long and you'll be able to search information like that from home."

"Huh?"

"You haven't read about it yet? The world wide web they are calling it. It's coming out of Britain. A way to link documents into an information system."

"Okay, you're a geek."

She laughed. "I'm a librarian. Of course, I'm a geek. I should be offended, but if the shoe fits, right?"

"Did you worry any about the shutdown of all computers on New Year's Day?"

She laughed. "The millennium bug?"

I nodded.

"No. I figured it was blown out of proportion. I had a few friends that were computer programmers. They didn't seem worried. But the scare sure did sell a lot of merchandise, didn't it?"

I thought back to a few months before Y2K and how the stores were stocked with items imprinted with that term. "True."

Behind me, the front door opened. Avery sighed and her face turned even whiter. Speaking more forcefully to the person coming in, she said, "Tim, I told you not to come by my work."

I turned to find a man about my age and same medium build. He had jet black hair slicked back and wore a business suit that was obviously freshly pressed. He put his hand up. "I just want a minute to talk."

Avery gave me an embarrassed look and then walked closer to the man. Just above a whisper, I heard her say, "There is nothing to talk about. I said we were done."

Tim's voice was several notches louder as he asked, "Is that why you moved here? To get away from me?"

Avery stepped back. Her eyes were wide as she looked down at Tim's hands. I looked, too. The man had both hands balled up in white knuckled fists by his side.

I took a few steps towards him. "Mr., I think it is time to go."

Avery waved me away. "It's fine."

Tim's eyes flared over at me before looking down at my prosthetic that stuck out from under my Bermuda shorts. The man smirked and asked, "Who is this? Is he why you left me?"

When I saw the librarian flinch, I got irritated and raised my voice, "Doesn't matter who I am, man. It is time to go."

Mr. Cocky got in my face. "This is none of your business, cripple."

I held up my hands. "No need for any of that name calling. Didn't your momma teach you better than that?"

The guy didn't back down. This was about to get good. A nice distraction and I'd get to fire up my muscles. Excitement caused me to laugh.

Tim pushed me and I heard Avery tell Ralph to head to the back. Just while I was getting ready to slam the dude's face in the table next to him, Avery came up between us. "Both of you stop."

She turned to the prick and demanded. "Go away now and never come back or I will call the police."

Tim looked from the petite girl to above her head. He eyed me. "We'll talk later."

Avery shook her head, and we both watched him storm out of the library. He got into his bright red Ferrari GTS and sped off. "Darn", I thought to myself, "My adrenaline was up and now I had nothing to use it on".

Avery murmured to me something about being sorry and then she simply retreated to the back of the building, waving for me to follow her.

She motioned for me to sit at an old oak desk next to the stacks of historical texts. I watched her run her elegant fingers over them.

She pulled out a few books and laid them in front of me. "These are the most accurate. There were a lot of different survivor accounts of the chain of events before and after the hurricane. I trust these sources more than the others."

"Thank you," I said. "But are you alright?"

Frazzled eyes down at me. "Of course. I mean, I had preferred Ralph not to have seen all that, but it is what it is."

"Oh, look, I'm sorry. I didn't mean to-"

She raised up her hand. "It's not your fault. I actually appreciated you standing up for me."

"It was my pleasure. No one treats women like that."

We both stared at each other for a moment until she turned to grab another book to add to my pile.

I opened the first one off the top.

Avery watched me and asked, "You're not from here, huh?"

I looked up at her. "Why? Because I don't take people's bs?"

"No, that's normal here. I mean because you don't know much about the hurricane." She gave me a small smile and added, "That and the accent. It's funny sounding."

I laughed. "If you heard your accent through my ears, you'd think you all didn't know how to talk correctly."

"Wow, that a shot?" she asked. Her soft skin on her forehead wrinkled but her pink lips smirked almost to a smile. "I love my accent. Get used to it if you plan to come into my library anymore."

I smiled. I admired her confidence. "Sorry, I'm a Marine. We shoot straight."

Avery nodded like everything was starting to make sense. She replied, "So do I, Marine." This tiny girl wanted to go toe to toe with me, too? Interesting. Not like Alexis at the bar who just likes to be a pain. This librarian was sure of herself in a way that was… attractive? What was I saying? I dropped the thought as quick as it came.

Avery continued, "Anyway, I can handle a Marine as a customer, even if he's arrogant, so keep coming. Books will do you good." She smiled back. Her eyes twinkled when she smiled just enough that I got distracted again. "Well, since you are not from here and you're interested in this part of Galveston's history, you should go see the Texas historical marker they erected on the corner of 69th Street and Seawall Boulevard."

"What kind of marker?"

"A statue in memory of the orphans and nuns that died during the hurricane. It was set up a few years ago on the exact spot of the original orphanage. Well, I got work to do."

Before I could inquire more, she headed back to her post. I thought a second about the historical marker and then turned to my research.

It didn't take long to find all the history about the Galveston hurricane of 1900. An eerie feeling passed over me as I read the latter part of the last article. There it was, "Of the 93 children and 10 sisters in the orphanage, only four boys survived. All ten nuns perished with the rest of the children."

CHAPTER 27
We Hail

I was overjoyed when I started to read Mr. Reynolds' reply. So much so that I stopped on the first sentence and smiled up in delight. "Mr. Reynolds wrote back!" My heart was singing.

I started to read again, but it wasn't the reply I expected. I held my chest as I read sentence after sentence about a hurricane. The poor man was really under the impression that I would die on September 8th because of a storm that would take out the entire island. He continually kept telling me to leave the island. If no one else would leave, at least I needed to.

I picked up the quill and prayed first before I began writing.

Mr. Reynolds,

How is everything? You seem distraught.

In regards to your request, I can't move the children, not without permission. And I won't leave them either. My duty was given to me by God and it was to care for the children first. So I ask one more thing. If this is truly our fate, please don't tell me any more details of this. As God is with me, I will not live in fear.

I am disheartened that you did not reply with more about you. Please let me hear about your day. Did you take my advice and leave the fireplace in one piece in the house?

****

I closed my diary without adding anymore to it. I couldn't believe that some rainstorm could do that much damage.

As I headed back to the orphanage, I thought about how upset Mr. Reynold's was. Did he feel the same about me as I did about him?

Sister Anna met me in the kitchen as I was pouring some milk. "Trey got them all correct again, Sister. Not a single child has ever done that well on that assessment."

"I am so proud of him!"

"Me too!" she exclaimed.

We both sat down at the wooden table in the center of the kitchen. She continued to talk about how smart Trey was, but I kept thinking about my Trey in the future. I interrupted Sister Anna. "Sister, did you say there were weather reports out of Cuba that were disturbing enough to stop incoming vessels into our port?"

"Yes, why?"

"I wonder. Do you think there is a hurricane?"

"If there is, it isn't very big. One trade ship came through yesterday."

"Oh. But what if it is a big storm brewing? Should we leave? Move more inland?"

Her usual squinty eyes grew big. "No. Inland is not safe. The fever, Sister. The Bishop would never approve of that. We have to think about the children. You are immune to the fever, but not many others are."

CHAPTER 28
The Morning Star

This time I slammed the diary shut. "Come on!" How does she not take this seriously? She brushed me off. Does she not believe I am here in the future knowing what is coming? Who did she think she was talking to all this time?

So, is that it? Is she just going to die in the next week? I rubbed my face as it hit me. In one week, she'll be gone. I can't live without her. Wait! What did I just say to myself? Do I need this woman that much?

I stood up, left the house, and headed out on my bike. I'd be fooling myself if I thought I could live just fine without her. She's the only one I could talk to, but she won't listen to me. I didn't know what to do. All she cared about was that I opened up more. Seriously? What kind of fool hears about their future and doesn't want to change it?

When I got to the bar, I noticed a scurry of people hammering boards over their windows.

I walked up the ramp, onto the sidewalk, and then entered the bar. Alexis was there cleaning glasses. She stopped and came towards me. "Sorry for being such a turd the other day. It was just something you said, and I had been dealing with a lot."

I sat down. "Seems like that's a common thing with both of us."

"What's wrong with you?"

I paused and thought of how to ask it. "Alexis, if you knew your future was that you were about to die, would you try to change it?"

She snickered at me. "Of course."

"That's what I thought."

Alexis turned to pull a few glasses out of a sink behind the bar. Her t-shirt was tied up at the waist. She rubbed one of the wet glasses on her shirt. "I don't understand. What is going on, Sergeant?"

"I have a friend. She takes care of kids. She's kind of like a teacher. Anyway, let's just say the kids keep getting her sick, so she needs to quit her job before she contracts something that kills her."

Alexis tilted her head. "Um, okay. That's like telling all teachers to quit their jobs."

"Well, her immune system is weak."

"Then let her doctor tell her. He will."

I rubbed my sweaty hands on my jeans. "Let me give you a hypothetical and then maybe you'd understand how hard-headed this woman is."

"Okay, shoot."

"You know those nuns that died during the 1900 Hurricane?"

"Yes, so sad."

"What do you think they would have done if someone told them the hurricane was coming?"

"Well, back then they didn't have weather reports. But if they did, they'd take those weather reports seriously like we do now. In fact, the Governor just issued a State of Emergency for Galveston County a few hours ago."

"For what?"

"The Cat 2 hurricane in the Gulf. Forecast models show it coming for us. You evacuating?"

I shook my head. "Cat 2 is nothing. But seriously, listen. What if a friend of the nuns had a vision about the hurricane and told one of the nuns?"

"Nuns are spiritual, Trey. They may think the vision is from God," Alexis added as she wiped another glass dry.

"Right! That's what I thought!"

She set the glasses down. "Um, what do you mean?"

"I mean, a vision from a friend is all they need to convince them to leave right?"

"So, you are asking if your teacher friend will follow a vision and quit her job?"

I nodded. "Basically."

"Probably not," she said adamantly and moved to wipe the counters down.

"Why not?"

Alexis gave me a heavy sigh. "Teachers aren't like that, Trey. Their students are like their own kids. They love them. They don't quit on the kids just like that."

****

I walked back to the old house deflated. I still hadn't figured out how to fix this.

I understood the situation with Margaret and how she did not want to leave the orphans behind. But she could convince them all to leave, right?

I got back to the room and opened the diary while thinking of a way to convince her. It was her that said the truth will set you free. Well, here I was trying to tell her the truth so she would be free to live.

I shook my head. No, that wasn't what she meant by the truth will set you free. How could I convince her, though? I needed her. She had to live.

I wrote another entry into the diary begging her to act. I told her to tell everyone that her friend had a vision. I knew that would do the trick. I put the diary in its place and sat on the bed thinking. How far was the orphanage from the water? Didn't I hear that the site of the orphanage was at that expensive hotel, The Flores?

Rubbing my eyes, I kept wondering and worrying. I knew I could have sat there for hours or days before she wrote back. There really was no sense in just sitting there and waiting on a reply. I decided I needed to get out.

I jumped up and grabbed my bike keys to head down to the beach. It was an especially hot day, but something was itching at me almost like a song I couldn't shake that played on and on in my head. I had to see what she saw. I had to gauge for myself how close she was to the incoming storm.

I arrived at the Hotel Flores. The driveway was lined with over thirty palm trees towering above the parked cars beneath them at a height similar to a three-story building. The whole landscape's set up looked like a welcoming tropical armada.

I continued around the car path and opted to park in the garage a few hundred feet on the west side of the property hoping it would be cheaper. However, it was still a whopping twenty dollars required to the man on duty.

I frowned before handing him half of the contents in my wallet.

"It's cheaper than usual," he told me. "Not many people visiting right now because of that hurricane warning."

I looked around. "What hurricane? It's sunny."

"The calm before the storm, gringo. The calm before the storm…" his voice faded out as he looked towards the ocean.

After receiving my vehicle tag from him, I headed back down the drive to the front of the hotel. The ocean breeze hit me immediately as I was removing my helmet and crossing the street. It felt nice.

I stopped at the valet station and turned towards the beach. The waves were puny and unremarkable for an incoming storm. And that was when I realized that it was just like that back in 1900 before that hurricane. Why would Margaret or anyone at the orphanage believe what I was saying? The weather was beautiful.

Just then, the wind picked up. A strong combination of salt intertwined with organic power began to drown out any other sound in my ears. I tucked my head and continued on while giving a nod to one of the valet attendants.

I walked into the lobby of the historic hotel. Nothing about it was old, per se. It had been well taken care of. The only parts that would make you think it had been around since nineteen eleven were the ornate curves of the top floor windows and smaller square windows stacked one by one from floors below.

The building itself was designed similar to an old mission style church, just ten or so times the footprint of a church. Yet, it had a terra cotta roof slapped on top of it that was almost too simple for the luxury below it.

I moved further into the lobby. All around me was more of that rounded wood work above interior windows and doorways. The walls had a calming, lemony paint color. I would have thought the color would have been too cheery for the space if it wasn't for the cherry stained interior doors and four layered crystal chandeliers lighting every few feet of the large room.

I smiled at the ladies at the front desk and noticed the bar area. That would be a good spot to rest.

I got to the first table I could find that was by a window. I sat down on the tan wingback chair and rubbed the thigh of my injured leg. Positioning my legs on a bike and relying on them to maneuver the little steel horse that I loved so much only further exacerbated my injury. Still, I couldn't give up the only thing that gave me a natural high.

A man dressed in a black button up shirt and formal slacks appeared next to me. "What would you like?"

"Amaretto Sour."

"Yes sir. Can I start you a tab?"

I shook my head. The bar tab at the hotel would certainly bankrupt me. Plus, I had to drive back after. I simply said, "That probably wouldn't be a good idea today."

He nodded in understanding and walked away. I turned and took in the view again. The ocean was gorgeous. The waves came in only a few feet apart and stopped short of the shore until they were just a flat line of water glossing over the sand.

Even with the hurricane warning, there were still families enjoying the beach. In my direct line of sight were about four kids on the beach building sand castles. They began utilizing the water by their feet to carve out the moats of their imaginary kingdoms.

Couples walked by hand in hand and skirted around the infantile masterpieces. I was too far to see anyone's face on the beach. I wondered if the couples passing the kids paid any attention to the hard work beneath them. Were they smiling at them? Were they smiling at all? Or were they in deep conversation about some stupid argument they had at lunch or over something in their past? I bet all that was distracting them from the experience only an ocean could provide.

Again, I was being cynical. After what happened between Emily and me, my faith in the whole happy couple scenario seemed like such a sham. But here I was. At a fancy hotel trying to find a woman that aroused something inside me that was surely aggravating every core of my soul. Or whatever was left of it.

A small glass with an amber colored liquid was placed on the table before me. "Anything else, sir?"

I took a sip. "This is really good."

The waiter smiled revealing a smidgen of pride. "Thank you. I made it. The bartender had to unexpectedly leave early."

"Why? Everything okay?"

"His elderly grandmother needed to be moved from the hospital here to one in Houston before the storm comes. Just a precaution."

"Oh, okay." I set the glass down. "I have a question. The brochure said that this hotel was built on the site of the St. Mary's Orphanage Asylum and that it was haunted."

The older man shook his head. "Don't believe those brochures. People from up north write that stuff and sell them along with their bogus tours down here. Yes, it is said that this hotel is haunted, but the orphanage was a little further down where Wal-Mart now stands."

I laughed. "Seriously?"

"Oh yeah, now there are some historians that speculate that the ghosts are some of the kids from the orphanage but only because after that hurricane, the survivors buried the dead bodies where they found them. There were so many dead and no one to claim them or give them a proper burial. They literally were buried exactly where they were found."

I got a chill and let my eyes drift back towards the ocean.

"Anything else?"

"No, I'm good. I'll take the check please," I said without looking back up at him. I sat there staring at the water and the kids finishing up their castles. I wasn't exactly sure where Margaret was before her storm, but I was pretty close to it. That dang ocean was seriously *right* there. Maybe two hundred feet give or take.

I took a few more sips of my drink when he came back with the check. I handed him cash. "Keep the change."

"Thank you."

"Oh, one more thing. I'm staying at a house more inland. Do I have anything to worry about over there?"

The man thought for a second. "The city built the seawall years or so after the hurricane of 1900 to help protect against future storm surges. For the most part, it's helped. Sadly, it caused massive erosion. Now, we have that narrow strip of beach."

"So, the orphanage was further back away from the ocean than this?"

"Pretty much, but it still wasn't protected by that wall."

"But does the wall really help?"

"Oh, um, heck yeah. You weren't here for Hurricane Alicia, were you?"

"No, but when was that?"

"1983. The Corps of Engineers were pretty proud of that wall. They estimated that millions in damage was avoided because of their wall. Alicia capped out at…" He lifted his eyes in thought. "Seemed like a Cat 3. But if we get a Cat 4 or 5 here, I'm not sure we'd be so lucky."

CHAPTER 29
Joyful Hearts

The next day, the response wasn't what I had hoped for. In fact, she told me that she mentioned it to the priest, Father O'Brien, and he told her that fear was the Devil's way of taking our happiness. The orphans were happy and prospering. To move them now after everything they had been through based on a vision from some unknown friend would only make them revert back to fear and worry.

I wrote back and begged her to leave by herself.

Her reply again was that she wouldn't leave the orphans. Yet, she asked me to share what was going on with me. It was like all she cared about was hearing about me, my troubles. For heaven's sake, the woman was about to drown in the deadliest hurricane in our nation's history and all she cared about was making sure I was okay.

I picked up the glass of vodka I had been nursing and threw it against the wall. "Ugh, Margaret!"

When I sat back down and tried to calm my nerves, it hit me. I referred to her the same way I did for my mom, my brother, and Emily. How could I have put Margaret in the same category with those worthless people?

Not Margaret. She was so much better. In fact, no one had ever wanted to check on me as much as this woman, even when her own death was on the horizon. Yet, all she cared about was me.

She shared things with me I never imagined a nun would share. And she said she did it because she felt there was something special about me. I, of course, knew the truth. I wasn't special. I was a wrecking ball that allowed everyone in my life to swing me wherever they liked no matter what it did to me.

But not this nun. She didn't ask of me something that would hurt me. She truly felt it would help me. A type of therapy. As a Marine, I didn't bother with those therapists that they referred me to. Marines are stronger than that. We don't need all that.

Yet, I sat there on the bed as my thigh cramped up from the prosthetic not being securely fastened, and I finally teared up. The reality hit me, I was really going to lose her. This could be one of the last chances I had to talk to her.

I took some ibuprofen to ease the pain in my leg and then picked up the diary.

Dear Margaret,

I write this with a sense of defeat. I'm pretty upset that you won't leave Galveston. I'm so scared to lose you. Yes, I said it. I need you. But you continue to be hard-headed. I will honor your wishes and not share anymore with you about the hurricane. Instead, I'll tell you something. You wanted me to be honest, so here it is. Because Margaret, if I had known then what I knew now, I would have changed things. Why can't you see that?

So, I think you need to know this. After the shootings on the base, our patrols got more serious. We were angry and dead set on finding every weapon we could find. I kicked down doors with no care in the world for my own safety. I wanted someone to pay. You know what for, Margaret? They killed Webster, Margaret. They took the life of that sweet boy, one of their own, by shooting at us. For what? What would it solve shooting at a bunch of Marines that were there to help them? They were cowards, and I hated them for it. But I could have saved him if I had known. Now, you are not listening to me. Margaret, I'm telling you how I wish to God I could have saved Webster. It kills me that I couldn't. I can't let the same happen to you. Take my advice and leave.

Dear Mr. Reynolds,

I am so sorry about sweet Webster. I know the pain of losing him is unbearable. I understand your concerns, but all I would be doing is saving myself because they will not let me leave with the orphans. They do not believe a storm is coming. I believe you, but I can't leave the children. I hope you understand.

Tell me more about what happened after you lost Webster. Please keep talking to me about these things.

Dear Margaret,

Again, I am upset. But that is why I love you. You're a good woman not wanting to leave the kids or children as you call them. We just say kids now. But anyway, I wish I could have found some proof that you could show them, but all my research showed was that there was no warning.

If this is our last talk, I want you to know everything. I hope you have time to get back and read this.

After the shooting, we confiscated a lot of guns and beat up the natives pretty good. No remorse. There, I said it. Margaret, I still struggle with no remorse. You wanted to know the truth.

And you know who I have no remorse for too? Emily. I don't care what my ignorant brother says about her. She's pathetic. You know what she did? She cheated on me while I was fighting that war and then had the audacity to write that eleventh letter.

Yeah, I remember it like it was yesterday. I came in one morning after an entire night of patrolling and confiscating guns. I was dead on my feet and missing Webster. Every morning, Webster would be hollering for me at the gate. Not that morning. What I did have waiting for me was the 11th letter from Emily. Guess what it said. She said she was sorry, but she was leaving me.

You know what is funny? For a moment, I wished Webster was there so I could tell him and send him away with that stupid twelfth letter from Emily that he thought I should have read that day of his death. I knew it was coming. So why did Emily feel the need to keep writing me letters? The 11th that I held in my shaking hand was plenty. I crumbled the letter up and screamed. Another Marine came in and had asked what was wrong. I remembered the anger in my voice as I replied...

"Ugh! I can't believe it. She left me for another man."

"Oh geez, I'm sorry," Lieutenant Marks said. He chugged down an entire water bottle and wiped his mouth. "Just sucks."

"My friend back home, Ricky, he had told me he saw her with the mayor's son. I knew it was coming."

Lieutenant Marks sat down next to me. Marks had been married for five years to a woman that religiously sent him letters without missing a beat. I was jealous. I needed that. "Then, good riddance to her. Look at the bright side. It is looking like the army will be able to handle everything now, so the rest of us can go home. We're going to be going home soon. Go find you a new woman, Reynolds."

I shook my hands. "The natives here hate the army guys. It's just going to get worse."

"No, it won't. Heck, you should have left when the other Marines left. Why did you stay?"

"Why did you?"

He shrugged.

"Anyway, I don't want another woman. They're all messed up, except yours of course."

"They're not all messed up. You just got one that couldn't handle being a Marine's girl. A lot of women have trouble with that."

"Trouble with what?"

"Having a relationship only through letters."

Suddenly, there was yelling everywhere. It was coming from outside our barrack. We both rushed out.

Once outside, we saw everyone moving swiftly around grabbing gear and supplies. A disturbing energy was all around. Our lieutenant was off to the left advising another sergeant. A young private rushed by me. He had just picked up his rifle and was headed out with his group.

I ran over to Lieutenant Harris. I had to look up quite a bit at him as he was a former college basketball player that had even gone all the way to the Final Four. I was short of breath as I asked, "What's going on, Lieutenant?"

My lieutenant looked down at me. "Reynolds, gear up."

Another Marine, a radio operator wearing his SAT phone equipment came up on the other side of the Lieutenant. "Sir, we're about ready."

My lieutenant nodded. "Great. Give me five. I'm joining."

The radio operator's eyes got big. "Sir, with all due respect, you heard the report that came in. Snipers are looking for the tallest black American because they know you're our commander."

Our lieutenant grunted and looked down at the radio operator. With a few rapid blinks of his eyes and a scowl, he added, "Son, I said, I'll be ready to go in five."

The other Marine nodded and then headed over to another group of Marines. I spoke up, "What's going on, sir?"

My commanding officer spoke to me while waving for another Marine to come over, "The army was on a mission to get the terrorist tribe's ring leader and it went south. We got a

Black Hawk down and many soldiers stranded. They are sending us in to help. We leave in five. Let's get it!"

"Yes sir!" I didn't ask questions. I nodded and turned around to get my things.

We geared up in a matter of minutes. Since we were at the Olympia Hotel, we were not far from the location of the first downed Black Hawk. Once finished with preps and about to head out, we got the rest of the intel from our commander. Our mission was to provide support to the Army.

Without delay, I led four other Marines with me out of the compound quickly and onto the streets of Somalia not knowing what to expect.

I had point as we ran from block to block trying to stay out of sight. We stopped at a building that looked to have been littered with bullets. I checked the compass on my watch. "Four more clicks to the east."

Lance Corporal Marks turned to the other three Marines. "Let's go, move out."

We made it two more blocks before we ran into enemy contact. Bullets skirted all around me. I heard *pop, pop, pop*, and then bang. We dropped down immediately behind a car that appeared to have been set on fire. In between enemy fire, I lifted my head the best I could to see what we were dealing with. "Only four combatants. Three o'clock," I hollered out.

We fired back. After a few rounds, all targets were neutralized. We all took a second to breathe to calm ourselves and also to make sure it was really all clear. "Alright, let's move out," I ordered.

We ran to the next block. I immediately saw something. I threw up my hand. "Wait!"

Off to the left of the street ahead of us was something small. I squinted my eyes to see. It began moving. I looked around. There was a woman lying dead on the street not far from it. "Is that a baby?"

Lance Corporal Marks replied, "Looks like it."

"Stay back with the men. I'll just be a second."

"Sgt., what are you doing?" Marks asked.

"I'm going to move the baby off the road and put him on that wagon right there. Then we continue north."

"We don't have much time, sir."

"I know."

I ran as fast as I could and then slid across the ground where the infant was. He or she was wrapped in a black blanket that covered not just its tiny body but also much of the ground. The little thing looked up at me with big brown eyes like Webster had.

Suddenly, shots rang out. My men returned fire. I quickly grabbed the baby and was about to run when a hand from behind me shoved me incredibly hard that I dropped the baby.

A loud blast rang in my ears and an intense feeling of burning traveled throughout my body, but more so below my waist. I felt like I was lifted up and then instantly slammed to the ground. My vision went blurry and the worst smell I had ever smelled lingered in the air.

Private Baker appeared above me. His movement was strangely in slow motion. I felt tugs on my body, but I refused to see why. As I was being drug out of the streets, I kept yelling out, "The baby! The baby!" Then, I passed out.

Weeks later as they flew me home injured, the men with me still could not tell me how I wasn't more injured than just my leg. And no one ever told me what happened to the baby. Nor would they tell me how Lance Corporal Marks died.

Margaret, I wanted to think I got the baby to safety. That maybe in the blast I was able to throw him away from the bomb. I kept telling myself that as they were giving me the news that I had lost my leg and was paralyzed. Let me at least hold on to the thought that I did some good in that pathetic place. I couldn't save Webster. And in some way, I am responsible for the death of

Lance Corporal Marks. I just held onto the hope that maybe I at least saved that baby. The truth is, I knew better. The bomb had been originally strapped to the baby. I hated the Somalians even more after that. What kind of evil would blow up a baby to the point that there was nothing left of him?

Please, Sister, let me convince you to get out of Galveston. Let me at least save you. I can't bear…

I stopped writing and dropped the diary. I started crying and crying. It was the first time I cried in years.

CHAPTER 30
Around Thine Altar

Dear Mr. Reynolds,

Thank you for sharing all this with me. I didn't realize that you lost so much. My heart is aching for you. You are one of the bravest men I have ever known. You have to know that God favors you. When you say that you felt like you didn't do any good in Somalia, nothing is further from the truth. What you have done for those poor people is proof that you are special.

There are things that happen to us in life beyond our control. Our problem is that we can't give up that control. God needs to be the one to not only guide us, but also to carry the burden for us. Let Him do that, Mr. Reynolds. If we try to take the throne from God and put ourselves there instead, we will struggle through life. I know firsthand because it is what I did until I met you.

I didn't tell you everything before. When I first read your writing and realized that someone had read my secrets, I prayed. No one needed to know the darkest thoughts of a nun. I worried what it would mean to the faith. I felt that I let God down. So, I prayed for him to give me guidance. If I got a reply from God, it would mean that I needed to burn the diary and confess my sins. But I didn't get a reply. Truth be told, I hadn't gotten a reply from God in a long time anyway. However, I took it as a sign that I needed to continue to write in the diary.

My point is, I trusted in a God that no longer talked to me. I put my worries aside about my secrets getting out and I trusted that God had a plan. And He did. And because of that, I will always choose to do God's work. I made a vow, Mr. Reynolds. I will do my work and stay with the children.

But now look at us and how far we've come. No matter what happens to me, please stop fighting for the throne from God. Sit back and let him take you on a journey that is out of your control. See where He leads you.

God bless,

Sister Margaret

CHAPTER 31
Grateful Psalms

Dear Margaret,

The only journey that I want to go on is with you. I don't know God's plan, but I wish it was the chance to talk with you for the rest of my life. Even if it is just through these short passages we share in your diary.

I stopped writing and remembered the diary my mom gave me before I joined the Marine Corps. We had been on our last vacation as a family in Colorado. I used to love going there. She had told me that writing in it would help me with my thoughts.

My dad laughed from the living room. "Put that down, Trey. Come on, Olivia, don't you realize that diaries are for girls?"

My mom ignored him and gave me a big hug. "I'm proud of you, Trey."

"Thanks, Mom."

I set down Margaret's old diary and pen before lying down. It felt good just to relax and think good thoughts for a change. Before I knew it, I was asleep and dreaming.

I was back in Colorado teaching some girl how to ski.

When she started to disappear from my view, I shifted my skis back to facing downhill and took off after her. The ski path was empty of people so far, so the snow was still soft, not half melted and compacted yet. Undisturbed ground after a morning of snowy downpours, make for fresh powder which is a skier's dream. I moved smoothly down the mountain taking in nature all around me. It was quiet and so peaceful. The sun was now shining just right to warm my body but not ruin the slope.

Feeling a sudden drop in temperature, I looked up and watched the clouds drift harmoniously by in the dark blue sky covering the sun. Untouched by man, they floated above clean and free. When I settled my eyes back down to check on the girl, I thought that she had blonde hair dangling out of what looked like a veil.

I blinked again wondering. Was it Sister Margaret? Had I been teaching her how to ski?

I decided to keep going with it. I noticed the little dare devil shuffling over to the ski lift to go back up again without me. I laughed and leaned forward in a rush to catch up with her.

When I got to her, she turned and gave me a big smile. Her hair was free of the veil now and her nose, red from the cold wind, was sprinkled with freckles. She was so beautiful. I reached for her and then woke up.

My body was drenched in sweat. I went into the bathroom and splashed my face with water. The dream seemed so real. I needed a breather and an ounce of hope. I thought I'd try to find it by going back to the library.

I grabbed my bike keys and headed out again.

****

I parked my bike on the side of the building to the library and watched drunk tourists dancing around with punch style drinks in colors of pink and blue. One of the women gave me a sly smile as she walked by me. Someone was a little too drunk.

I turned to see that library lady coming out the door with a sign in her hand that read, "CLOSING EARLY TO EVACUATE FOR THE HURRICANE".

"Hey! Remember me?" I asked as she taped the sign to the window.

She looked me up and down. "The Marine?"

"Yes. Can you show me those books again?"

"Sure. I haven't put them back up yet. Give me a sec. I'll meet you inside."

The air conditioning in the library was blowing colder than last time. Still, it was a nice reprieve from the humid heat outside. Ralph was in his usual spot reading a book about tornadoes. He nodded at me, "What's up?"

"What's up? What does that mean?" I asked, grinning at him. He was a cute kid.

He shrugged. "Just something people are starting to say."

"Are you always here with your mom?"

"Nah, my babysitter couldn't watch me again. She already evacuated."

Behind me, Avery walked in. She skirted her desk and moved some folders out of the way. "Here you go. Anything in particular you are looking for?"

I took the books from her and smiled. "Just seeing if anything changed."

"What do you mean if anything changed? They're the same history books," she added sarcastically.

"I don't know. Just trying to understand."

She lifted a brow at me. "Are you interested in all this because of the timing?"

I looked up at her. She had her hair pulled behind her head this time, no braids. It further accented her long neck. "Timing?"

"Because this hurricane coming is making landfall in the same place *and* on the anniversary of the hurricane you're researching." Avery spoke with a questioning tone but was making more of a statement.

I flipped through a few pages while half ignoring her. "Look, I'm gonna go sit over here and read. Thanks for this."

She gave me another strange look. "You're welcome. Just set them back on my desk when you are done. I'm closing soon, by the way."

"Yeah, I saw, you're evacuating."

"Yes."

"But I thought the seawall could handle a storm the size they reported it was up to."

"You need to learn how hurricanes work. It only takes a warmer than usual pocket of air for it to cross and then boom, it can explode into a bigger storm than predicted." She looked over at Ralph who was now sweeping the floor for her. "Plus, I've got a kid, you know? Can't take any chances."

"I understand."

I headed over to a table and began looking through the books.

Pretty much nothing had changed in history since the last time I read these books. All the children's bodies were found still attached to the sisters via the clotheslines they used in an attempt to keep from losing any of the children in the flooding.

The only change I read was that many Galvestonians, even in present day before a storm, reported a ghostly figure walking on the beach not far from the Hotel Flores. Witnesses said that she was dressed in nun's clothing. The patrons that see her and don't evacuate, report that she is a vision warning people of incoming Tropical Storms and Hurricanes.

I walked back over to the librarian. She was watching the weather report on the television before she looked up at me.

"Look is there anything in any books showing that the people of Galveston knew the 1900 storm was coming?"

"We didn't have radar back then, sir." Her eyes showed something different. Some doubt. "You need to take this storm serious. You're not from here. The evacuation is mandatory for Galveston county. Surely, you understand what that means?"

I shook my head impatiently. "Right now, I just need more information, please."

"You seem desperate."

I calmed myself. "I just need to know."

She thought for a second. "There may be something. But after this, I'm closing. Promise me you will evacuate with the rest of us."

"Yeah sure," I flippantly responded.

But it was enough for her to leave her desk and head to the back of the library. "There was something."

In the fourth row of stacks, she pulled out a thin book. The title was 'Gulf Coast Hurricanes.'

She flipped through it and read it out loud verbatim, "The station's climatologist, Isaac M. Cline, was notified by telegraph that the hurricane had passed over central Florida. On the following day, Cline noted in his journal that the winds at Galveston were becoming stronger and the seas were rough, but he did not see any of the usual warning signs of an imminent hurricane."

"Thank you," I said and ran out of the library. I could hear her behind me say, "That's all you needed?"

****

I got back to the Gaines house right before dark and ran up the stairs. I didn't know how it would help, but I would try.

Dear Margaret,

I found something. I hope you read this soon. There was a man. His name was Isaac M. Cline. He was the climatologist or something like that. Anyway, he had gotten a telegraph that the hurricane had passed over Florida. If I'm looking at the calendar right, he's already gotten that telegraph. Find him, please. Get him to talk to the Bishop or heck, anyone. You don't have much time, because only a day after that notification, the weather changed drastically in Galveston as the storm approached. God, I hope you get this in time. Please find him. Please.

I closed the diary and saw that I had been shaking as I wrote to her. Tears filled in my eyes. "Please Margaret, please get this."

Thunder rumbled outside, so I rushed to the window. More lighting lit up the now dark sky and rain had started falling. I placed the diary into its hiding spot and grabbed the remote for my little bedroom TV to turn on the news. They were already reporting warnings and saying that the first band of the hurricane had come on shore.

I sat back onto the bed and just stared at the floor where the diary laid below it. Weather alerts continued to go off for hours, but I wasn't leaving. I stayed in my room all day and every hour, I checked Margaret's diary for some sign that she got my message. Still, there was no response.

I fell asleep at some point after nightfall with hopes that it would all blow over, the storm here in 2000 and the storm in 1900.

When I woke up a few hours later, I couldn't believe the sounds coming from outside. I went to look out the window. It was pitch dark and the wind was pushing the trees over at a ninety-degree angle. I had never seen anything like it.

Splashing sounds caught my attention, but it wasn't from outside. I headed over to the bedroom door and opened it. I couldn't believe what I saw. The first floor of the house was starting to flood. "Oh no."

I went to pick up the phone and call the police department to get an update or any kind of advice on what to do. I knew from my research that if I tried to walk out into flooding water, I could get pulled away by the current and possibly drown. I also knew that there was no way I could take my bike or any car for that matter. Nothing could drive in flood waters this high. Plus, my bike was probably gone by that point.

No one answered at the station. I turned on the television. Nothing. I was on my own. I sat down on the bed and debated my options. I had never been through a hurricane.

A howling wind, almost like a freight train, shook the windows of the bedroom. I stood up and went to the window. I opened it to get a better look at how bad everything was. Sure enough, everything was flooded by several feet. I guessed the seawall didn't hold this time.

And then I saw it.

CHAPTER 32
Down the Nave

I couldn't explain the light. I had heard about it in some of the haunting stories. It floated up through the rising water in the form of an orb. When it got almost to the surface, I heard a female voice, raspy and low. She said, "It is done. Go and be happy."

I fell backwards in fear and knocked over a few boxes that I hadn't unpacked yet. Several things fell out of the boxes. I tried to grab onto something, but I slammed the back of my head into something. When I looked up from the floor, I saw that stupid seashell covered chair. Blood was dripping from its arm rest. Then I passed out.

When I woke, the storm had passed. For the next few days, I helped those that stayed behind. There was so much to clean up outside. The streets were covered in debris and every now and again, snakes slithered around. I was warned to watch my step.

The National Guard showed up to assist. Since the power was out, we lined up at the National Guard tents for MREs and water. And the heat. It was unbearable as an uncanny amount of humidity engulfed the city after the rain stopped and the flood waters receded. It was ridiculous. It didn't help that there was no electricity to power our air conditioning. I felt like I was back in Somalia. Honestly, everything about Galveston looked just like the ruins of Somalia. It gave me an eerie feeling.

A few weeks later, after helping everyone clean up after the storm and seeing that the power had come back on, I headed back to my own residence to clean up.

As I was shoving things back into boxes upstairs, I saw it. Laying among the trinkets and newspapers that had fallen out, was an envelope addressed to me. On the top right corner, in Emily's handwriting, was the number twelve. The letter I never opened but for some reason kept with me all this time.

My hands shook as I opened it to read it.

Hey Trey,

I haven't heard back from you so I thought I'd just try one more time. I know you're mad at me because we broke up, but I have news. I had the baby. And the crazy thing is that I think he is yours. So, I named him Joshua after your brother that passed when he was a baby.

Anyway, I know you're still reading letters because Ricky is getting letters back from you, but I see you don't want anything to do with me and I can understand that. But I was pregnant and I didn't know what to do. I'm so sorry about everything. I won't bother you. If you want anything to do with Joshua, I'll wait until I hear from you.

Again, I am so sorry.

Emily

CHAPTER 33
Never Our Faith

I didn't know why I flew back over there. I did have some things to sort out at my dad's house. But I could have done it long distance. Instead, I went back. Back to that pathetic place I called home once. I guessed that after everything that I learned from Margaret, I started to see Emily differently. Or maybe I just wanted to confront her one last time.

My thoughts were conflicted as I stood outside the rod iron and huge walnut wood built front door that belonged to Emily.

When she opened the door, she had a look on her face of astonishment. She fidgeted with the blouse she was wearing while looking around outside and then back at me. "Trey?"

"In the flesh."

"Um, come in."

I followed her in as she picked up a few toys off the floor of the foyer. "I heard Galveston got slammed with another hurricane. Were you there for it?

"Yes."

"Are you okay?" she asked timidly.

"Maybe. Let's cut to the chase. I have a son?"

Emily swung back around to me. A plastic caterpillar toy she clutched in her arm started playing an annoying song. "Okay. Let's have a seat."

She motioned for me to sit on the couch across from her. As she turned off the caterpillar and placed the rest of the toys on the seat next to her, I scanned over all her family pictures. Emily, Carlton, and a little girl in Easter attire. Another of the happy family with Santa. On the wall behind Emily that was adjacent to the kitchen, a huge black and white portrait hung of Emily holding a baby. The baby had a huge smile.

"Nice little family you have here. Nice home. You really achieved what you always wanted." I smacked my gum impatiently.

"What are you talking about?"

"You know what I mean. You found a way for a rich man's son to marry you, so you could be rich, too."

"I married Carlton because he was there for me. He knew Joshua wasn't his baby and he stayed with me anyway."

My left brow lifted. "You used him then?"

"You are even more paranoid since your time there. I'll give you grace because you lost so much, but why are you here?"

"Isn't Carlton everything you ever wanted? You got him."

"Everything I ever wanted? Everything I ever wanted was you, Trey! You!! But you left to go play hero and please your dad!"

She picked up a blanket off the couch and began folding it out of nervousness. "And then you stopped talking to me."

"But you broke up with me!"

"Just…" She put her hand up. "I don't want to hash all this out now. It's too late for that. But I have a question. Why now? You didn't ever write back to me even when I kept writing you. But now you come here."

"Kept writing me?"

"Twenty or so letters."

I looked down at my hands. Each line on the inside of my palm and fingers still had dirt or debris traces from the cleaning up I had to do after the hurricane's flood waters ruined the first floor of the Gaines' house. "I stopped reading after your 11th letter."

"Then how did you know Joshua was yours? I put that in the letter after the 11th one."

"I just pulled out the twelfth one and read it a few days ago."

"Oh geez. So, you missed it completely. Did you get any of my other letters or read them? I sent you pictures of him."

"No, but how is it possible that he's mine? All this time, I thought he was Carlton's."

She sucked in her lips and said, "I missed my period and didn't think much of it because I had always had irregular periods. When I was four months late and went to the doctor to see what was wrong. That was when they told me I was pregnant. Then, when he was born, it became more obvious. He was yours, Trey."

"Was?"

Emily's eyes teared up.

I looked back at the family pictures. Only a little girl was in them. "Oh God. The baby you buried after its birth was mine? Joshua?"

"Yes, the doctors thought it was a genetic flaw. Similar to what happened to your brother who I named Joshua after."

We both sat there in silence for a moment.

Emily wiped her tears and stood up. "I have more pictures if you want to see them. You can take some with you."

"You do?"

Emily walked out and then a few seconds later, came back in. She handed me a handful of pictures.

"I made a lot of mistakes, Trey. But when I had Joshua, I finally felt the full impact of those bad decisions. I guess I continued writing you in hopes that you'd want anything to do with him. After a few more letters unanswered, I gave up. So, I left you alone." She sighed. "But you know what, the past is the past. My only regret now is that you never got to hold him."

I stared at the picture in my hand. Light brown hair, brown eyes, and a big smile just like mine. "He really was mine? He's adorable."

"Yes. I'm so sorry."

"Me too. I'm sorry, too. I know how I get. The war does things to you. Male pride is always an issue but then you add war on top of that. I shut down on you and my son. I am so sorry, Emily."

"Thank you for that, but Trey, you shut down on people way before the war."

****

I didn't stay long. I thanked Emily for the pictures, gave her a hug, and decided to leave her in peace. She had a new life now and I did not want to jeopardize that. I walked down the driveway and got into my rental car. I didn't leave yet. It began to rain. I just sat there listening to the cold rain slap against the windshield. The air inside the car was sterile as was my heart at the moment.

I clutched the pictures of Joshua. Tears ran down my cheeks. I thought of Margaret. I wished I could have told her about Joshua. Some of her last words filled my mind. As I was sitting there in emotional agony of losing her and then learning that I had a son of whom I lost too, I remembered Margaret's words. She had said life was a journey to be lived and to live it the best we could.

At the time, my ignorance clouded my choices. No way could I look back and hate myself for anything. I did live through my situation the best I could. Margaret had been right. She was always right.

The rain let up and splashes of sunlight hit the windshield. I looked up. Across the pinkish sky was an array of colors that I hadn't seen in years. A rainbow that stretched from the apartments across the street and all the way out into the sky above the factories. It was beautiful. I marveled at it, not wanting to take my eyes off of it. I needed that feeling. I needed to feel good again and fight through my broken heart. I needed to do this for Margaret. I needed to do this for Joshua. More so, I needed to do this for me.

I looked up and spoke aloud, "Margaret, I wish I could show you this picture of my son. Tell you all about it. Tell you how right you were. But maybe you've already met him up there in Heaven. If so, please give my son a hug for me." I sobbed for a minute and held tightly to the picture.

Finally, I put the rental car into gear, looked in my rearview mirror, and let my eye catch on the crucifix I had started carrying around with me.

"Margaret, I have one more important stop to make. I owe this to you and God."

The Ford Taurus jerked as if the gear had slipped. When it began to move, I took a turn down Amsterdam Street instead of Williams Street. My destination was one I hadn't planned on when I flew up here, but it was now a must.

CHAPTER 34
Thy Sweet Power

My mom greeted me at the door. A few more wrinkles had gathered around her hazel eyes. "How are you, baby? I heard about that hurricane. I was worried sick for you."

"I'm good."

"How are you holding up after your father's passing?" she asked as we made our way to the kitchen.

"It was hard at first." I laid my hands flat on the marble counter. "Did you know that Emily's son, the one she had buried, he was mine?"

She froze. The silence was tricky. It was almost like she wanted to cry, but her disbelief was stronger. "What? Of course not. What do you mean by yours?"

I took a picture out of my pocket. It was damp from either my tears or the rain soaking through my jeans when I got out of the car. I handed it to her. I continued talking, "Emily had irregular periods. It's obvious that he was mine. He even passed away from the same genetic disease Joshua had."

Her eyes examined the picture and then she raised her hand to her mouth. "Oh, my goodness. I am so sorry."

"It's okay. I'm just glad I know the truth about that now."

"His name?" she asked as she leaned down onto the arm of the sofa.

"Joshua, too."

"Oh." She started crying. "How could we not know?" she could barely ask.

"I don't blame Emily for anything anymore. Nor do I blame you."

"For what?"

I took the picture back and looked down on the angelic face of my son. "You and Dad. I know it wasn't all your fault now."

She stood and took my hands. "Trey, you have been through so much in your life. I hope you know that I am so proud of how strong you are." She wiped her tears. "You really have changed. How?"

I smiled. "Thank you. I had a pen pal to help me lately."

"Pen pal? From what Japan or something?"

I laughed. "No, but with a nun."

"Oh?"

"She taught me a lot. That is why I am trying to see things differently. Mom, I just want to tell you that I am so sorry. I am so sorry for treating you the way I had."

She cut me off. "Stop. You don't owe me an apology. I'm just glad you are here with me today. If I had lost you in that war and then in that hurricane, I don't know what I would have done."

"Well, I'm here. God willing, He's keeping me around." My heart hurt for Margaret. After the hurricane, she never entered anything else in the diary. She was gone.

My mom took my hands again. "You should write all this. The hurricane, your pen pal, the war. Something. You need to share your experiences with others. You never know, it could really help someone else."

She stopped talking and turned towards the window. Her voice came back almost as a whisper. "So, I had a grandson."

"Yes."

She turned back towards me. "Trey?"

"Yes, mom?"

"Remember Mark Shepperd?"

"From school?"

"Yes. He went into the Army not long after you."

I fidgeted with my shirt sleeve. My elementary best friend, Mark had joined up? I couldn't believe it. He was always the one that hated playing war at recess. In high school, we didn't hang out much, but he helped me out one time when I really needed it. "I didn't realize."

Mom nodded. "Betty, his mother, and I are friends. Mark had a son before he left. Betty comes around and brings little Will with her sometimes. Her sweet grandson."

I felt bad for mom now, too. "Oh."

She raised her hand up. "Trey, Will made it back after his tour, but he had problems. He got into drugs and they kicked him out."

"Out of the military, huh? That happens. Where is he now? I'll go check on him."

"Well, you see, that's the other problem. When you're dishonorably discharged, you don't get any psychiatric care. Trey, Will took his life a few months ago."

I didn't know what to say. My legs were trembling. Or was that anger for Will's weakness? All kinds of emotions came over me. Will was the guy with the fastest car in high school. He actually let me borrow it once so I wouldn't be late for a football event out of the city. I balled up my hands remembering how kind he was. I never even knew he joined and now I'm hearing that I lost another friend.

My mom came up to me and took my face in her hands. "I prayed for you every night when you got back home."

"Why when I got home?"

"Because that is when it is the hardest, Son. I learned after Mark's death that whole twenty-two a day. Veteran suicide is…" She paused and tears filled her eyes. "I didn't want to lose you."

I removed her hands from my face. "You never had to worry about me, Mom."

"I did. And I'll keep worrying and praying because the way you used to talk it sounded like you were fighting it."

"What?"

"A battle that shows no physical wounds. In fact, it's a harder battle to fight." She smiled up at me. "I'm glad you met someone to talk to. Sometimes that's all a person needs. That and to be able to write out how they feel. So, write!"

I nodded while thinking about what she was saying. Suicide crossed my mind every single freaking day until Margaret. It still crosses my mind sometimes, but I feel I'm getting better.

As my mom began to make us some lunch, I stood in her little kitchen thinking about everything and Margaret. I could write about my time with Margaret. Write it like it was a fiction or maybe paranormal story. That a way, I could keep Margaret alive in my heart just a little while longer. I could, but fear crept in at the thought of writing it all out. I still wasn't ready.

CHAPTER 35
Falter

After I flew back home from Pittsburgh, I focused on completely finishing the remodel on the historic home that survived yet another horrible hurricane. In between my trips to the hardware store once it opened back up and many late nights of staring down at a diary that continued to show me what I already knew, I finally decided to put the diary in its spot to rest.

It was about eight o'clock the next morning when I heard a knock at the door downstairs. I rubbed my eyes and lifted myself from the bed. My back was sore from laying the laminate floors in the kitchen last night.

The knocks continued as I made it down the stairs. I opened the door to a familiar face. "Larry? What ya doing here?" I asked while squinting against the bright sunlight coming in from behind him.

He was dressed decent this time in pull-over sweatshirt and dark blue slacks. He was wearing an Army cap and a big smile. "Yup."

I motioned for him to come in. "Come on in. I was just about to make coffee."

"Sounds good," he said as he looked around the first floor. "Nice. I knew this place flooded again. What's that like the fifth time and it still stands."

"Yep,"

"You didn't take long to fix it back up, did you?"

I was already headed to the kitchen. "Nothing better to do." I pulled down a can of Folgers and put a heavy scoop into the filter in the pot.

Larry followed me in and gave an approving nod at the floor. "Great choice in flooring. That stuff lasts."

"I heard. So, what brings you here?"

He leaned up against the white washed cabinets that I had just painted last week. "Alexis."

"She okay?"

He nodded. "Oh yeah, she just said something about you going into the bar right before the hurricane. You seemed all upset."

I thought back over that day. I was upset, but I didn't want to talk about it. "I'm fine."

"You see? You keep saying that. And buddy, that's okay. You probably are. But do you want to be just okay or do you want to try something?"

I set the coffee cups onto the counter and took a breath. "Not following you." His change of tone and words reminded me of Sister Margaret.

"What ya got going on today?"

"Resting."

"Come with me on a little day trip over to Louisiana. Not far… maybe forty-five minutes. The border between Louisiana and Texas."

"Why would I do that?"

He leaned in and tapped my shoulder. His taller form appeared more intimidating this morning than it did at the bar that first time I met him. Or maybe because I was sober. "Because I said so. Just come spend a few hours with another combat vet." He removed his hand. "Plus, the food is good over there. You'll love it."

I remembered Sister Margaret's voice in my head from the night of the hurricane. "Trust others. Be happy," she had told me. I realized then that I had been so busy putting together the pieces about Emily and my son and then diving right into fixing up the old house, that I still hadn't taken Sister Margaret's advice. "Alright." I didn't recognize my own voice saying it, but I didn't regret it.

Larry smiled. "Perfect. Get dressed. We'll grab some donuts on the way."

$$****$$

A few hours later, we were duck hunting in the middle of a swamp. Me, Larry, two other Army vets by the names of Terry and Mike, a Navy vet named Henry, and another Marine veteran named Antoine. It was a blast! We laughed, teased each other, saw alligators, and ate deer sausage that Antoine served everyone when we got back to the one room shed that the guys called their duck hunting camp.

I sat there watching them tear into the sausage and laugh at themselves and each other. I had missed that. The comradery between brothers.

Just before sunset, Larry lit up the bonfire a few hundred feet from the camp. Off to my right, Antoine had begun untying the American flag from the tree where it had been flying all day while we hunted.

I followed the group and stood with them just staring at the bonfire. We watched the flames get bigger as the sun began to disappear leaving darkness at our backs. Henry called us to attention and then began speaking while holding the flag, "This flag has served its nation well and long. It has worn to a condition in which it should no longer be used to represent the nation. This flag represents all of the flags collected and being retired from service today. The honor we show here this evening for this one flag, we are showing for all of the flags, even those not physically here."

All the men nodded in agreement. I had heard about retiring the flag, but I never saw it done like this.

Antoine began cutting the flag into several pieces and handed each of us a piece of it.

Henry, holding a paper in his hand only lit by his flashlight, continued the speech, "I am your Flag. I was born on June 14, 1777. I am more than just a piece of cloth shaped into a colorful design, I am the silent sentinel of freedom for the greatest sovereign nation on earth. I am the inspiration for which American patriots gave their lives and fortunes. I am the emblem of America. I have led our troops into battle from Valley Forge to Afghanistan. I have been there through the Civil War, Two World wars, at Gettysburg, Korea, Vietnam, the Gulf War and many other missions. I walk in silence with each of our honored dead to their final resting place beneath the silent white crosses.'

'I have flown through peace and war. Through strife and prosperity, and amidst it all, I have always been respected. My red stripes symbolize the blood spilled in defense of this glorious nation. My white stripes symbolize the burning tears shed by Americans who lost their sons in battle. My blue field represents God's Heaven under which I fly my stars, clustered together, unify the fifty states as one for God and Country. I am "Old Glory" and I proudly wave on high. Honor me, respect me, and defend me with your lives. Never let our enemies tear me down from my lofty position. Keep alight the fires of patriotism, strive earnestly for the spirit of democracy, and keep me always as a symbol of freedom, liberty, and peace in our country. When comes the time when I am old and faded, do not let me fly in disrepair, rather retire me from my duties only to replace me with a new flag so that I may continue to symbolize our country." He lowered the paper in his hand and looked around at all of us through the dim light. "At this time, anyone who would like to speak in memory of someone, please do so."

Larry was the first to talk. "I retire our flag for my brothers, Private First-Class Miguel Jones, Specialist Walter Reeves, and Corporal Simon Russo, who lost their lives in Kuwait." He walked up to the fire and dropped his piece of the flag into the flames.

Next to me, Terry began talking, "I retire our flag for Sergeant Rick B. Williams who took his own life two weeks ago."

I couldn't focus on what Terry did next. My mind was on what my mom told me just the other day. And how she would continue to pray for me.

That night at my mom's house, my brother had shown up. He gave me a brochure for mental health of all things. I had gotten pissed. My mom calmed us down and reminded me that they were just trying to help. I had told them I was fine. Then, my brother did something he never did before, he said, "I believe in you and I'm proud of you." After that, he just walked over and hugged me.

My eyes were blurry with tears thinking back on that day and thinking of all my time with Margaret. Everyone seemed to genuinely care about me. However, my breathing began to speed up. Just as I was changing my thoughts back to how I was a pathetic excuse of a Marine to be so vulnerable, Larry touched my shoulder and nodded at me. Every inch of my body strangely relaxed.

Another guy at the bonfire retired his piece of the flag after saying his friends' names. I watched him shed tears, too. At that sight, I couldn't believe the peace that washed over me.

I squeezed my portion of the flag and took a breath. Then out of nowhere, I began to speak, next. "I retire our flag for **Lance Corporal Tyler Marks** and **Private Brian Lopez,** both died in Somalia. I retire our flag for my friend from school, Mark Shepherd. Mark committed suicide not long after getting back home. Also, for Sgt. Harris, who committed suicide in San Diego not long before I came here to Texas. And…" I choked on my words. Larry patted my back.

I took a breath and continued, "I also retire our flag for the boy I loved and miss to this day. The boy I met in Somalia that I put in danger by letting him in the compound with us. I should have been able to save him. I couldn't." I teared up on the last word.

Still, I continued, "He was only ten. His name was Webster," I said and immediately dropped my part of the flag into the fire. A flame engulfed it completely. The fire seemed to singe my face, but I didn't move. I just stood there with tears rolling down my cheeks and stared at the red and orange colors of the fire retreating and flaring back up.

When the other guys began to move around, I didn't look at them. In my head, I heard something else. Something unworldly. This new voice and strange voice still seemed to be familiar. A chill passed over me as I heard, without ears, that voice whisper into my ear saying, "It is time to be at peace, my son."

My shoulders relaxed as I dropped down to my knees. Larry's hand stayed steady on my shoulder as I went down.

When I looked back up above the flames and into the dark sky, I thought I saw something. The silhouette of a woman slowly swirling in the smoke. The image was lit up dimly by only the fire of the bonfire. I smiled then. I did it. I took Margaret's advice and shared my heart with others. In doing so, I also opened that same heart up to God. And He came in. I had never felt more alive than I did that night.

And that was when I realized. Just like Margaret had helped me, I needed to do something for her. I had to tell her story.

****

A few months later, I was back in Pittsburgh. I had finished their story. As I sat there in a literary agent's office only a few blocks from Holy Trinity Church, I thought of how my family used to attend that church but no longer do.

The agent in front of me leaned over onto his five-foot-wide desk and regarded me oddly. The balding man asked, "Why write a book now?"

"I used to write all the time. I stopped when I got older. But just recently, someone inspired me."

Mr. Phipps sat back and laid his hands over the armrest of his large black chair. "Look, I'm going to be honest. You're a new author, no street credit. Tell me why I should invest in you and in this."

"You shouldn't." I clasped my hands together. "But you already did."

"I beg your pardon."

"You read it, you called me in here, and you hadn't declined it yet. It has to be because of what those nuns did at that orphanage that touched you, too. Plus, it's a bit of a paranormal story. People love that stuff. Throw in my expertise of renovating old historic homes and bam, you got the perfect package."

"I won't lie. I liked the title. That made me read further. *Historic Homes are the Souls of our Towns*. Perfect title. But then you tell us that story about the hurricane survivor down in Galveston. A cute Victorian that stood through the 1900 hurricane and again through seven more. Wow." He sighed. "Now, the nun's diary and their story… icing on the cake. Bravo. I never knew the selflessness of those nuns. I never knew much of that hurricane in particular either. I still don't know."

"Of all the people that could have found that diary, it was me that found it. I ask myself every day, why me? Why not some other war-torn soul? Or why couldn't it have been an alcoholic who needed to hear the Good News or a parent who lost a child? And you know what conclusion I came to?"

"What's that?"

"God knew I'd take it and write about it. And in doing that, it serves two purposes. One, I would start writing again. And two, the nuns and the orphans from that terrible day would be remembered more personally than as some names of people that died in history. You see? We have to get this published. Whether I do it through you or not, it's getting out to the masses."

The man rubbed his large nose with the back of his hand, but he smirked instead of remaining indifferent. "Um."

"What?"

"Because you're Olivia's son, I'm going to take a chance. Of all my son's years in school, she was the best dang teacher he ever had. She really believed my Jeffrey could succeed, even with Autism. That's a good woman, your mom. They don't make them like that anymore."

When he said that, I realized. I had said that same thing about Margaret. Why did I hold such a high standard on my mom and resent her so much? She went through the trouble of setting this up for me. And she *was* an amazing teacher. "I know."

He took his glasses off and leaned in. "So, where is this diary?"

"Hidden and safe for a reason."

"What's the reason?"

"Her words helped me. Just like they will help others. But I don't want the diary to get ruined."

"Is it at some old house still in Galveston?"

I leaned towards him, meeting him half-way across his desk. With a firm voice, I added, "Not saying?"

He shifted back and began laughing. "You're a serious guy, aren't you? Trust me, I never had any plans to touch it. I was just curious. But seeing your reaction tells me there is something special going on here. And you inspired me to looking into renovating an old home here too. Oh, the mysteries I could find."

"Exactly."

Mr. Phipps rolled his chair over to a filing cabinet. He pulled a folder out and rolled back behind his desk. "I'll draft up the contract."

CHAPTER 36
Mother of God

Larry grabbed my last suitcase. "Ready to go?"

I eyed the empty foyer of the Gaines' house. I came to Galveston in July of 2000 as a completely different man than the one that was now standing inside that same historic home. I survived a hurricane and met a woman that I would never forget, so much so that I memorialized her and all the nuns in a novel that has sold over twenty million copies.

I nodded. "Yep. No need to be a contractor anymore. Now, I'm just going to follow what the other contractors uncover."

"But San Antonio? That's hotter than here. Don't get me wrong. I know you like your history stuff, but I'm going to miss you."

I smiled. "I'll miss you too but there is a beauty of a home getting renovated down there right now, and it's close to the Alamo!"

I followed behind him. I needed a new start. I couldn't stay around hoping Sister Margaret would just magically appear and I would live happily ever after for a change. Nope, she was gone. So, I needed to be, too.

Larry walked out first. As I turned to lock the door, I heard a soft voice behind me.

"Trey Reynolds?"

"Yes. Can I help you?" I asked while securing the door. When I turned around, there was a woman with blonde braids and big blue eyes. "Wait a second. You?"

"Yeah, the librarian."

"That's right."

"May I come in for a moment?" she asked demurely. Her only shred of makeup was a pink lip gloss that shined in the sunlight. She was definitely a pretty lady. I could make time.

"Yes? Why? And I never checked out those books. How do you know my name?"

"Your book arrived at the library. I read everything new that comes in. And then I saw your picture on the last page."

"So, you have an interest in me now, why?"

"My family and you are connected. Can you give me a chance to explain?"

I eyed her for a second. Her son, Ralph, walked up behind her. "Hey, it's you!" he exclaimed.

"Hey, Ralph."

I sighed and went ahead to let her and Ralph in. Avery sent Ralph into the kitchen to play his favorite card game, Solitaire. Then, she sat down on the malt-colored couch that I replaced in the living room after the hurricane flooded the entire first floor. "So why become a Marine and now a writer?"

"Do something good for my country." I didn't bother explaining the writing part.

She fidgeted with something in her bag. "I actually come from a long line of military people."

"That's nice."

Her brows lifted. "A long line of Texans with our roots starting here in Galveston."

"I kind of got that impression from our short talks."

"But you don't know my full story. Give me a few minutes to tell it and then I'll tell you why I'm here."

"Okay."

Larry walked back in and set my bags down. "Hey, buddy. I'll give you two a minute. Gonna go get some ice cream."

"I shouldn't be long," I said as Larry nodded over at Avery. Then, he gave me a look. As he was walking out behind her, he mouthed. "She's beautiful."

I shook my head at him and looked back at Avery. "As you were saying."

"There has been a tradition in my family dating back to my great, great, great grandfather that would occur at their will readings mostly. When the will was read, a package was passed down from father to son or father to daughter. Whichever child was first born. We all referred to it as a time capsule."

"Time capsule?"

"Yes, because it was something put together by Trey, my ancestor, that couldn't be opened until 2000."

"What does that have to do with me?"

"Inside the package there was a letter addressed to the descendant, which would be me now. The descendant would receive the package. It gave instructions that on October 1st 2000, we were to deliver it to this address. To a man who bears the same name as our great, great, great grandfather."

"Not following. It's 2001 now. So, who got the package?"

"No one yet. I… um, I stuck the package in a storage unit and thought it was stupid. Until, I saw a book come into the library. A book written by a man with the same name the package was intended for. And to make it even more odd, it was a book written about a nun during the Hurricane of 1900 and your face was on the back cover. That's a lot of coincidences."

My hands started to shake. Could it be?

She leaned forward with wide eyes and asked, "So, Trey Reynolds, my question is, are we related?"

I played around for a second. "Wait. Is this some way to get money now that you know I'm a best-selling author?"

She tugged at her ear and asked, "Still arrogant, huh? Nope. So, I'll leave the letter with you because it's addressed to you and you do as you wish with it. Believe it or not, but I have no agenda. I just believe things happen for a reason."

"I never asked, whatever happened with Tim."

Avery eyed me cautiously. "What about him?"

"He come around again?"

"No."

"Why did you ever date someone like that?"

Avery pulled out an old folded letter and it held close to her while she replied, "Get back with me when you have no family left, Trey. I guess you could say I settled because I thought I could grow my family."

She looked down at the letter and then handed it to me. It was, like she said, addressed to me- *Trey Reynolds*. There was no denying it. It was even in Margaret's handwriting.

My body went rigid. "How did this happen?"

"I'm not following." She frowned. "I just thought it was because we were related."

I ignored her and with sweaty palms, I slowly opened the letter.

Mr. Reynolds,

A light rain started a few hours ago. We continued our day as usual with mass followed by having the children begin their school work. As the day went on, a heavier amount of rain came. I had been staring out towards the sea thinking of what you had told me about this storm. The waves had been rising higher than I had ever seen and were beating the shore with an intensity I had never knew possible before that day. I thought of you, Mr. Reynolds, and I clenched my rosary tight to my chest. I knew what it was. I also knew that I did not have time to head into town to write in my diary or read your words again, so I write to you on a few empty pages of a class journal. You will never see these words, but I write them anyway as my candle is starting to run out of wax. I will finish writing this quickly whether you get it or not. I will let God decide if it makes it to you or not.

I wanted to tell you how much I appreciated our time together. You showed me things that opened my heart to life in general. I hadn't laughed until I met you. And not long after I laughed, I heard God again. Trey, it was not because God hadn't been talking to me all along. It was because I wasn't listening to Him. I was afraid. After I met you, I learned how to be courageous and to listen again.

The most important thing I learned through all this was that I never took the time to talk about what had happened in my life as Amelia. I never took the steps needed to heal myself first before I took my vows to be a nun. That was my biggest mistake. God knew that and he found a way for me to do it. It was through my friendship with you, Mr. Reynolds.

I want the same for you. I want you to listen, not just to God, but to everyone. And keep talking. Talk to anyone who will listen. Maybe even talk to Emily. We go through life thinking we know everyone's feelings and intentions, but we know nothing. Everyone has a story that is rooted in love. Don't be clouded by worthless judgement but be free from willingness of temper.

Your time at war has greatly shaped your thoughts on people. Don't let the good you did helping and protecting others as a soldier, steal the happiness that God always wanted for you. Therefore, my last prayer as this storm blows out my candle and I finish writing in the dark, I will pray that you get this letter and heed my advice. I pray that you let more people in like you did with me. And more importantly, that you let God back in.

I closed the letter.

Avery was still sitting there. She lifted her brows. "I guess I just have to know and then I'll leave. Are we related?"

"No, we're not. Not really." I shifted in my seat. "Avery, how did your Trey Reynolds survive the hurricane?"

She looked puzzled. "Like the other three orphans. They swam to a tree."

"I know that but weren't they tied to the nuns?" I asked. All the while I was thinking to myself that I never told Margaret about how that was the reason the children and nuns died. All it took was the flood waters to pull one kid under and then the rest went down too.

The door opened and Avery's son, walked back in. She pointed to the chair. "Just sit there for a second. I'm almost done, sweetheart."

Then she looked back at me. "All I know was what was passed down. Sister Margaret tied the kids to her, but my ancestor, Trey Reynolds, was usually always right next to her. This time he remembered that she entrusted him to be at the end of the line. He said she stuck something in his pocket, that he later realized was not for him but to be passed down, and then she told him, 'Trey, I need you at the end of the line with me at the beginning and all the rest in the middle, because Trey, you are my soldier, and you know what good soldiers do? They protect God's flock'."

My mind shifted back to our correspondences. Did she know not to tie the rope? No, he had to have been tied. Maybe she just didn't tie it tight enough or maybe. Did she know? How did she know he would live? I never even told her that I found out that the orphan she named after me had lived through the storm. So how would she know? Was it God? Did He tell her now that she was hearing Him again? She said He used to speak to her all the time, but stopped. That was why she was upset the last year. Did He finally speak to her and tell her to not tie the rope so tight on Trey? Oh my god. My mind was racing.

But Avery's son gently touched my shoulder and said, "Mr. Trey, you are a soldier too, aren't you?"

Avery reached for his arm. "Ralph, go sit back down."

"No, it's okay." I smiled over at him. "I guess, Ralph. Or I used to be."

Ralph's face beamed with a new kind of joy. And then he said something I'd never forget. He said, "So, that's what you do. You protect God's flock like my really old grandfather did."

I teared up from this child's innocent words. He got it, why hadn't I? I smiled at him and then folded up the letter.

CHAPTER 37
Upon Sea and Tide

I didn't know what else to say. I sat there for a few minutes stunned as I continued to put the pieces together. "Avery, can I tell you something?"

"Yes."

I motioned to Ralph. "But can we talk in private?"

She gave Ralph a look. "Go back into the kitchen with your cards.

After he walked out, I told Avery everything about the diary. "Like in your published book?"

"Yes."

"So, you're saying that was real?"

"Yes."

She had a look on her face like I had lost my mind. But in contradiction, she said, "Like I said before, I believe things happen for a reason."

"So, you know what this means?"

She nonchalantly shrugged. "What?"

I motioned for her to follow me upstairs. We both moved slowly, as if in deep thought, until we reached the threshold of the room.

Once in the bedroom, I pulled up one of the boards of the new flooring I had installed. It killed me to do it, but I wanted her to see it. I pulled the diary out of its hiding spot and handed it to her. She flipped through the first pages, but I took it back from her before she could see where I wrote in it. "Sorry, I just wanted to show it to you. The rest, I'd like kept private."

"No, I understand. But wow. It's real, huh?"

"Yep. And Avery, if all this is true, then that means I changed things. Originally before I came to Galveston, your ancestor, with the same name as me, either had a different name or he didn't survive the hurricane at all."

She looked down at the diary and covered her mouth. "Oh my God, that's right." We both stood there for a minute. We couldn't deny that it all was true. But the most haunting of all was what Avery realized next. But instead of being serious, she laughed. It was the cutest laugh, I couldn't deny it. She hiccupped when she did it.

"What's so funny?" I asked.

Avery continued laughing. "It's crazy, I am here today because you were a pen pal with a nun from another time." She kneeled down by the hole. "My life began because of *that* book in your hands that was hidden in *there*?" She stopped laughing and looked back up at me. "God works in mysterious ways, Trey. Mysterious ways."

I nodded and looked back down at the empty space below the subdeck. A shimmer caught my eye. "I almost forgot. The quill. I don't know why I'm just now seeing it." I picked up the small object and wiped it off. It still was an off-white color with specks of gold on it. I lifted it to show her and said, "We both wrote with it. Look at it. It's beautiful."

Then, I handed it to Avery. When I placed it in her hand, she squeezed it strangely and her eyes glossed over. With a soft voice, she said, "Yes, very beautiful."

"Sister Margaret said it was given to her by one of the tenants in this house before the hurricane. Ms. Davenport, I think I remembered her saying. And something about the ivory on this quill being around for centuries before as a -"

She cut me off by saying, "Rosary."

"Yes. How did you know that?"

Avery didn't reply. She tried to hand the quill back to me.

I shook my head. "No, you keep it. It's the least I can do. Just promise not to tell anyone where the diary is. Can you do that?"

"Yes. Thank you."

"I had been debating how to handle the privacy of the diary and originally thought that leaving it in its hiding space was the best. But now, I wonder about how easy it can be found. I'm going to still leave it here, but I'm going to run to the store for supplies, so I can seal the plank. That a way, it can't be removed so easily. I'll tell Larry. I'll have to wait and leave on a different day."

She seemed to tune me out but headed over to the nightstand by the bed. While she was perusing that piece of furniture, I closed the floor back up and made a mental note to change my flight to San Antonio until next week. I wasn't ready to leave.

I turned and thought I saw Avery pop something back into place under the nightstand. Maybe the door came unhinged. "Thanks," I told her.

She seemed to be processing a lot of information. I couldn't blame her. I walked over and touched her hand. "Look, I'm not in a rush. I still need to do this to keep the diary safe. But since apparently we're connected, how about we go get a bite to eat?"

Distant eyes looked up at mine. "Yes, please."

CHAPTER 38
For Where it Comes

Avery took us to a neat café not far from the house. I didn't realize until we walked into it that it was that place that made the great pecan pies, GG's Diner. Ralph and I enjoyed our sandwiches. Avery barely touched her shrimp gumbo, even though she had said it was her favorite at the diner.

I pretty much talked the whole time while Avery either stared at me or around the diner with child-like eyes. She was acting strange ever since the letter and revelations were revealed. She still talked and smiled at Ralph, so I was beginning to think I had done something wrong or offended her or worse, maybe she thought I made it all up. That I had fabricated a diary and acted like I was something special. It didn't matter. God and I knew the truth. Heck, that was all that mattered anymore.

Ralph took his last bite and said, "Mom, can we go down to the beach? I want to show the Sergeant something?"

She smiled over at him. "The Sergeant?"

"That's what he is, isn't he?"

I chimed in. "Was?"

"Nah, you'll always be a hero."

I didn't know how to take that, but looking at Ralph's face light up with fascination was just so dang sweet. "If you say so, young man."

"I do. Now, let's go to the beach."

Avery sat back in her chair and looked up at me. "Do you have time?"

"Of course. I already moved my flight."

"Great!" Ralph exclaimed.

After that, I paid the check and followed the little family out to the street. Avery stopped outside the door and turned around looking up at the windows to the second floor of the diner.

"Everything okay?" I asked.

She smiled. "Just still taking it all in."

"Come on, Mom. Let's go!" Ralph yanked at her wrist and she followed laughing.

When we got to the beach, Avery seemed to relax a little more. After Ralph ran off again, she spoke softly, "Remember when we first met in the library and you asked about the painting I was staring at?"

"Vaguely."

"And I said that it was odd timing that someone wanted to read books about the hurricane."

I nodded. "Yes."

"And I just told you that it was a special day."

"That's right. What was the occasion?"

Avery took a deep breath. "That picture is a painting my ancestor made of his memories of Sister Margaret. And the day you came in was the five-year anniversary of when I found God. I wasn't always religious. I had lost my way. That's why the package from my inheritance ended up in storage when I inherited it ten or so years ago."

"Why?"

"I did not believe the stories. I did not care anything about the fact that a nun took in my ancestor and taught him unconditional love, which my family tried to pass down to me. Nope. Instead, I rebelled, did some drugs, lost my way. Five years before that day that you walked into the library, I had found the old painting of Sister Margaret and the rosary that came in the package. For some reason and a few years before that, I took it out of the package and shoved it under my bed before I stuffed the rest in storage."

"And?" I asked.

"So, what I'm saying is that even though I didn't believe in the family history about a special package to be delivered to someone with the same name as my war hero ancestor, I still for some reason kept the painting and the rosary. Like I said, I shoved the rest away, not wanting to continue what I thought was a stupid tradition centered around a made-up religion." She took another cleansing breath. "But why did I keep things about her?"

I shrugged.

"Five years before you showed up and when I was at my lowest, I was on the floor of my room in tears. I saw the edge of the painting. I pulled it out with the case that held the rosary. When I stared at the painting, I felt moved to open the case. Lifting up the rosary in my hands and staring at the crucifix dangling on the end, I just started praying. It was really… I never felt like that. It was almost like I felt a presence."

She sucked in her lips. "And after that, I never stopped praying. I call that day my redemption day. Therefore, it was odd that a man from another state came in asking about the hurricane that changed my family's life, which ultimately led to my salvation."

I smiled. There it was again; Margaret's hand was in everything with God's intervention.

Avery's son, with his hair spiked up from the salty water, ran along the beach with seashells falling out of his hands. "Mom, look! A rainbow!"

I followed his eyes up to the sky. My gut reaction was to snicker and ignore it. Like I said, I hated rainbows. But when Avery smiled sweetly at me, my breathing slowed down and I thought of Margaret's words to me. "It's the journey," she would tell me. "Good, bad, or even unplanned, you need to enjoy the journey."

I marveled back up at the rainbow. Maybe that was the last part of my story that I was missing. The journey. Now, here is this rainbow. Not long ago, I still thought of a rainbow as nothing special. Today, that mirage of different color palettes was breathtaking.

Well, this was the good part of my life. I'd honor Margaret by taking her advice and enjoying it. So, I decided to start today under that beautiful rainbow. It reached out from the shoreline all the way across the sky to a shallow oil well off to the East. "Thanks again, Margaret," I thought to myself and wondered about how she stood on this exact same beach one hundred years ago watching these same waves but with peace in her soul. I never thought I would feel that way, too. But as I felt the ocean breeze pick up, I wondered if she was in that breeze. Or was she pointing me out to God so that He was there watching me and my new little family. Maybe He sent the rainbow. I guessed I was tired of looking at earth's cycles as anomalies. Those thoughts didn't do me justice. Then, I thought to myself, "Did I just say *my little family*?"

I smiled over at Ralph and Avery as they sat next to me hugging and looking up at the rainbow. Where would little Ralph be now if Avery didn't exist in this world to be there to adopt him? Or actually, where would Ralph be if Avery hadn't felt God's grace on her life so much so that she felt worthy of being a mother to such a sweet blessing as Ralph was?

Then, I thought of God giving me grace. Avery was obviously worthy of it, but I was a harder case. Yet, here I am. I'm a new man. I'm finally free of the anger towards others. I finally feel worthy of God's love and this new life he has given me.

As I pondered over that, I felt the softest touch on my hand. I looked over and saw the most beautiful smile on Avery's face as she marveled at the rainbow, too.

She looked over at me. "Thank you," she simply said. I was about to ask why she said that, but then sunlight began to shine a soft hue over her face. I never noticed how beautiful she was until that moment. She was a little rough around the edges, feisty, and independent. But the woman was sweet to the core with the most stunning blue eyes. I coughed to clear my throat.

"Are you alright?" she asked.

"Yeah, I just… You and Ralph. I'm just glad you both are here."

She squeezed my hand. "We're glad you are here, too. You're our family now."

I nodded and realized that I had just thought that same thing a few seconds ago. I added, "Thank you for that. I feel that, too."

"Thank you, too," she replied.

And then I remembered something and leaned back on my elbows to see Ralph. "Hey, Ralph."

The young boy lounged back to see me around the other side of his mom. He saluted and said, "Yes, Sergeant!"

I smiled. "You said you had something to show me at the beach."

His thick, dark brows lifted. "I… I did?"

"Yeah, at GG's Diner. You wanted to come to the beach. You said you had something to show me."

Little Ralph tilted his head at an odd angle. Then, he looked at his mom for a second before smiling.

"What is it then?" I asked.

He didn't reply yet. He kissed his mom's cheek and looked back up at the rainbow. Then with a strange and goofy tone, he said to me, "I think I already showed you." Ralph continued to smile up at the rainbow.

It took me a few seconds, but this crayon eater finally got it. Or maybe it was my heart that got it first. Either way, I finally realized what had just happened.

****

As Ralph went back to swimming, Avery and I sat there quietly for a while. She seemed to be content just watching her son. It felt good just being with them both and enjoying mother nature. I'd be lying if I said I didn't miss Margaret. I wondered if she stood in that same spot one hundred years ago thinking about me before the great storm hit. I looked over at Avery, who seemed to still be acting strangely. Even her words weren't as rushed as before, more thought put into every comment. Like she was still in shock and trying to reason out everything.

"I miss her so much," I said.

Ralph ran up a dune alerting me to the washed-up seaweed that the hurricane had brought in.

"Who?" Avery asked.

"Sister Margaret. God was probably who Margaret always thought of while she was on this beach, not me, right? And that is okay, because I miss her, but through all this I realize, I had missed God more. Does that make sense?"

Avery looked at me blankly. "God wasn't who she always thought of."

"What?"

She sat up straight. "Oh, just… people think about all kinds of things, don't they?"

"True, but does it make sense, all of this?"

"Yes, Mr. Reynolds," she answered with a hint of joy bubbling up in her voice.

Avery admired the woman too, just as I had. Avery even had the same disposition. And when I was in Avery's presence, I felt that same warm feeling I felt every time I opened Margaret's diary.

And then my breath caught. Something odd was nagging at me. I turned to Avery. "Did you just say, *Mr. Reynolds?*"

Avery's blue eyes widened. "Did I?"

I turned towards her. "Yes, in fact. I may not have known you for long. But you are acting differently. I thought it was just shock. But you're really acting strange."

"Strange?" she asked with guilt in her tone.

"Yeah, did something happen during the hurricane? I never asked how your home did after the hurricane? Is everything okay? Do you need anything?" I slowed my speech with the next question. "Did you do something?"

"Something?"

"You just seem upset."

She smiled over at me. "We had damage, but it didn't take long to fix. The library took the longest, but I had help."

I nodded. "So, you are okay?"

"Why certainly."

I sat up. "See? That! That right there. No one talks like that anymore."

"I have no idea what you mean," she said and turned back to face the waves.

I studied her profile and then looked down at my feet. I drew a circle with my index finger into the sand and said steadily without even looking up, "Avery, the craziest thing in my life happened just a year ago. Something supernatural. Something I can't explain. But it's brought me peace. Still… I question everything. I'm still not as trusting as I was before I went to war." I looked over at her. "Something about you is off."

"I'm just stressed."

"Okay, and?"

No answer. We just submerged ourselves into silence.

A minute or so later, she spoke again. "Just because you cannot explain something does not mean it could not have happened."

"Right. I know."

"I am gathering my thoughts and doing the same," she said.

"I know. It's tough to wrap our minds around it, huh? Or around anything that is impossible."

"Or possible." Avery replied but kept her eyes forward. Now, her face was unreadable. "What is perplexing is that I never thought I would ever see what you really looked like." She looked at me.

"What do you mean?"

Avery looks away again. "Nothing."

"There *is* something."

She turned to look at me again. Her eyes were squinting against the sunlight. "You are just as handsome as I pictured you."

I didn't know what to say, but my patience was wearing thin. "What do you mean, Avery?"

She continued, "You said, the correspondence back and forth between you and Sister Margaret was how things changed. Basically, the only way that I was born."

"Yes, but I'm not following."

Avery smiled again. "It's me, Mr. Reynolds."

"You, what?"

She looked back at the ocean and then behind us towards the sea wall. "Everything has changed. I see it through Avery's eyes and also through Margaret's eyes."

I stood up too quickly. My right leg was shaky on the sand. "Is this a joke?" I asked and fought with my prosthetic to stabilize myself on the uneven sand.

She stood up and shook her head. "I'm both. It all came back to me. I saw everything from my life in England to my life here in Galveston with my son now. Everything."

I took a step back. "That can't be."

She moved closer to me. Her hands were shaking. She lifted them with her palms up. "You told me about Emily."

"Wait. How do you know about Emily?"

She smiled. "You told me about her when you wrote to me in the diary."

I rubbed my head. "What is going on?"

Then, she took my hand, almost like a child would. Her hands were cold but strong. "I will understand if this is too much. I will take with me the touch of your skin, a feeling I had dreamed about for so long, and I will go. You have only just found yourself and your purpose. I will not ruin that." She let go of my hand.

"I need…"

"Explanations?"

"Yes, I guess." I rubbed my head.

Her nod and sweet smile seemed to break the thick atmosphere we had just created. She sucked in her lips. "I need time, too. It is okay. I understand." She looked at Ralph playing in the waves. "This is not easy for me either."

"Wait, wait, Avery. Do you really think you are Sister Margaret? Did you read where we talked about Emily when I handed you the diary?" I held my head with my hands. "There was no way. I took the diary back before you got to that page. What's going on, Avery?"

I was the one shaking now, but she remained ever so calm and collect. She was almost too calm. "I do not want to bring you distress. I will go." Avery turned and called for Ralph.

I grabbed her hand. "This can't be. Tell me."

"No. Nothing else to say," she replied without looking back at me. "I need time, as well. I know this is a lot for you and it is for me, too."

Ralph had begun to move out of the water. I shook my head. "This can't be. Avery, just stop."

Her reply came back with a hushed tone. "I will, and I will go." She looked back up at me. "But before I do, tell me if you finally talked to Emily?"

"What?" I stepped away and noticed that Ralph was almost among us. "Yes… yes, I did. I got closure."

She smiled and repositioned her purse on her shoulder. "Good."

My heart longed for it to really be Margaret, but no matter what I had seen in the previous year, I still couldn't believe that it could be. But then Avery said, "Was it the twelfth letter that you never wanted to read from Emily or from your time with me that made you realize that the hurt was not worth holding on to?"

I didn't respond. I just stood there.

She didn't expect a response. Her eyes were already somewhere else. Not on me. Not on this moment. But then again, my mind had drifted to. As I watched her and Ralph walk off and up the steps of the seawall, I thought of that one detail she had said. The letter.

I frowned and gazed at the sun cresting across the silver tinted water. I thought back to the night of the hurricane. The night I imagined that I saw Margaret's face through the water. It was the shock from that vision that had made me fall back into my old boxes, which later helped me find Emily's letter. How could Avery have known? There was no way she could have known everything she knew.

CHAPTER 39
AVERY

I got to the library and opened it up for the morning. As I looked around the large world I had lived in for years without realizing who I really was, I was overwhelmed.

The portrait behind my desk was the first thing I gravitated to. The resemblance was spot on. Little Trey painted my likeness well. All this time, I had stared at that picture as Avery wondering about the woman of who I actually was.

I picked up the rosary and rolled the beads through my fingertips as I prayed, "God, you really orchestrated something amazing and intricate this time. Why would you do that for me?"

Suddenly, I felt the rush of water that wasn't there. I heard banging on windows all around me that when I looked, were perfectly still. The night of the hurricane came crashing into my senses. I closed my eyes and all I could remember was the fear.

Falling to the floor, I squeezed the rosary tighter as I heard a sign from the shelf next to me fall to the ground. "Please God, please. Save the children!"

The water was so cold and dark. There were hard tugs pulling at all sides of my body as I continued to pray. Their little eyes looking to me for strength, so I held tight to them and continued to sing.

"Mom! Are you okay?"

I opened my eyes to a bright light coming through the windows. I wasn't in that hurricane. It wasn't storming. The sun in all its beauty felt like a rebirth.

Ralph came up to me. "Mom?"

"I am fine. Just praying."

"Okay. Well, I'm going to go restock the books that came back. Looks like they are all dry now. Next time, are we going to move them to a higher floor? It was a pain restoring them after the storm. And we lost a lot of them."

"I know, hun. We'll see."

As I was going to stand up, I heard the entry door open. "Avery? Avery?"

"Yes, Clara, I'm back here."

Clara was the original librarian before I came. She taught me everything I knew. After the hurricane, she was the first person to show up and help me get things back in order.

Clara walked down the aisle with her hands on her hips. "That dang hurricane. I still can't believe it flooded this poor building again. It looks like the restoration crew did pretty good, huh?"

"Yes. Clara, can I ask you something?"

"Sure."

"Why did you retire so early? I mean, I always wondered. Not that I'm not thankful to have this job, but you are still fairly young."

Her face seemed distant as she lifted the sign off the floor that I had knocked over. "I don't know. My husband was already retired. You know, disabled from the war. Just one day at church, I was watching the pastor talk about spending more time with family, and then I suddenly felt something."

"What?"

Clara put the fallen sign back onto the shelf next to us and added, "It was like God was telling me to spend more time with Frank. And then the next day, we got an inheritance from my long-lost uncle. Just out of the blue. The money was exactly what I needed to be able to afford staying home. I believe it was God's plan."

I looked around the library. If she hadn't decided to retire, I would have never come back to Galveston. It was the job ad that brought me here instead of the job in Beaumont. Did all this happen after God changed things because of Trey's writing to me? Chills ran over me.

Clara placed her hand on my shoulder. "Are you okay, Avery? You seem different."

I nodded. "Just overwhelmed."

"You need a break. You've been working hard getting everything back together." She moved in front of me and embraced my shoulders. "Take the day off. Let me cover for today."

"No, I can't."

"I'm not asking." She smiled over at Ralph. "Ralph and I can keep doing the stocking. I'll keep an eye on him."

I nodded and looked over at my tennis shoes that had been dropped next to the door from after my last workout. "You know what, Clara? I think I will take you up on that offer." And with that, I grabbed my sneakers and headed off to the gym.

****

When I walked through the door of the gym, I had mixed emotions. The last time I was here was only a week ago, but I wasn't here as Margaret. I stepped on the treadmill thinking I would run my usual three miles, but started to get nervous. As Avery, I knew my body was used to three miles several times a week. But I stood there with the consciousness of Margaret who had never run more than a few minutes in her life.

Another woman got on the treadmill next to me and gave me a motivational smile suggesting that I could do it. I always loved the atmosphere at the gym. Everyone was always so supportive and positive. But who am I? Am I Margaret or am I Avery? Or am I both? And if I'm both, how does that work? Do I continue to be a gym rat working in a library or do I go back to being a nun?

I turned the machine on and began a slow walk. I couldn't be a nun anymore. I had Ralph to care for. Plus, I was no longer really Margaret. Margaret died serving God. But did He bring me back or did some old quill laced with magic bring me back?

Turning up the speed on the machine, I began a slow jog. My legs felt like Avery's, but my mind was still fighting my body as Margaret. As I began running faster, my feet just took off. I watched the mileage counter go from a quarter of a mile to half a mile. Before I knew it, I was at the one-mile mark. That was always the point in my run when I would really start feeling good. And I did. I felt great.

The woman next to me had since stopped and headed over to the weights. I kept running. When I made it to the end of my third mile, I slowed the speed and began to walk to cool down. I didn't know who I was or what identity should take precedence. What I did know was that I felt really good and was thankful for the chance to have this life. The grace and knowledge Margaret had combined with the beautiful life Avery had made, could not be any better.

As I was leaving the gym, I thought of Trey. Through my eyes as Avery, he was a hot-headed but extremely cute Marine. Through my eyes as Margaret, he had my heart in a way that I never knew I could give. I had been married to the church and God only. How could I have fallen in love with a man?

I got in my Volvo and adjusted the mirrors again. For some reason since I became both women, I couldn't decide on a comfortable driving position. It was all too weird. As I put the car in gear to head back to the library, I thought over about how it would take me time to become acclimated. Either way, I still thanked God.

CHAPTER 40

When I arrived back at the library, Trey was there talking to Ralph.

I shook my head. "I do not question God's ways anymore, Mr. Reynolds. Goodbye." I moved to walk down the aisle away from him.

He followed right behind me. "Just talk to me. Let me explain."

"I'm busy."

"Doing what?"

I shook my head and pulled out another book. "Just checking on everyone. To see who all survived."

"Avery, they all died. All the nuns."

"No, not them. Rebecca Sampson of Sampson Manor and Georgiana Pierce, the caretaker of the Tenant's House you were in."

"Both structures made it, so yes, most likely," he added with a deadpan expression.

"What do you mean?"

"Both the buildings withstood the hurricane. So, both women were probably safe."

I nodded slowly in recognition. "Oh, that's right."

He grabbed my hand and spun me around. "Just stop and listen. I went back in my mind and something stood out to me."

"What?"

Trey looked around the room before bringing his eyes back on me. "I do think it is you, Margaret. But how, I don't know. So, I thought back over something you wrote to me in the diary."

"I'm listening."

"You told me the scripture that you chose for becoming a nun."

"Yes."

He continued, "You told me that it spoke to you but there was something that you didn't understand."

I lowered my head and thought back. "Yes, the last line." I began to say it all aloud, "It said, 'Until when, Lord?' The Lord said, 'Until towns are in ruins and deserted, houses untenanted and a great desolation reigns in the land, and Yahweh has driven the people away and the country is totally abandoned'." I took a step back and my voice got hoarse as I continued to recite the rest, "Then it said, 'And suppose one-tenth of them are left in it, that will be stripped again, like the terebinth, like the oak, cut back to the stock; their stock is a holy seed'." I gasped.

Trey touched my arm. "That was Galveston after the hurricane of 1900. You can't think it's a coincidence that the bible verse you chose upon to become a nun had directly referenced what was to happen to Galveston." He then squeezed my arm gently. "Margaret… Avery, sorry. I don't know what to call you, but what I do know is that you were called to come to Galveston. To be here for these people. You were the one who taught me to trust in His plan. I'm trusting in it now. You *are* Margaret. Do you understand what I am saying? I believe God could have done this. I believe He can do anything."

I shook my head as tears filled my eyes.

He got closer. His cologne activated my senses. "You did your job already, Margaret. You can be Avery now. Whichever you choose. I just wanted you to know that. I wanted you to know that I believe you."

****

That night, Trey took me to dinner. He was still slated to leave soon for his new book. He felt we needed more time to talk out what all we had gone through. Truth be told, he was worried about me. Now that he knew what I was truly going through, he didn't want to leave until he knew I was okay.

We opted for outside dining on the patio while listening to the ocean waves crash along the shore. Not many restaurants were opened back up yet. We lucked out that Tres Monet's hadn't sustained too much damage. It stood strong during the storm like GG's Diner had. And I liked that there weren't many people there either. Usually people on the coast enjoyed seafood and frequented those types of places. A French restaurant wasn't usually the main attraction.

Trey ordered us an appetizer of bread and cheese. I watched his eyes study me while I ate the warm bread and decadent cheese. I swallowed and said, "I feel like a science experiment. Stop looking at me like that."

"I'm not… I'm just wondering how you're feeling. What's going through your head?"

I took a sip of a sweet red wine Trey swore was the best on the island. It was pretty good. "A lot. Believe me." I set down the wine and leaned back in my chair. "Tell me what I don't know."

"What do you mean?"

I folded my arms over my chest. "After the last time we wrote each other. I mean, look at you. You wrote a book and you seem happier. Did you make peace with your family? With your ex fiancé?"

He set down his glass, too. "You can say that. The night of the hurricane, this recent hurricane, something happened."

"What?"

He licked his bottom lip. "I thought I saw you."

"Avery or Margaret. Because as Avery, I got the heck out of dodge, all the way to Dallas."

He smiled at that. "I thought I saw you that night as Margaret."

"Oh."

The traffic along the seawall rumbled on by. Trey's attention followed it. "You're different than Margaret in some ways, more confident. But then she changed. You changed. It was like your two personalities were already converging. Like with the flowers. As Avery, you hated flowers, of which you never told me why."

"Not any big story about that. I just hate how quick they die. The thought of death, especially when you have such a short life, sickens me."

"See? That is why I think you were always connected to Margaret. The subliminal feelings hidden inside over the death of the young orphans and even your life being cut short. It changed your personality as Avery to where you hated flowers and as Margaret, you loved them. But where you are both the same is your love for children." He smiled.

I took his right hand. "Yes, but that's all fine and dandy, but you began to tell me something and dropped it. Are you embarrassed? After everything we both experienced?"

"No."

"Then, tell me the vision you saw of Margaret the night of the hurricane."

Trey looked back and took another sip of wine. "You came up under the water as an apparition or something. It scared me so much that I fell and knocked over an old box that I hadn't opened since I packed it up back in Somalia."

"What about it?"

"That was when I knocked over the old box holding the twelfth letter. You know, the one from Emily?"

Our waiter walked up. "What will you two be having tonight?"

Without looking, I handed the young guy the menu and abruptly said, "Anything with pasta."

Trey laughed. "She'll have the special with alfredo sauce and grilled shrimp and I'll take the same."

I nodded and as soon as the waiter walked off, I urgently nudged Trey along, "And did you finally read it?"

He smiled. "Yes. I did. After that, I went home. Back to Pittsburgh."

"Good. And?"

"In the letter Emily told me I had a son. So, I went to confirm it." His gaze held mine. "Margaret, I did have a son."

I sat up straight. "You did?"

"Yes!" he exclaimed and then pulled out a few pictures. His hand jetted out towards mine and three pictures fell onto the table. I studied the chubby cheeks, the big smile, but most importantly, the big round brown eyes. Just like his daddy's. The little boy was adorable. He looked just like Trey. In one picture, someone had put a camo hat on his head.

But then it hit me. "Did you say you *had* a son? What does that mean?"

Trey's jaw tightened. "He died."

My hand went to my mouth. "Oh no, I'm so sorry."

Trey reached and took my hand. "Thank you. But at least I know now. If it hadn't been for you I would not have ever read that letter. I would have never known the truth. I thank you, Margaret, with all my heart. And I thank God for him bringing me to you."

I smiled. "I'm happy that you found out, too."

"Thank you."

But then I pulled my hand away, almost like I needed him to see that I was taking all this serious, every word, every moment, every revelation. I started to speak but had to clear my throat first. "It's incredible, God's works and His timing. You know, it had all come back to me when I touched Mrs. Davenport's quill that you found under the floor. My quill…

pen… whatever. I didn't notice anything different when I touched the diary or scanned through it, just that pen."

"The pen? Wait, yes, the pen." His face lit up. "Could that have been it all along? The writing with that pen in particular?"

"Be careful. Do not take credit from God."

"I don't mean to, but the pen is the constant in all of this. And didn't you say that Ms. Davenport's family had it made out of a rosary they passed down for generations?"

"Yes."

"Wow. And that was why when I tried to put a picture of me in the diary, you never got it."

I laughed. "You did?" She frowned. "Wait, that is right. I remember you said you tried to."

We both sat there for a second thinking. When our dinner arrived, we both had become silent. Deep in our thoughts, we'd smile once in a while at the couple next to us that seemed to kiss every five minutes.

After our plates were taken away, Trey grabbed my hands again. "So many nights I wondered what it could be like to touch you. So many lonely nights."

"Same here, but I see now that God needed us to find Him again first before we could truly find each other."

He nodded and sat back. "I agree."

I pulled away from his hands again. This time, he frowned at the gesture. I ignored it and added, "So, Trey, here is the thing." I took another sip of wine. I was close to finishing a second glass, which was unheard of in my past life. However, as Avery, my body could handle four before I was a goner.

Trey refilled my glass. "Here is what thing?"

"I debated when I first realized what was going on. I didn't know how to tell you. When I finally got the courage to tell you, I felt lost. Confused-" The waiter came up interrupting me. "Anything else?" the young man said.

I sighed. "No, thank you."

Trey took that as a chance to grab my hands again. "What are you saying?"

"I am so happy to be with you and you are everything I ever imagined you to be, but I haven't found myself, my whole self, yet. I'm trying to make sense of all of this. I'm glad you believe me, but you have to know what I'm going through right now."

"What is that?"

"Trey, I am not living my life as Margaret anymore. I'm Avery."

He nodded solemnly. "I can see that. I can see that it would be hard."

I looked up at those deep brown eyes of his. "I really did dream of what this would be like."

"Am I a disappointment?" he asked with a new tone in his voice, almost childish.

"No, no… it's just…" I sighed. "You were my closest friend. I know you like I know the back of my hand. But now there are two perspectives, two lives, lots of history inside me. And it's not only that."

"What is it?"

"You are a good man, Trey Reynolds. You have sacrificed a lot and had always kept a good heart. But…"

"But what?"

I frowned. "I know you, but I don't *know* you. And honestly, as Margaret… I… I love you. But as Avery, I don't. I have a son to worry about. He is my priority."

Trey's eyes drooped as his entire face exuded loneliness. He had to know what I was getting at. He took a deep breath. "I'm sorry that I didn't believe you before. But I do now. Will you at least let me help you navigate all this?"

"What do you mean? Navigate how?"

"I wrote to you. I disturbed your diary, disturbed your way of life, and in doing that… I brought you to a life one hundred years into the future. One of which, you weren't prepared for."

"Trey, it's not just that."

"It's the whole reincarnation thing, right?"

"I won't say I'm sure about how it's possible. I'm not. But I am also unsure if it is possible. But it is. It's a wonder. I'm just-"

He interrupts me, "-Here. You are here."

"Yes, but biblically…"

Trey leaned towards me. "Why do you still question things? God is capable of anything. Haven't you learned that yet?"

"Yes, but…"

He shrugged. "I understand. This is a lot. Life is hard. Faith is hard. Miracles are complex. I'm not going to sit here and push you. I'm not going to rush you. Heck, I don't even know what to call you. Avery or Margaret." He seemed to be getting aggravated. I needed to leave. I didn't want to see him upset.

But then he rubbed the back of his head and took another breath, this one more cleansing. "You know that bartender at the Anchors Aweigh?"

"I don't go to bars."

"So, you don't know Alexis?" he asked and waved to the waiter for the check.

"No."

"Well, anyway, she told me something one time. It was actually pretty good. And I thought about it after you and Ralph left me on the beach. It resonated with me because of what I went through and I think it could help you, also."

"What?" I asked.

"She said most people have several sides to them. One they show the world and one or two they keep inside them that they hide. Sides to them that they try to understand, control, or maybe even get rid of. Either way, they utilize every side of themselves, inside and out, when they make decisions in their life. It affects everything. Once the person reconciles who they really are, they accept all their different sides and find a balance."

He handed the waiter his card and continued, "But it's not an easy process. I am going to give you space to do this. I'm going to go off to San Antonio and start that next book. I'm going to research and write and hope to find more incredible stories from our past. I'm going to drown myself in the next chapter of my life. But you know what I'm also going to do?"

"What is that?"

"I'm going to always think of you and pray for you. When you are ready, I'll be here. You're not the only one who has juggled with different sides of themselves. I firmly believe that is all this is. So, decide who you're going to be, even if it's half Margaret and half Avery."

I nodded and was almost moved to tears.

The waiter brought back his card. "I'm going to go. I'll just take a taxi. Thank you for bringing me to dinner."

"Thank you for paying."

"Of course, I was gonna pay," he said and stood up.

"I can bring you home."

He shook his head. "I got this." As he went to turn to leave, he stopped. "You were the one that always said we need to trust in God's plan. Avery, I'm trusting in God now. Because I have never been as happy as I am now. Whatever happens, I want you to know that. Thank you for everything you did for me as Margaret and for taking the time for me now as Avery."

He went to leave and I lifted my hand to stop him but didn't say a thing. When I heard the bell on the door chime, I looked down at my hands. They were shaking. The wind was blowing in my ears so loud even my scream wouldn't be heard. A memory began to come over me…

****

I was back at the orphanage and the storm was blowing in. A longing feeling entered my heart as I closed my bible and headed back outside of the orphanage. I knew I'd never talk to Mr. Reynolds again, so I cried silently. An even stronger breeze came and seemed to lift my body up. It pushed me into the wall. I stayed pinned to the masonry and tried to catch my breath.

Erratic movement came from my left side and a hand touched my shoulder. "Sister Margaret. Do not linger in this rain. You risk becoming ill," Sister Mary said and helped me rebalance myself on my own two feet. Then she rushed off now holding a blanket over her head. She stopped short of opening the door to the boy's dormitory and turned around towards the ocean with a distant look. "The seas are so unsettled this afternoon."

I followed her eyes out to the beach. "Yes, Sister. I feel it will not end anytime today."

"Then, we must finish our rounds." Her skirt slapped at her ankles as she disappeared into the safety of the building.

I stood there watching Mother Nature build and build her strength. I wondered how big of a storm and how much damage would she leave behind when it was all done. Would I see the results before the light of day was extinguished? Or would I ever see it at all?

When I got back to my room, my head had begun to hurt, probably because of the impact I experienced on the hard wall. I was glad all my duties were done that day and that I could turn in early to get some rest.

My sleep was short as I awoke to screams from down the hall. The fear in their voices reminded me of my sister's plea with Henry the first time he beat me with a horse whip. The poor child thought her own body could stop the onslaught of evil, but nothing could.

I threw on my habit and rushed out of my room towards the others. There was a new noise all around. The sound was coming from outside the orphanage, and it was like nothing I had ever heard before. But it wasn't just a sound. There were deafening bangs all around, almost like shock waves ravishing the walls of the asylum.

Up ahead and where a window should have been, glass was shattered all over the floor. Rain was blowing in almost horizontally and fiercely.

Outside, several men ran across the lawn. I hollered out to them, "It is not safe out in the elements! Come inside. Seek shelter."

The taller and wider shouldered of the three stopped to reply to me, but he struggled to even balance himself. I could see his pants were torn below the knee. Further down to his ankles, I couldn't see the rest. His lower limbs were completely submerged in dark water. "Thank you, but we're looking for the rest of our family."

"My prayers are with you. If you need to, bring your family here."

"Thank you, Sister."

I started to worry about Georgy and then Mrs. Sampson and her children. "When did it start flooding?"

A gust of wind forced him to fall over into the water. I gasped. One of the other men briskly rushed back to help him up. The taller man came back up and looked to be covered in a sticky black mud.

His friend helped him upright and hollered over to me, "Sister, you and everyone else in there needs to move up higher. I fear the flooding will get worse. Now, we must go."

Then, another man came drudging by through the water and his words to the first two men were bone chilling. "The ocean has connected to the Galveston Bay! Seek higher ground, everyone!"

Fear crept in leaving my knees shaky and my throat dry. The island was no longer above water. We were no longer on an island. The rain picked up again and stung my face with each droplet.

Rushing down the narrow hall behind me, I saw Sister Mary again. "We need to get the children away from all windows and up a floor."

"Yes, I agree."

Her eyes were full of tears. "I do not understand this weather. I have never seen rain become so violent."

I squeezed her cold hands. She was not much different than me. Her birth home, France, only ever experienced cold winters and an occasional blizzard. Nothing like what Trey said this storm was going to bring. "My sweet Mary. You must listen to me. It will get worse before it gets better. Help me wake the other sisters and children. We need to move quickly." I decided not to mention the flooding yet. It would only scare her.

Sister Mary nodded and headed down the hall towards the south side of the building.

Mother Gabriela and Sister Anna were already dressed when I reached their rooms. Mother Gabriela placed her hand on the door jam. "You were right, Sister Margaret. What you told Father O'Brien was true."

"You don't know that for sure."

"Yes, I do. There was another storm that hit not far from here just weeks ago. Father O'Brien did not tell everyone. That storm completely devastated that entire town. The Gulf of Mexico brings many hazards that we are not familiar with. Father O'Brien said the usual storms could be brutal, but this is more than I feel he meant."

I didn't know how to respond. Why did Father O'Brien not act when I went to him? Why did he keep the information about the other storm from us? "Mother Gabriela, there were men outside looking for their families and the water was already up to their knees. They said the entire island was flooded. We need to move everyone to a higher floor."

Mother Gabriela rested the back of her hand against her top lip. "Yes. And Sister Margaret, tell Sister Mary to move all the boys from their building into here."

"Why?"

"That part of the asylum is older and not built as solid as the girl's section. Now, hurry and do not scare the children. Tell them we are just relocating for the night."

"Yes, Mother Gabriela."

Mother Gabriela was right. Later in the night, the boy's dormitory succumbed to the relentless winds and water. It was a terrible thing to see its collapse as parts of it were carried off in the water.

We continued to try to stay calm. We said prayers and sang hymns to help the children. Little Trey was my lookout. Every half hour, he went down the stairs to gauge the water level. Sadly, it was rising faster than we had hoped.

We sang and prayed hoping that the storm would end and that the waters would recede before it got any worse. However, Mr. Reynolds swore to me in his correspondence that it wouldn't. In some ways, I wished I didn't tell him not to share more. But I wanted to have faith as Father O'Brien. I wanted to continue to trust in God's plan.

At what should be the earliest hours of the next morning, we moved to the third floor. I felt helpless and unable to protect God's precious children. I became angry with myself. Trey came over and sat with me. He took my hand and asked, "Why are you upset?"

"The answer to that is not an easy admission."

"I don't understand."

"I made a good choice, the right choice, but sometimes the unselfish choice is hard to make and it hurts."

He touched my face and said something that reminded me of Mr. Reynolds. Mr. Reynolds also always talked using percentages. And little Trey had just learned percentages from Sister Mary last week. He squeezed my hand and said to me,

"Sister Margaret, no one can be one hundred percent unselfish all the time. God will understand."

The last remaining lights flickered off and we all lit our small candles. Sara, one of our first orphans to come to us, laid her head on my shoulder. I kissed her forehead and thought of Mr. Reynolds. My time on this Earth was done. I prayed that I helped him as much as he helped me. I pulled out the writing instrument and turned back to the empty pages of the classroom journal I found. I continued to write. After I finished, I ripped the pages out, folded them and wrapped them in the leather binding from the bible. Then, I handed them to little Trey.

"Miss? Miss?" My waiter was shaking my shoulder. "Are you okay, ma'am?"

"Just had a…"

"I understand," he said and topped off my water. It was the first time all night that I really looked at his young face. He had a wide forehead and thin lips over a mouth full of braces.

I smiled at him and began to stand as I wiped the sweat from above my brow. The memory was intense.

My waiter helped me up. "Your dinner date left so soon? We have really good dessert here."

"Yes, he has a flight to catch. He's an author."

"Oh, that's neat."

I smiled while thinking of how proud I was of Trey. "Yes, it is. He used to be a soldier, actually a Marine."

The young man nodded. "I figured that. He had that way about him. Is that how he hurt his leg?"

"Yes. Actually, he lost it."

"Oh, I'm sorry."

"He's a special man. He's come a long way," I said as the waiter helped me out the front gate and towards my car.

"My father served. He had so many nightmares. They call it PTSD. He would have flashbacks right in the middle of the day."

"Really?"

"Yeah, it kinda reminded me of what you were doing. The other waiter said it was probably just because you had two glasses of wine, though."

I unlocked my car and turned towards him. "Oh. No, I'm fine. I'm just getting a headache." I never thought of my memories as flashbacks. I never realized that what I had gone through could be so crippling. I went from my life as a mother and librarian in the year two thousand to a woman that was now reliving a horror. A trauma when at the time of the hurricane in nineteen hundred, I was on automatic pilot in an effort to save the children.

As I got in my car to drive away, tears filled my eyes. Trey had been living with these kind of memories for years before he found peace. Now, even with my strong relationship with God, I will still have to work through my past in order to fully find my own peace. The battle with PTSD for a brave and extremely tough-minded soldier is not easy. How would someone like me rise above it? But I knew God had His reasons. But God help me. This is tough.

CHAPTER 41
AVERY

Passing by this part of the beach hundreds of times to go to Wal-Mart and not once did I pay attention to it. It had only been placed there a few years ago anyway.

I pulled into the Sonic parking lot across the street to order my favorite dessert, a chocolate milkshake. As I waited for them to bring it out, I stared over at the historical marker on the beach side of the street. It was one of over two hundred historical markers in Galveston. It was no wonder that I never really paid attention to it, even though my ancestor had lived in that orphanage as a boy. I never felt pulled to it until now.

Of course, now I had an even more of a reason to find it. But my limbs went numb and my chest tightened. When the teenage girl came bopping out with my shake, I managed to steady my breathing. "Thank you," I said and set the drink in my cup holder. I knew I had to do it. "I'm going to go take a quick picture of that landmark. Is it okay if I leave my car here?"

She looked over my shoulder. "Sure."

After I locked my car, I checked the traffic and ran across the street. The marker looked like most of the others on the island and stood almost as high as my height of five foot. I was enthralled in the moment that I didn't see the joggers in my peripheral. It surprised me when they ran behind me that I quickly moved out of the way but lost my balance. I fell over and caught myself with my right hand on the cold stone of the memorial.

One jogger stopped. "Hey, you okay?"

"Yes, thank you."

"Alright. Didn't mean to scare you," he said and turned to run again. His fancy white New Balance running shoes slapped the cement of the man-made sea wall's walking path.

I stood back up and finally let myself read the inscription. I did not read it with Avery's eyes, though. I was all Margaret at that moment, and it was terrifyingly all true. It read:

"Children orphaned by a yellow fever epidemic in 1867 were cared for temporarily in Galveston's St. Mary's Infirmary by the Sisters of Charity of the Incarnate Word. In 1874 Galveston Bishop Claude Dubuis bought the 35-acre plantation and home of Farnifala and Laura Green located between this gulf front and Green's Bayou for use as a permanent orphanage. In early 1874 the Sisters of St. Mary's Infirmary founded St. Mary's Orphan Asylum by housing 28 children here at the site of the Greens' former residence. A 2-story facility for orphan girls was built nearby in October 1874."

"The girl's dormitory was all that remained of the orphanage after the storm of 1875. A new residence for boys was built by 1879. St. Mary's was caring for orphans from throughout Texas at the time it was granted a Texas charter in 1896."

"The catastrophic storm of 1900 completely destroyed the orphanage. Ten nuns and at least 90 children were tragically killed despite the nuns' valiant efforts to save the children by securing them to their own bodies with clothesline. Four orphan boys rescued at sea were the only survivors. St. Mary's Orphan Asylum reopened at 40th and Q streets in Galveston City in 1901 and remained there until closing in 1967."

When I read the last words, another memory came back to me. And this one was after I wrote the final letter to

Trey and handed it off to little Trey. However, it was not like all the other memories. I knew that when I remembered it, that it would be the very last thing I would ever recall from that horrible night. And for that, I was thankful.

I had just finished the letter to future Trey and handed it off to little Trey when the storm outside howled like nothing I had ever heard before. Mother Gabriela had come back up the stairs and ushered all of the adults together. She whispered so that the children could not hear. "The floor below is flooded, too, Sisters, and the water continues to rise."

I felt the building shake and heard the crumbling of walls all around us. Mother Gabriela continued, "It will not cease. We need to protect the children. If the building gives way to the onslaught of the winds and flooding, we need to make sure that we do not lose any of the children. Most cannot swim and would be easily pulled out into the tide only to drown alone. I feel it would be prudent to continue with the plan to tie them off to us so we don't lose any of them."

The other nuns nodded. Not a single one showed fear as they turned around and made haste to begin tying the clotheslines around their waists.

I stayed standing there in front of Mother Gabriela. My hands were trembling. She took my hands in hers. "I know you tried to warn us. I do not know how you knew, but I ask for your forgiveness since we did not listen."

"No, don't."

She could tell I was panicking. She touched my cheek. "Don't fear, Sister Margaret."

I shook my head. "I should have listened to him and left."

"You would not have left the children."

"But I knew," I said.

"There was a reason why you knew and maybe that is why you are scared. Don't be. You struggled with your faith for way too long. Here's your chance."

I shuddered. "How did you know?"

"I just knew." She squeezed my hands. "Let me just say something and listen closely."

"Yes?"

"The fact that you had your doubts about your faith and then were told that you could possibly lose your life in this storm, but yet you stayed anyway tells me that your faith is more devout than any of ours is."

"Never."

"Remember your bible verse that moved you to this calling."

I lowered my eyes and felt a warmth rush over me, almost surreal.

She continued, "To sacrifice yourself for those less fortunate than you is the greatest thing a nun or anyone can do."

"Sacrifice? How do you know our fate?" I asked.

Mother Gabriela shooed me and looked around. The other nuns had already begun tying themselves off to the children now. They sang while they worked to help keep the children calm. These women that I had admired and now thought of as my true family were so beautiful to watch. I didn't deserve to be among women as amazing as they were.

I stepped away from Mother Gabriela. "I'm nothing like you and them. You, not me, will be remembered…"

Mother Gabriela raised her hand up at me. "No more talk like that." She clasped the cross hanging around her neck. "Either way, my heart feels that it will be you that will do that for us."

"Do what?"

"Remember us, my dear child."

"How? My fate is the same as yours."

She smiled slightly before saying again, "Remember us."

A ringing in my ears pulled me back from that nightmare. Next to me, a car drove in, parked and was blaring loud rap music. "You okay, girl!" the man behind the wheel hollered out of the lowered window.

"Yes, thank you."

"Okay, but you are white like you saw a ghost." He then laughed. "That wasn't supposed to be a pun. I know, rude, right? With all the ghost sightings going on lately, that was harsh. But seriously, you don't look good."

The sweat was pouring down my face and back. "I'll be fine," I said and rushed back across the street. I got back to my car and turned on the air conditioning to cool my skin. God, I loved the invention of the air conditioner.

But I couldn't believe what had just happened. I had been back there again and feeling all the fear and pain. As I pulled out of Sonic and onto the main strip, I started to feel guilty that I was given this second chance at life when the orphans and the other nuns weren't. Those women were worthier of it than me, but they were not given this opportunity. I could barely drive. I cried all the way to the stop sign at the corner as I kept remembering their beautiful faces.

A convulsion in my stomach made me slam the car in park. I opened the car door and threw up the few sips I had taken of the chocolate shake. As I leaned over the road, I began praying. "Why me, God? Why did you do this for me? Please, I don't deserve this."

That same warm feeling I felt as Margaret during the storm came over me as I sat back in my car. Then, I thought I heard, "Because I can. You were there when my children needed you. All I ask is that you will let him be here for you."

"Him?" I asked. Was he talking about Trey?

"And that you will continue to be there for him," the voice added.

I sat at the stop sign for several minutes with my head rested back on the seat. I was taking in the message my Father was giving me. I heard Him this time. Loud and clear, but all that I could think about was how did Ralph fit into this.

CHAPTER 42

Pulling up to GG's Diner felt different now. Even though I was there with Trey the other day, it felt funny. Maybe it was because of the reason that I was there this time. I parked my car in the street. I had a hunch and I just had to know if my hunch was right.

The closed sign was in the window, but when I realized the door was unlocked, I walked in. I heard a pounding sound of a hammer. "Hello! Anyone here?"

A voice echoed from the back. "Yeah, come on through. Watch the nails. I haven't finished the flooring."

"You were just open the other day."

A young man was putting up fresh sheet rock but the voice came from down the hall. It replied, "Yeah, but it wasn't a good effort. I knew I would have to fix it better soon, but not this soon."

"What happened?" I asked following the voice.

A man about my age with dark, curly hair appeared. He added, "Had issues with the city about the permits." He laid down the hammer he was carrying and asked, "Can I help you?"

"This diner?" I asked.

"Yes," he prompted.

"Who owns it?"

He lifted his arms out. "That would be me."

"Oh. You're young."

"You don't recognize me?" he asked with a smirk.

"No."

He smiled and added, "You've eaten here before."

"Yes, but I don't remember you."

He smiled even bigger with big white teeth against dark skin. "I made the shrimp gumbo that you raved about."

I thought back. "Oh, my goodness. That's right. Remind me, where did you get that recipe?"

"Handed down for generations."

"From?"

He eyed me while wiping his hands on a red cloth. "I got it from my great, great, great grandmother and her family. She brought it with her from a plantation in Mississippi."

"So, your ancestor is Georgy?"

He looked surprised. "Yes, of course."

"She did it then?" I asked more so to myself.

The guy put his hands in his pocket. "Did what?"

"She survived and finally opened her own restaurant."

"Survived?" he asked and frowned.

"The hurricane."

"Yeah, well. The diner didn't." His stunned eyes landed on me. "Wait, we're not talking about this building, are we? Are you asking about *the hurricane*?"

"Yes. By the way, I am Avery. I'm the librarian."

He shook his head. "Remember? I know." He reached out his hand. "I am Gregory."

We shook hands and I added, "Nice to meet you."

"The pleasure is mine. But yeah, Georgy did survive it. How else would she have started this diner? Everyone in town knew that, pretty much. I thought you did, too."

"Do you have a picture of her?" I asked, almost interrupting him.

Gregory wiped the sweat off his neck with the same red rag and asked, "Why all this interest?"

I smiled coyly. "I admire good food."

"Well, thank you, but no pictures made it after the flood of 1937."

"Oh. Okay."

He dropped the cloth. "You know what? I do have something that was special to her that she passed down." Then, he winked. "Besides her great recipes."

My jaw went slack. "It wouldn't happen to be her first coin she ever earned, would it?"

He studied me for a second. "Not many people know that."

I fell silent. When the awkwardness lingered too long, I finally said, "I assumed. I guess."

His caramel eyes watched me and then he shook his head. "You're really into all this, aren't you?"

"Yup."

"You know, it may be cool to show you since you seem so interested in her. But honestly, I keep it in my office. Safer there."

"Can I see it?"

The side of his mouth turned up. "Why not? Come on." He walked into another room, and I followed right behind him. Inside the room was a desk and a few cabinets. The desk had tons of family pictures. Lots of couples with lots of children. And then there it was. On the wall above his desk, I saw it. He must have noticed my excitement because he pointed up at it. "Yup, that's it. Her precious coin."

It was the same exact coin Georgy kept hidden in Mrs. Davenport's night stand. The other day after Trey had given me Mrs. Davenport's quill that made me realize who I was, I checked the secret compartment in that night stand and didn't find the coin. At that moment, I felt that Georgy had survived. She would never leave her coin there unless she died in the storm.

"That's really neat," I said.

"Yes, it is."

"She was a very special lady."

"Thank you. But you didn't know her."

I snapped out of it. "In a way, yes, I did." I looked back up at the coin. That coin on the wall proved it. My friend survived and got to live. And look what amazing things she did with that life.

He was frowning at me again. "Don't understand."

I smiled at him but didn't respond. I simply turned to leave and said while walking out, "Love the pecan pies more than the gumbo, though." The happiness inside me was growing.

CHAPTER 43
TREY

I got back to my hotel room exhausted. I dropped onto the bed wishing my prosthetic could come off with a push of a button. There were a few people partying in the room next to me and the elevator right outside my door seemed to ding every few minutes.

I sat up on the bed and unstrapped my prosthetic while thinking of my son, Joshua. It is sad how we let life pass us by because of our anger and pride. I wondered about him as I laid back down in bed. Would he have been a pain like me? Would he have joined the military, too? For that matter, would I have married Emily?

I shrugged and sat up again. I needed some sugar. I hopped over to the minibar and pulled out a Cola. Dang, the carbonated sugar drink sure did taste good. The bubbles tingled my throat as I finished the entire can.

No, I'm actually glad I didn't marry Emily. Not because of who I thought she was, but because if I had, I would never have met Margaret.

I set my empty Cola can down on my nightstand and lifted my good leg onto the bed. How long until I check on Margaret or Avery, whichever? How much time do I give her? I sighed. It may mean I have to give her longer than I could stand. And if that was the case, maybe I should just move on. I couldn't fathom that yet.

My hotel room phone rang. When I picked up, I immediately recognized my friend's voice. "Hey, Larry!" On the other end of the line, I heard motorcycle engines. "Where are you?" I asked him.

"A biking event. I was just going to check on you."

"How did you find me?"

Larry laughed. "Your agent."

"That's good. I'm glad to hear your voice."

"Yours too. Hey, I was wondering when you'd be back around to Galveston."

I shrugged. "Dunno."

"I saw Avery today."

I sat up. "Oh?"

"Yeah, she was coming out of GG's Diner."

"Oh, okay. How is she doing?"

"Funny, she asked the same thing about you," he replied.

I laughed.

"Give her a call. She's a good lady. And hot."

"Stop, Larry. She's a little young for you, old man."

He started laughing then. "No, seriously. Marines don't give up, remember? Call her."

I sighed and rubbed at my thigh. "I may come around for Mardi Gras. Will you be around?"

"Miss that craziness? Heck no. I'll see you then, buddy. But keep in touch."

"Will do."

I hung up the phone. Larry was right. Marines didn't give up.

I started thinking, maybe I could just check up on Avery as a friend. See how she was acclimating to her new life. My stomach growled, so I dropped the idea.

I picked up the phone again and had the unwanted urge to order a vodka tonic when the room service lady answered. I fought against the craving. "Yes, I wanted to order a hamburger, fries, and a chocolate shake please."

"Room number?"

"1012."

"Give us twenty or so minutes."

"Sure. Thanks."

I hung up the phone and thought about what my agent said, "Go to Vegas, sign some more books, and then start your new one. There is plenty of time for you to write about Marilyn Monroe. Heck, everyone has written about her already. But I bet you could put a good spin on it."

I shook my head. Yes, I needed to keep writing. It would keep me busy. I hated how I overthought things like I did earlier today. I was meant to write, right? I had already planned my new book, so why not? And I did good research on this one this time. Back in England, there was a small inn where Marilyn stayed while filming a movie there. They swore up and down that it is haunted. I had already booked my tickets and was leaving Las Vegas on the first international flight out after the new year.

I began to doze off when I heard a light knock at the door. Was it my food already?

I stood up and hopped over to the door. No sense in putting on my prosthetic just to open the door.

I let the guy in. He set my food down and said, "Thank you for your service."

I frowned. "How did you know? The missing leg?"

He smiled. "Oh no. You're wearing a USMC shirt and it's obvious in your demeanor." Then, he pointed up, "And the hairdo, know what I mean? Anyway, my father was a Marine. The training sticks no matter how long you've been out."

"Ah."

"So why you here in Las Vegas?"

"Just a book tour."

"Cool. Where you headed next?"

I debated how much to tell a stranger. "Denver."

"Ah, that's perfect timing for Christmas."

I guessed I hadn't realized it was Christmas time already. "Right. Yeah, forgot about that."

"The Christmas lights everywhere didn't give it away?"

I rubbed my head. I had gone back to the military cut for ease, but I had really missed the feel of it on my hand when I touched my head. "Maybe. I don't really have a reason to enjoy the holidays."

"No family?"

I rested my hand on the table to balance myself better on one leg. "No." Then, it hit me. Avery and Ralph. They didn't really have any family left either.

"You okay?" the guy asked as he lifted the cover on my food.

"Yeah, I'm good. You just gave me an idea."

"For your book?"

I smiled. "Maybe. It will surely be a twist." I tipped him and let him out before rushing to my phone to call my agent. "Hey, Sam. I need your help with something."

"Sure thing. Shoot."

CHAPTER 44
AVERY

I opened the door to a familiar and handsome face. It was Trey, but his typical grown out beard and longer hair was cut short. He had a military crop now. He looked good. My dog jumped up and planted his paws on Trey's thighs. Trey smiled. "Cute dog."

"Little Bit, get down." I sighed. "We haven't had him long. Still in training." I looked back up at Trey. I had really missed him. "What's up?"

"I have a proposition for you and Ralph."

"What?" I asked.

"I have a book gig in Colorado and wanted you two to come with me. Just a week."

I shook my head. "But that's over Christmas."

"Let me treat you. A vacation."

"Why are you wanting to do this for us?"

"Because if it wasn't for you, I would have never known the truth. Or anything that I learned. You helped me so much. Let me help you guys."

"Oh."

Ralph walked up and shouted, "Hey, Mr. Trey!"

"Hey, Ralph."

He looked between Avery and me. "What you two discussing?"

"Bringing you and your mom on a trip to Colorado."

I was about to wave for him to be quiet, but it was too late. Ralph smiled really big. "Yes! When?"

"I don't know about this, Ralph," I replied.

Trey grabbed my hand. "Let me do this for you. What do you have to lose? And you'd be doing me a favor. I'm tired of trips alone. You're the only close friend I have. Someone who really knows me."

Ralph shoved at me. "Mom, I have always wanted to see the mountains. Please. Let's get out of this hurricane messed up town for a little while."

"He's right. You need a fresh slate to help you maneuver through all this. New memories." Trey smiled big. "That's it. If anything, let's make new memories together."

"I'm in!" Ralph exclaimed.

I looked around my apartment. "Wait, what about Little Bit?"

Trey smiled. "Bring him, too. I rented an entire house for you. After all, it's partly because of you that I was able to write that book."

Ralph rolled from his heels to his toes. "Mister, I'm not sure how my mom helped you with a book about nuns, but we'll take it. Come on, Mom, let's go!"

I shrugged. "Okay."

****

Four days before Christmas, Trey, Ralph, and I were unloading ourselves off of the Continental plane and headed into the Denver International Airport's lobby. I was tired from being nervous about the flight. It was my first time on a plane. I tried to hide it from Trey by sneaking into the restroom to vomit once. I had Dramamine for the trip. It didn't help one bit.

Then, poor Ralph. He was a stress ball on the plane, too. He tried really hard not to show it in front of Trey. It broke my heart, but I knew it would all work out once he saw snow. The plane flight was a good experience for him. He still looked over at me at one point on the flight, since we shared a row together, and said, "This may not have been a good idea mom. I'm freaking out." So needless to say, the vacation didn't start out easy.

Also, to make matters worse, when Ralph wasn't fidgeting from nerves, he was saying he was bored.

Well there I was on a trip with Trey. A trip that I was already hesitant to accept. I had to remind myself that it would be okay to be this close to him on a vacation. It wasn't just about me. This was good for Ralph, too. He had only been on maybe two vacations in all, I thought.

Trey was jerking the luggage off of the conveyor belt and seemed to be getting annoyed. I wondered if Trey would make it through this whole week. I told Trey to go get the rental, and I would stay with the luggage to make it easier on him. He smiled and took my offer.

Leaving Denver, CO to head up to Breckenridge was time consuming. The traffic was bad. I cringed as cars jumped over in front of us, some slammed on the breaks without warning, and many wouldn't let us over into a lane. "These people are rude," I said while grinding my teeth.

Trey raised a brow. "You're not in Kansas anymore, Dorothy."

"Excuse me?" I retorted.

Trey lifted the corners of his heart stopping lips. I couldn't help but watch his mouth as he spoke. "You're from the South, as in Galveston, but you are also from England, Avery. You, more than anyone, knows what it's like to see how different people act in different areas."

I grabbed my seatbelt in thought. "I still can't believe I agreed to this."

Trey grinned. "Why did you?"

"Because it's Christmas and you had a point. I was struggling between two lives. Getting away from both could do me some good." I shifted in my seat. "How have you been?"

"Good."

"I mean, really been?" I pressed.

He smiled. "Really good."

"Still talking to Larry?"

"Actually, yes. He called the other day. He said he ran into you outside of GG's."

I thought back. "Oh yeah. He did."

"Did you find what you were looking for there?" Trey asked as he slowly turned his head towards me. His eyes were a lighter brown in the sunlight. A hint of green around the irises drew me into his eyes even more. "At the diner?" he asked.

I smiled. "Yes, I did. I found her."

He smiled a knowing smile as my attention began to hover in front of us. In the distance, I saw the enormous outline of what looked like mountains. "Mountains!" I said excitedly. "My goodness. Ralph, look ahead!"

Ralph was sitting behind her listening to his music. With his bright green earbuds plugging his auditory abilities as well as his brain, he was missing the sight.

I turned to shake his leg. "Ralph, hey!"

Ralph's perturbed and uninterested brown eyes looked my way. "What mom?"

I pointed ahead and replied, "Mountains!"

His eyes got wide for just a second. "Cool." Then, in the next heartbeat he was back to his musical prison.

I paid it no mind, I was so enthralled at what I was seeing. I palmed for my camera in the pocket of my wool coat until I could get it free from the tiny pocket. Finally, with nerves racing, I had my camera up and ready for a pic. I began to speak softly so Ralph couldn't hear me. "I can't believe it. I've never seen anything like this since I was a kid in Scotland."

Trey kept his eyes forward as a tiny little white car swerved into his lane. "Get ready, there's more to see."

I knew I was all smiles. "They look so close. So, we'll be there fairly quickly then?"

"Oh, no. That's an illusion. We're still over an hour till we start up the passes."

"Really?"

Finally, the petulant child sitting behind me came alive. "Mom! I see snow! Cool!"

Trey addressed him without turning, "Just wait, Ralph. As we get up the mountain, you'll see more snow than you can shake a stick at." Trey smiled over at me.

Warm feelings entered the place where I had first felt doubt and sadness. "Yeah, Ralph. This is going to be a really neat trip. So, are you looking forward to skiing?"

Ralph shot back, "Of course. But what I'm really gonna enjoy is watching my mom ski!"

I turned to my teen. He had the hood of his jacket pulled down low to his brows. His dark hair was sticking out around his forehead. He looked much older like that.

My baby was growing up too fast. One day soon, he will be an adult and leaving home. I didn't like that thought at all. I remembered having that same thought about my older orphans at St. Mary's. I never wanted any of them to go. Then, I cringed. I lost all of them but four. "Change your thoughts, Avery," I told myself.

Trey turned on the radio. "Ralph, I am sure your mom will do fine."

"That's right. I'm going to be skiing circles around you!" I told Ralph.

Everyone in the car laughed. Things were looking up.

****

Two hours later, Trey woke me up from a deep sleep in the passenger seat of the Toyota SUV. The stress or excitement must have zapped me because one moment we were talking about snow; the next moment I was out. I quickly wiped the obvious drool that had escaped during slumber from off the side of my mouth. I was so embarrassed. It appeared that the useless Dramamine had kicked in too late.

As Trey pulled the rental into the driveway of the most picturesque cabin I'd ever seen, I shook it off and was in awe. The large log cabin sat on the side of a huge ski slope. The cabin and everything around it were covered in blankets and blankets of snow. I noticed immediately the massive wrap around porch and gas lights on both sides of the oak front door.

By that rustic front door was a three-foot bear carved from a tree trunk. It was holding a cute 'welcome' sign. Scattered all over the rest of the immensely large porch were dark wood rocking chairs beckoning me to sit and have morning coffee as the sun comes up on a new day.

Trey brought our luggage in and turned on the lights revealing the most beautiful fireplace I'd ever seen. It was a masonry fire pit with huge stone pieces stacked one on top of the other all the way up to the crown lined vaulted ceiling. The couches in the living room were a soft brown leather and the floors were a dark solid wood with plush crème carpet laid out only in the bedrooms. And the kitchen! It was huge with windows all around it and a stove to die for.

"Can this get any better?" I pondered. I opened the cabinets to find they were fully stocked with only the best pots. The most important feature of all was the larger coffee pot on the counter under one of the enormous windows. Opening the walk-in pantry, I noticed that it too had all the staple. Things like chips, beans, paper plates, condiments, rice, and pasta!

I thought of cooking one of my favorite English dishes that I was taught when I was younger. My sister, Cecilia, always loved when I made it. I stood there taking in all the food thinking how Ralph had never eaten my family's favorite recipe. Ever since I realized who I was, I had been too busy to cook anything for us anyway. It had been take-out at the library every night. The image of us all around a dining table made my heart sing.

"Mom, come see!" I made my way towards Ralph. He was in an adjacent room to the living room. He was pointing at a beautiful black grand piano sitting beside a two-story high single pane window.

Trey walked up beside me. "So, what do you think?"

"Wow."

"Glad you got away now?"

"Yes. How did you get this?" I asked, still in shock.

"My agent found it. Fully stocked and ready for us. Neat, huh?"

"Yes, it is. But why here? Why Colorado?"

"My family brought me here once." He put his hands in his pockets. "And recently I had a dream."

"A dream?"

"Nothing." He shook his head and turned on the lights to the hall. "Over there should be the master. Why don't you check it out? Ralph and I will sleep in the other rooms downstairs."

Ralph came running up. "Mom, we need to get a Christmas tree!"

I stood taller. "Of course! I love shopping for Christmas trees!" At that, Little Bit barked and wagged his tail.

I glared at the little dog. "Little Bit, it's freezing out there. Do you have to go that bad?" The dog circled around in place giving me his answer.

Back out the front door, Ralph and Little Bit escaped outside. Ralph hollered out, "Mom, it's snowing again!" The hyper dog jumped all around with him.

I stepped out the front door to see what was falling gently from the sky. So many puffy, white snowflakes. There was about one hour left till complete darkness, so I was glad to be able to enjoy the vision of seeing my son play in the snow. It was surreal!

I ran outside with him and opened my mouth to catch a flake without hands. A small one landed right on my tongue and gave me a tiny tickling sensation. It felt so good after all the heat in Galveston. I hadn't been in snow since I lived in England.

From off the porch, I heard Trey laughing at us. He was grinning with that pretty smile of his. I frowned and said, "Hey, stop that. It's been too long since I've been in snow. Leave me alone. It's beautiful".

Ralph stopped playing and addressed me. "Mom, you've been in snow before? I thought you never saw mountains and never traveled farther north than Dallas."

I froze. "Oh… Well…"

Trey jumped in to save me. "It snowed in Dallas a few years ago. Didn't it, Avery?"

I swallowed. I had been good about being careful around Ralph. Moments like these, I felt bad about lying to him, though. "Yes, it did. Once."

He nodded. "That's awesome. I bet it wasn't like this."

I laughed. "Nope. Not like this at all." I closed my eyes and went back to enjoying the feeling of the cold, feather-like precipitation. I smiled and spun around in place. I needed this. "Trey, it's beautiful!"

CHAPTER 45
TREY

It's beautiful? Dang it, no, Avery's beautiful. But what am I saying? I thought about everything while I laid in bed the next morning. I couldn't help thinking about how cute Avery was acting while playing in the snow yesterday with Ralph. Neither mom nor son had put back on their coats before dashing outside. So needless to say, within a few minutes, they were freezing. But I liked how Avery's cheeks and lips were a deep candy apple red color when exposed to the cold elements.

Then, when Ralph threw a snowball at Avery, it hit the back of her head sending her blonde locks dangling down over her shoulders. I liked her hair down. I had always just seen it parted into two braids. In the snow, she let it swirl all around her as she danced blissfully to the music in her head.

I sat in bed wondering how much of Margaret was in Avery at that moment.

Suddenly, I heard the clanking sounds of pots and pans and forced myself to get out of bed to go see who was awake. The shimmering sun was barely coming up over the mountain and there was a light brushing of snow falling in spite of it. There was no one in the living room or kitchen, but I thought I heard singing outside. I grabbed my coat and stepped outside to find a makeup free, relaxed, and happy Avery rocking back and forth on the porch sipping some good-looking coffee.

"Good morning," she said. "Want some coffee? I made plenty." Her little dog was nestled on the chair beside her.

"Yeah, hang on. I'll get me some and be right back." I scurried in to pour the Community Coffee that Avery must have found in the pantry.

Then, with happiness in a cup, I headed back out. "It's nice today. It'll be a good day for Christmas tree shopping." I leaned over and rubbed Little Bit on the head.

Avery smiled. "I agree! I'm so excited."

I loved how the littlest of things got this girl excited. She acted like Margaret, not a spoiled bone in her body.

Avery smiled over at me. "This place is gorgeous. I can't get over it. Thank you so much for asking us to come."

I sat down on the seat right beside her. "Don't thank me. I'm glad you came." Her delicate hands grasped her coffee cup tightly.

I continued, "So this is a new experience for you at a ski resort? You and your life as Margaret?"

Her eyes lit up. "Yes! The snow is so much prettier here." She looked behind us at the windows. "I have to be careful. But when we first got here, I was going to say something about snow back in England."

"What about it?"

"When it snowed there, as soon as it hit the ground it was a muddy mess. Nothing like this."

"Then, this was exactly what you needed and that makes me happy." I gazed ahead to watch the white precipitation fall from the sky. I still preferred a beach life, but this was nice.

As I stared off, I thought about my dream again. Over the year as I've worked to heal, it was comforting to have a dream that was not about my time in Somalia.

The girl beside me shivered. I wrapped my arm around her. I wasn't going to tell Avery about the dream, though. I wasn't even sure if it was Avery or Margaret skiing. But something inside of me told me that if I thought it was Margaret, then I brought Avery here for the wrong reasons.

Avery crossed her legs and turned towards me. I removed my arm from her shoulder so she could fully face me. Her eyes were soft as she said, "Trey, I'm her but I'm not her."

It was as if she read my mind. I studied the quiet mountains in front of us. "I know. Is that why you avoided me?"

"Yes. And the fact that I tend to jump into relationships too quickly."

"Like with Tim?"

Avery elbowed my side. "I was hoping you forgot all about that."

"Nope."

She took a breath and the loose strands of her hair lifted up with the cool breeze. "Trey, I figured out something important."

"What is that?"

"That my life as Margaret is over."

"But she's still you."

She shook her head. "You still don't understand. Do you even want to know me as Avery? Because that is who I am now. I don't -" Avery stopped talking when she saw me look down. "I don't know what you want from me, Trey."

"Nothing. I just want you to be happy."

We stopped talking for a few minutes and then I broke the uncomfortable silence by turning to face her dead-on. "Your writing to me and me being able to write to you helped me. It did, Avery. And then after the hurricane, Larry had come by. He took me on this duck hunting trip with other veterans. Avery, it was beautiful. I shared…" I caught my words.

"Shared what?"

Then it all poured out. "Everything. Everything I could only do in writing to you. After writing it all out, it felt okay to share for real. To talk to people about what all I went through. And the guys, they all had similar stories. It just felt right."

She smiled big. A warm dimpled smile that made my heart skip a beat. "I'm so glad," she added with excitement.

I reached out and took her tiny hand in mine. "I do want to know you as Avery. So, please, tell me more."

"What do you want to know?"

I stretched out my legs. The cold made the thigh the prosthetic was on harder to move. "For one, why didn't you ever travel further than Dallas?"

She tapped one delicate finger to her narrow chin. "I don't know. I guess it was just how my family was. I was actually only in Dallas for my mom's funeral. Her family was originally from there. They were Hispanic. My dad, of course, was all Texan. His family, being the Reynolds and all, could never leave the home of the great war hero of WWI."

We both laughed at that. Why we laughed, I didn't know. The orphan turned soldier became a hero. However, at that moment, the thought of where she came from seemed humorous to us now. Like we had accepted what had happened and were trying to move on and be at peace with it. Of course, we'd never forget the tragedy. I let my finger travel across her hand and said, "I think we both needed this."

"What?"

"Avery, it feels like we've been through so much. This will be my first Christmas genuinely happy."

She smiled and just stared over at me.

I took a sip of my dark coffee. I noticed the coffee had some bite to it. I liked that. "So, you are part Hispanic. I guess I didn't realize."

She giggled. "The blonde hair and blue eyes, right?"

"Maybe."

"Before you ask, no I can't speak much Spanish. Just the little you've heard that I remember my mom saying from time to time. I've learned a few other things here and there, but my dad was against me learning it conversationally."

"Really? Being able to speak Spanish nowadays is big time beneficial down in the South. Companies and schools give stipends or extra pay for that."

"Tell me about it. I'm getting there and using it more and more now. But I can speak French well!"

I about spit out my coffee. "What? You kidding me, right? From your time in England?"

Avery's flawless skin caught my eye as she spoke, "Bonjour, je m'appelle, Avery."

I laughed. "Cute."

"No, not from there. Texas. We had to take at least two years of foreign language in school, just like you guys did in Pittsburgh. French was the oddball class. I always liked doing things off the beaten path. It does help that both French and Spanish are rooted in Latin. So, they are very similar."

"Languages of love, huh?"

Avery's light blue eyes studied me. "Yes, see you know more than you let on. Anyway, Ralph wants to take Spanish. He's signed up for it for next year."

"That's good." I leaned in closer. "How often do you slip up about your past to Ralph?"

"Not much. Just when I get excited or frazzled." She rocked a little in her seat. "He can't know all that. He'd never understand. He's too young."

"I agree. But do you think he should know when he's older?"

"Trey, I don't know. See? That was another part of what made this hard and maybe why I avoided you."

She turned towards me. "Trey, I am a parent first. Ralph is my priority. When he's grown, I'll make that decision. Not now. But I really appreciate you not giving it away either and by also bailing me out yesterday."

"You're welcome. I figured that was what you were trying to do. I would do the same."

She looked down at my feet to her dog that was twisting and turning on my boots. She scolded the little thing.

"Little Bit, if you can't stop shivering, I'm bringing you in."
The dog barked at her, so Avery stuck her tongue out at him.

I sat up. "Let's finish our coffee inside before your dog
turns into a furry ice cube," I said, and we both laughed.

****

When we got to the tree farm later, I waited until Ralph
was distracted so that I could get to know Avery more. "So,
what made you decide to be a librarian?" I said while touching
the blue spruce Ralph first ran to.

Avery waved that question away and addressed Ralph,
"That one sheds its needles too much. What about this one?"
She walked over and touched a Frasier Fir.

I glanced at the smaller tree. "That one is nice. So
seriously, why? What would make a person want to work
around books all day."

"You're one to talk. You're an author who writes
books."

"Touché."

She waited until Ralph walked off. "I'll sum it up. My
mother left us when I was young and then my father had
issues ever since. As I told you before, I started my teen years
with the wrong crowd where I found drugs and made a whole
lot of mistakes. Not long after I found out about Sister
Margaret…" she stopped and shivered. "Well, I guess that
was when I got my act together and turned to reading as my
escape instead of drugs."

"Wow, I'm sorry." I kicked the snow at my feet. "You
know we have more in common than I thought?"

"What's that?"

"Messed up childhoods."

Avery stopped walking and turned towards a large tree. She gestured all around it. "This one!" She looked around. "Ralph! Where are you? Come see!"

Ralph ran up and frowned. Then, he decided to chime in, "A flocked tree? That's so girly." Ralph shook his head. "Come on. Let's find another one, Mom. This one is stupid."

Avery turned. "I'm sorry, he's moody now that he's a pre-teen," she explained. "It's like he's PMSing. I read boys can sometimes act like girls do when they PMS," she sassed back.

"Whatever," he said and walked off.

I lifted my brows and gestured for her to look at the next row of trees. "Oh, yeah. That is completely normal. He'll be trying other things before long, too."

"Oh no, I forgot about that stuff."

"You know what Avery? He may need to get 'the talk' pretty soon." She stopped walking and put her hands in her pockets.

"Yeah, I know. I just don't know how to do it. Who wants that to come from their mom?"

"Let me do it. He respects me, and I care about him like a son. I'll help you with that. It's the least I can do."

Avery noticeably tensed up. "No, I couldn't ask that of you."

"You are not asking. I'm offering."

After a few seconds, she nodded her head. "Okay. That would be great, if you are sure."

"I am sure. I was back and forth about popping a cap this trip anyway. We have time. I could go and take him. Has he ever shot before?"

"Are you serious? No, he's never shot a gun!"

I nudged her with my shoulder. "I'm surprised. You know, him being the great, great, great grandson of a legend."

We both laughed.

I tapped my chin. "Let me introduce him to it. I can show him the ropes. There is a shooting range close by. Let me take him there in the morning."

Avery's mouth flew wide open. "Oh, my goodness. I know he'd love that!"

Sweet! I thought and said, "Yep! Nothing better for boys than burning through some lead rounds."

She put one hand on her hip. "Okay. If you think so, but don't show him too much of those Marine skills. I'd rather not be a military mom. I can't imagine worrying about him constantly while he's off at some war. That is too much for a mother."

When she said that, I immediately thought of my mom and all her care packages that I just gave away. I felt horrible.

"What about this one?" I said and pointed to a Douglas Fir.

I liked how her accepting eyes sparkled when she looked up at me. "I think that one is perfect! And it'll look great in that room."

I admired her high rosy cheeks and cute smile. When she looked like she did at that moment, I thought she looked like an excited little girl. But I couldn't shake the fact that she was making it obvious who she wanted to be, or rather, needed to be. And Avery was not the woman I was in love with.

Avery touched the limbs of the tree with her pink gloves. I knew she knew that, too. That was what she was trying to tell me back in Galveston. I was just now fully realizing it.

Avery licked her lips and yelled out, "I think we have it, Ralph! Come see!"

He came around a row of trees. "Where?"

She pointed to the one we found. "This one. What do you think?"

"I like it!" he exclaimed with a big smile.

"Good."

"Sir, we'll take this one," I said waving over at the tree farm attendant.

He nodded and walked over. "I'll get it tied up and loaded. Where's your car or truck?"

"Side lot. It's a red car. Enterprise rental sticker. I'll follow you and show you."

He pulled out his clipboard. "Okay. Let me get some information and payment, and we'll have you on your way."

"Sounds good. Here's my card."

The man took it and started writing the numbers down. Then he stopped and looked up at me. "Trey Reynolds, the author?"

I stammered for a second, but my agent said I should never miss an opportunity to sell myself, no matter where I was. "Yes. You read my book?"

"No, but my girlfriend is going to your book event in Denver. Isn't that why you're here?"

"Yes. You should go, too."

He handed me back my card. "I may. After she read the book, she told me all about what those nuns did for those orphans down in Galveston. Amazing women."

I looked over at Avery whose eyes were cutting back and forth from one side to another nervously. I smiled at her but directed my comment to the tree farm attendant, "Yes, they were. The bravest."

The guy handed me a ticket. "So, is that why you're doing your book event in Colorado? Because the Sampson family moved up here after the storm?" he asked. "I know not all the characters were based on real life people, but my girlfriend said it was obvious that the Walters family was based on the Sampson family."

I saw Avery's eyes light up and she said, "The Sampsons all survived?"

He thought for a second. "No, but most. I don't remember the details."

Her shoulders dropped. "Oh." She lifted her chin back up. "So, they were here?"

"Yes. They were a big deal in Denver for two generations. Their two children, that were born after that hurricane, were both mayors at one point."

Avery smiled at that. "That's good to hear."

I patted her back and smiled over at Ralph. "Hey, Ralph, you know what?"

He was watching his mom's face closely and frowning. "Yes, sir," he said without taking his eyes off his mom.

"How about some hot chocolate and double stacked chocolate chip cookies?"

"Yeah!" Ralph responded. And just like that, everyone was happy again.

CHAPTER 46

A few hours later, we were back at the cabin decorating the tree with all the silver and blue ornaments we purchased after our hot chocolate sugar rush. Ralph was responsible for the low hanging ornaments, and Avery offered to go up the step-ladder to hang the high ones for me. It bothered me for a second letting her do it, but I wasn't sure how I'd manage climbing a small ladder with my prosthetic. I had a large contractor's ladder when I was renovating the house in Galveston, and that was difficult enough.

I stood there for a second watching them do their thing. Avery had Christmas music playing on the old record player. When she moved up the ladder with a shake in her hips that mimicked the beat of the music, I laughed to myself. It was cute. I hung a few ornaments on the tree where I could reach and then added candy canes all around it.

"Want some eggnog?" Avery said and rushed off into the kitchen before I could reply. She came back and handed me a small glass full of the velvety smooth looking drink.

"Looks good." I motioned for her to sit down with me. I was tired, and it looked like Ralph could handle the rest of the decorating.

"What's for dinner since you didn't want my cooking tonight?" I asked her when we sat down on the couch in front of the warm fireplace.

"A family recipe," she replied.

"Really?"

She leaned over and whispered, "I used to make it in England. It was my sister's favorite meal."

"Really? That sounds good." I took a sip of the drink and grimaced. "This is strong."

She ignored my critique of the drink she concocted. "You'll like my dinner more."

I sat forward in my seat to be closer to the warmth of the fire. "I like British food." I said and rubbed at my thigh muscle again. The cold was really making it hard. Carrying in that oversized tree through the doorway was a bigger feat than I had expected, too.

"I'll be right back," Avery said and walked off to her room. She came back a moment later and was carrying an old ornament that looked like a wooden stocking. It was about three inches tall in the shape of a candy cane and was painted in red and white. She added it to the tree.

"That's cute," I said.

Avery smiled over at Ralph as he frowned. "Really, Mom?"

"What?" I asked.

Avery turned back towards me. "I brought it just in case. It's the ornament Ralph made for me when he was in 2nd grade. I hang it on the tree every year."

My heart warmed instantly. How could I forget that in my selfishness of wanting Margaret, I was trying to erase Avery? She was a good mom. Through everything she had been through with the drugs and losing her mom at a young age. Still, she got herself together and adopted a son. She wanted to be the best mom she could be.

Ralph sat down on the leather couch. His feet bounced on the floor as he marveled over his work. And he should have. The tree was beautiful.

I watched Avery head back over to the tree. The humongous thing almost covered the entire room. It was decked out with perfect decorations.

The moment was amazing. It felt good. Really good. But what felt even better was that I was getting to know

Avery now, not just Margaret. And I realized just then that I was mesmerized by them both.

The funny thing was, I went to bed that night thinking about only Avery.

CHAPTER 47

About eight in the morning, Ralph and I headed out to the shooting range. Avery had made us a breakfast of pancakes and sausage before we left. On the way, I drank the black coffee Avery sent with me in a silver thermos. I thought of the girl from that ski dream and wondered over it off and on. I wondered if God was sending me a message. It surely was how I got the idea to bring Avery and Ralph here. But was it just some dream and I was stupidly putting a mom and son into my life to hold on to the memory of Margaret?

I sipped Avery's brewed coffee slowly and was hesitant to start anything other than a surface conversation for now with her son, Ralph. For the most part, we rode for a few miles just listening to Hank Williams, Jr. and Willie Nelson. Ralph made fun of me saying how he never pegged me for a country boy, especially since I was raised in Pittsburgh.

I asked Ralph a few questions. Nothing big. Questions about Ralph's school activities and band concerts. When Ralph answered, I noticed how polite and respectful the young man was. I hadn't really paid much attention to Ralph's manners until that trip. Ralph made eye contact with every response, just like a Marine. I was proud of him, yet he wasn't my son.

We strolled into Top Gun Shooting Range and was greeted by a gruff man in his fifties, presumably the range owner. I introduced myself and the boy while this enigma, named Bob Smith, eyed both of us with a weary, yet intense stare.

Mr. Smith, which was probably not his real name because he most likely was paranoid about the government, held nothing back. "That green horn know how to shoot?" He said with a voice like sand paper while pointing an arthritic finger at Ralph. "He's too young."

I answered honestly, "He is. I brought him here to teach him. We all gotta learn sometime."

Smith, who looked a whole lot like R. Lee Ermey, paused. It was a long, deliberate pause.

"Is that going to be a problem, sir?" I asked with a deadpan stare.

Ralph did not say a single word as us two, ex-Marine guys, had our stand-off.

The blunt older man looked down at Ralph with beady dark eyes. "Humph, well pay close attention to the range rules posted here." He pointed over his shoulder, but kept his sharp eyes on us and all the rest of his customers walking around.

I guessed I could I have told him I was a Marine, too. But that wouldn't have been any fun. I'd rather the old guy think I was some idiot city folk and then let him be surprised when I started shooting. "Thank you, Mr. Smith," I just said.

An older grey-haired man came up slowly behind us carrying his rifle outside its case. Mr. Smith said a few choice words at the newest customer and then added, "No way you're shooting that old thing around my establishment".

I didn't hang around long enough to see how that went. Once I was through getting checked in, I led Ralph out onto the grounds of the range.

Ralph finally spoke as soon as we were clear of the unruly man. "Ahem, Mr. Trey?"

"Yeah, Ralph." Oh, here it comes.

"I don't think that guy wants us here."

I held back a smile. "Why do you say that?"

"He was an a-hole."

"Watch your mouth."

Ralph smirked.

"Smith is a typical Marine. He doesn't fool around when it comes to safety. He was on you because you were young and you looked nervous. Hold your head up and always remember, no matter what, to attack life head-on."

"Yes, sir."

"And that's how those guys are Ralph. Every gun shop and gun range owner that I've been to from Pittsburgh down to Texas has been like that man in there. You just have to know how to take them."

Ralph had a quizzical look. "Oh."

We were assigned to bench #5. The guy next to us was shooting an AR-15 and it took Ralph off guard. I handed him his ear protection that almost swallowed his younger head. "Okay, you with me." I pointed my fingers at his chest. "Watch what I do and then I'll show you each step." Ralph was very inquisitive throughout the entire demonstration and even asked important questions as I showed him how to load, aim, and fire the 6.5 Creedmoor I had bought on the way to the range. Ralph was a quick learner.

The sun was high in the sky now and blaring down on the young boy's face. The shape of his face was narrow but with larger features. His wrists were wide too. Ralph's biological father or mom must have been big boned. The budding teen was even sprouting out splotchy facial hair and a juvenile zit or two around his small mouth.

"How is your mom holding up after the hurricane?"

"She's good. I just worry about her. She's so lonely all the time. She works, comes home, takes me to my school functions, and rarely does anything with friends. She can't be happy. And she did change a little after the hurricane. Something is different about her."

I could understand how that would be confusing for a child that knows nothing about what his mom was struggling with. What God did for her should have been a blessing, but in a way, could it be more like a curse?

"She is happy because she has you," I told him.

"I guess. I just want more for her."

I was amazed by this young man's empathy for his mother. Usually kids that age were selfish, self-centered. This was a special kid standing before me. Or at the least, he had an extraordinary mother that raised him that way, all by herself.

I watched as Ralph shrugged and I added, "You're a good kid, Ralph. She is blessed to have you. Ready to try again?"

"Yes, sir. Am I getting any better?"

I wasn't sure how to answer that one. "Better than when we started. But you have a little ways to go."

CHAPTER 48
AVERY

I closed my eyes to feel the cold breeze brush against my cheeks. The swirling wind reminded me of the beach. But the chilly air was soon replaced with a warm gust of an ocean breeze as I thought back to a day on the beach as Avery. I was sitting there in a blissful state and watching my parents laugh and kiss.

I was making sand castles and had my Barbie dolls all lined up around the castle like princesses. I remembered looking up and seeing my elegant mother sunbathing in the blaring sun. She was wearing a black two-piece bikini, and her long flowing brown hair was down to her waist. To me, my mother was the most exquisite woman I'd ever seen.

The memory began to go out of focus as thoughts of my other mother from England came into view. I was standing by her bed and holding Cecelia. Her pale face was washed out by the low lighting of the room. I had lost both mothers before I was ten.

Two completely different lives, yet two similar backgrounds.

I squinted my eyes tightly and I was back on the beach watching as my Hispanic mother came up and sat next to me. "Good job, Avery." She fluffed up my sand powdered hair and proceeded to help me build a bigger and better sand castle. Thinking of that moment with Margaret's perspective included, hit me hard. My heart was confused. As Avery, I always thought my mom was too self-consumed to want anything to do with me. But maybe my mother really did love me. Maybe, as Avery, I had just pushed all of that aside to dwell on the negative.

"So, what do you think so far?" Trey asked, intruding on my reflections.

I opened my eyes and felt the chill again. All the heat from the beach was gone. "I love it. It's relaxing up here."

I told Trey that I didn't want to ski, but he asked that I at least ride the ski lift with him so I could see all the sights. He said I'd enjoy it. And he was right.

I turned towards him. "Your parents took you here to ski a lot?"

"Yep." He looked down at his leg. "Those days are over."

I felt sad for him as he tapped at his prosthetic. "Trey, you said in the diary that you did a lot of sports. And that your dad was a big supporter?"

He nodded his head and cut his eyes over at me. I resisted the urge to hold my breath. He really did have adorable expressions for a grown-man. He appeared almost boyish sometimes.

Trey smirked at me. "I guess you could say that. I was his athletic son, so he was involved in everything. He coached my little league team, took me to Boy Scouts."

"I'm sorry for your loss."

Then Trey looked forward with a bemused smile. "I remember the time when I was Ralph's age, and I first skied. I fell and rolled down most of the mountain. It was crazy. But I got back up and tried again."

I liked seeing him talk about his childhood. His dreamy eyes would get brighter, almost like a caramel color. Even his full lips moved in a way that made me mushy inside. I liked seeing the happy Trey.

For most of the ride up the mountain, we sat in silence taking in the view again. I really liked Trey's company. I was so thankful that Trey took Ralph out for a man to man day.

Ralph came back that afternoon talking all about the guns and the rude, yet funny, gun range owner.

I knew there was no way I could take Ralph to experience anything like that. "I was glad that Ralph got a moment like that with a man. And he came back super excited! You don't know how much that means to me. Thank you again."

"You are welcome, but I enjoyed it, believe it or not. He's a good kid, Avery. You've done well by him."

I smiled with pride. I was truly happy at that moment. Or was it because Trey seemed to start looking at me more as Avery?

Trey put his arm up on the seat behind me to get more comfortable. He was staring off at the mountains in the distance. The corners of his mouth raised slightly. Something I hadn't seen him do. Maybe he was just as appreciative that me and Ralph were here as I was. I was so glad to see him like that. I wanted him to be happy, too.

Then, he shifted and noticed me looking over at him. He made a funny face at me that made me giggle. He laughed back and playfully poked my side with his free hand. It was like what friends did, right? After all, Trey and I shared something that no one in history had ever shared. We couldn't just write that off as fantasy. It really did happen. We changed history and now here we were.

Trey continued to laugh and I realized then that I had never been close friends with a guy before, not as Margaret nor as Avery. It seemed kind of neat. However, I couldn't help but think how good it felt to have him close to me. New things inside of me were coming alive in his presence. I squeezed my water bottle and looked away. Was it Margaret or Avery feeling this?

CHAPTER 49

Christmas mornings with my son were so incredibly joyful, even though they were usually spent alone, just the two of us. Now at thirteen, Ralph was not my little baby anymore, but a young man trying to learn himself as best he could without a father figure. This Christmas morning, I was extremely thankful because Ralph and I would not be spending the holiday alone.

At about six in the morning and out of sheer excitement, I wanted to get up before anyone else did. I walked into the living room that was dimly lit by only the tree's lights. A small amount of the sunrise was making an entrance into the room that helped guide me through the space.

I sat on the living room couch facing into the room with the black piano. Through the tall glass windows of the piano room, I saw that the snow was falling hard and covering everything left of color into a white existence again.

"Good morning," Trey said as he came into the living room with a yawn. He was dressed in grey sweat pants hanging low on his waist and no shirt!

I averted my eyes without being obvious as he walked by to head to the coffee pot. "Good morning," I said softly and took a sip of my coffee. Trying to catch another look at the sight after he walked by, I kept my lids low and coffee cup high while turning back towards him. I couldn't not ogle that chest, abs, and sculpted shoulders! Wow, Marines are that good looking? I was definitely seeing him through Avery's eyes. It was crazy.

Ralph woke up, came in, and he too made a v-line for the coffee pot. "Mom, can I have some coffee?"

I replied, "Sure but just one fourth coffee to three fourths milk, okay?"

"Yes ma'am."

Trey leaned over and whispered to me, "I hope you don't mind, but I put out a few things under the tree for Ralph after you went to bed."

"Trey, you didn't have to do that. I brought plenty for him. You're gonna spoil him. This trip, taking him shooting, and now gifts."

Trey smiled over at me with his coffee in his right hand. "I enjoy doing it."

I took a breath. Who was I kidding? I was still in love with this man. But I was going to be strong. If we were to be a couple, he had to love me as *Avery* and with my son included.

Then, I worried that if Trey couldn't take the whole package, would it hurt Ralph at this point? He was getting too attached to Trey. I reminded myself that Trey was a good man. It would be okay. But also, was this spoiling Ralph? No, Ralph needed this. I decided and let it go.

But then I looked at all the gifts Ralph was tearing into that weren't from *me*. I felt a little bad but continued to fight the sensation turning in my gut. It's just a few gifts, I thought and watched the red and gold wrappings fly into the air.

Trey was coming back into the room putting a shirt on while he walked. I waved over at him. "You wrapped very well."

He plucked fuzz off his wrinkled shirt. "Are you kidding? The mall ladies did all that."

"That's pathetic, Trey!"

He just winked at me.

Everything felt good. I was making new memories and finally everything started to make sense.

CHAPTER 50
TREY

That next night, Ralph went to a party at the country club down the slope with all the other kids. I planned to get some rest off of my leg and take it easy. Maybe even write. I was happy that Avery seemed excited to be here. After getting some more logs from outside for the fire, I entered the warm cabin with hopes of a quick shower and maybe a few beers to dull the pain from my leg. Christmas day had been fun. The best!

As I closed the front door, I heard a soft melody and started to head towards the lone piano room. As I approached the room to see if it was a record playing, I was struck by the vision in front of me.

In the dark room, that was barely lit but by a few dripping candles placed sparingly around the top of the black baby grand, I saw something entirely different. With long blonde, wavy hair tumbling down on an elegant neck and thin shoulders, a woman of immense grace and talent was playing the piano.

As my eyes adjusted to the dim light, I noticed it was Avery. Avery plays? Maybe it was her memories as Margaret?

To not disturb the utterly fascinating image in front of me, I stayed off to the side and watched her hands gracefully flow from one ivory key to another in a way that moved my senses and took my breath away. The moment was so ethereal in nature that I rooted myself in a spot a few feet away from her and couldn't move another step.

The music she was playing had a quiet and almost sad sound to it. It strangely paralleled my mood from when I was

deployed and alone on my bunk dreaming of getting home. A
chill ran down my spine.

Avery played each key as if she was trapped in the
throes of a struggle more deeply and spiritually than I could
have ever imagined. Her pouty bottom lip twitched a bit with
each upward motion of her wrists. And when her playing
slowed down, her long dark eye lashes fluttered over the tops
of her cheeks. Then, she leaned forward rocking in sync with
the rhythm as her playing sped back up. I'd never seen
anything like it.

She was wearing a white nightgown with a satin robe
over it that covered her petite body. I frowned, clamped my
jaw, and looked away. I wasn't thinking good thoughts. I was
ashamed for a sec.

I looked for the quietest way to slip away without being
noticed. I thought to myself, Avery didn't want this, so I
shouldn't try, right? But how do I not? How do I not think
about her laughter on the ski lift? How do I forget the beauty
I see now, the curves, the rise and fall of her chest? Awe man.
I clasped my hands together.

Risking one more glance back, I saw her close her eyes
again as she did a decrescendo of the piano's heavenly sound.
My heart stopped. I rubbed the back of my stiff neck trying to
analyze what was going on. Always analyzing and trying to
make sense of things. This I couldn't explain. This intense
feeling tightening up in my chest and making my fingers tingle
with an urge to touch her hair, her face… Heck, the urge just
to fall into her comforting arms and no longer feel alone. No
more stress or bad memories of what all happened in Somalia.
No sadness from the loss of a son I never knew. This woman
brought me to peace. I knew I should give all credit to God,
but I still needed this woman.

The moment was amazing. So much so, I wanted to
always have it now. Experiences just like this, always and
forever with her. "Crud! What's going on?" I looked down at
the wood paneled floor to steady my thoughts. I rubbed my

thigh above my prosthetic and then went to turn. But when I looked back up there were wide, blue eyes staring straight at me.

"Hey, I'm sorry. Am I disturbing you? I'll go back to bed," she said with a sweet and embarrassed tone as she went to stand while trying to cover her body as best she could with the delicate robe.

I held up my hand and with the most confident voice I could muster at that moment, I said, "No, no, stay. I didn't know you played."

"Well, I play a little. I learned the piano when I was a child."

"Back in England as Margaret?"

Her face and shoulders deflated at that question. "No, when I was young in Galveston, we lived by a pianist that taught me. Actually, she taught me almost everything I know because my mom wasn't there. Mrs. Miller was like a grandmother to me."

I felt horrible. How could I just assume that the best parts of Avery were because of her life as Margaret? No wonder she didn't trust our relationship. I stood there not sure if I should leave. I was hoping I wouldn't have to. "Avery, you play beautifully," I said and lowered my eyes to the floor.

"Really?" Her face lit up from the compliment.

"Yes, really. What was that?"

"Oh, just Mozart."

"Just? It was awesome."

"Well, yeah the piece is. I used to play this one when I um…." she paused appearing to look for the right words, "… when I had trouble sleeping. Anyway, this song is his Piano Concerto No.23 in A Major."

"Wow, that's a mouthful," I said to her.

"Yeah, I guess." Her eyes were dancing. Or was that the flicker of the candle light?

I paused again trying to think of what to say next. I was at a loss for words and she appeared to be, too.

For a moment we just stared at each other. Finally, the mesmerizing woman in front of me asked, "Want me to show you something?"

"Yeah, sure."

"Sit." She patted the spot beside her.

I slowly moved to the piano bench to sit on her right-hand side. When my shoulder brushed hers, a subtle heat moved through my arm and down my body. And that was when I noticed her smell - a soft and powdery, floral scent. Was it from her hair, her skin? I spoke timidly, "Now, you should know that I can't play."

"I'll help you," she said while flashing a bright grin my way. "Just hit this key three times. Then these, then back up to that same one another three times like this." She showed me with her long elegant fingers.

"Okay." I followed her lead and recognized it immediately. I remembered how Tom Hanks danced on a huge piano in a toy story while playing this number in Big. I could do this.

Avery began playing a few keys to the left of me in perfect unison with a unique and upbeat style. I was a little nervous that when she nodded for me to join her, I stumbled the first time causing the gorgeous woman by my side to giggle. I shrugged and added, "I'm a Marine, not a musician."

She continued to laugh. She was precious, and I couldn't help but mess up again and again just to hear her laugh over and over. Out of not wanting to be too much of an idiot, I finally put in the effort and we played harmoniously.

Avery showed me a few more notes for the next progression and before I knew it, we were making music together. Literally and metaphorically in a sense that made me feel bonded to her in a new and more intimate way than just as friends. Something was changing. But did she notice it?

And if not, what would I do? I couldn't live through another broken heart. I just couldn't.

Dread hit my stomach once the thought came up. And sure enough, without realizing that I was starting to project my inner struggle, I slipped on the keys and ruined the last measure. "Sorry, I think I'm just getting tired."

She looked up at me and smiled a sweet, yet nervous smile that looked like she knew what I was thinking. "Yeah, me too. I may have overdone it. Big day. I'm tired, too."

I partly heard what she was saying, but was captivated by her glowing eyes set off by the candle light. So much so that I was swimming in them into a deep abyss as my gaze dropped down to her soft lips.

She noticed it and parted her mouth ever so slightly, like she did it without thinking. I was drawn to her. Not only was she kind and a good mother, but she was suddenly breathtakingly gorgeous. I felt uncomfortable and was about to get up when she touched my hand and lifted her chin up towards me. Then, surprisingly, she brushed her sweet lips against mine. My heart dropped. Is this real? I nervously wondered to myself.

As if sensing my apprehension, she hesitated for just a second causing me to question the situation. I thought to myself, do we do this? Oh, screw it, it feels so right and you don't have to ask a Marine twice.

I then kissed her back by starting with her bottom lip. When I heard her sigh, I moved to her top lip. Next, I kissed her cheek and her chin. She smelled amazing. I noticed her shiver, so I returned up to her mouth.

I grabbed her face so I could press hard against her lips. I was losing myself and couldn't stop. The pleasing sounds she was making were driving me *crazy*.

She moved as if she was wanting to get even closer, but her elbow hit the keys, startling us both.

We both separated from each other instantly. We were breathing so hard, neither of us could speak. A few seconds passed. Finally, she smiled at me with a gentle expression. "I'm sorry. I don't know what I was thinking."

Standing up and balancing on weak legs, I shook my head. "No, no, it was partly my fault. I'm sorry."

Avery bit her lip and kept her eyes down.

I cleared my throat. "Thank you for teaching me to play. It was fun." Fun? I couldn't believe I said that.

I put my hand on her shoulder as her wide eyes looked up at me. "Trey…" she paused. "Trey, it's okay."

I sucked in my bottom lip. "Um, why don't you go get some rest. I'll wait up for Ralph."

"Alright. Thank you and goodnight," was all she said.

"Goodnight." I quickly added and walked away sheepishly. I got to the window and took in the snow falling outside. It was freezing out there, but I knew I needed fresh air and a cold something.

I donned my black North Face ski coat and made my way onto the back porch. After lighting the small pit outside and brushing off the accumulated snow from the wooden bench, I sat down and took in the dark sky. White flakes were saturating the landscape. I couldn't deny that my mind was not going to be at ease tonight. How could it? There was a sexy, astounding woman inside who wanted to be with me. But would it be long term? I had to have long term. I couldn't handle another situation where the woman didn't know what she wanted.

And then the door opened. Avery came outside and sat right next to me. "Pretty crazy, huh?" she asked.

My jaw dropped. I didn't know what to say. I grabbed her hands in mine. "Avery, what are you feeling right now? What do you want?"

She sighed. "I'm not teasing you if that's what you're worried about."

"Then what? You know my history. I just want to be loved by someone who loves me."

She looked down at both our hands. "You have shown me a life separate from Margaret and Avery. I feel like here, on this mountain, a new life has begun. And I'll be honest, that is exactly what I needed."

I squeezed her hands and stood her up next to me. "I have something to show you. I was back and forth on giving you this because I didn't want you to be upset with me."

"Give me something?"

"Your Christmas gift."

She shook her head. "You should not have gotten me anything and why do you think I would be upset?"

"Because it is from your previous life. Come inside," I said and led her back in and down the stairs to my room.

She paused.

I shook my head. "No, it's not that." I began to question what she really thought of me. But instead of continuing to debate who we really were anymore or what the ladder of our lives led to now, I just smiled. "Avery, argue with me or not, but I feel no matter what, you will always be Margaret *and* you will always be Avery. You can't deny it. You have the same soul. So, I got this for you. Come in."

I led her into the room. She cut her eyes over to my bed. "Typical Marine. Your bed is perfectly made."

I turned the knob on the closet door and then stopped. I wanted to preface what I was about to show her. I began to say, "My agent set up this speech engagement and book signing in Denver for a reason. I'm being honest in that this was set up with a purpose."

I watched her eyes dart around, but I continued, "Remember when you told me that Rebecca Sampson did some kind of artwork?"

"Yes. It was of large animals or something."

"Well, it turns out that after she and her family came here, she changed her style. No one knew why. Many thought it was because of what happened to her two children, but it wasn't?"

"Wait, you know for sure that Rebecca Sampson lived? I asked around in Galveston, checked the library history books. Nothing."

I nodded. "Yes, she lived."

"But what happened to her children?"

"During the Hurricane of 1900, the Sampson Manor held together. It was well built."

She interrupted impatiently. "I know, I knew that much."

"Well, most of the family lived because they stayed upstairs in Rebecca's art room. However, two of her kids had gone into the other wing looking for their dog that wouldn't come when they called him."

She mumbled, "Paris."

"What?"

Avery clutched her hands together. "Their dog was named Paris."

I nodded. "Oh. Well, the dog freaked out over the storm and ran into the adjacent wing. The two kids followed. It was later in the storm when it happened."

"What happened?"

I took a breath and delivered the news. "The weight of the rain on the roof and the hurricane's strong winds made that part of the mansion collapse. Those two kids were lost."

Avery gasped and threw her hand to her mouth. "Oh God, poor Rebecca. Why are you telling me this?"

I took her hands again. "Because your friend was a strong woman. She searched and searched after the storm until she found both of their bodies so she could bury them herself. Even when her family had given up, she didn't. She buried them in Galveston in the ground below where they were found."

Avery began to cry. "She was amazing."

I touched her shaking shoulders. "Yes, she was."

Avery's sad eyes looked up at me. Her voice shook when she asked, "Which two children?"

"Um, I think the kids' names were Mark and Claire."

Avery's shoulders dropped. "Clara."

"Huh?"

"It was Mark and *Clara*. Poor Rebecca. Those were her only two children that adored music like she did. But it doesn't matter which ones you lose, right? It's the tragedy of losing any at all. My heart is broken for her as my heart is still broken for my fellow sisters and all the children we lost."

Avery sucked in her lips. "But thank you for telling me."

"You're welcome. Anyway, the rumors say that is why the Sampson Manor is haunted."

"Oh. I see."

"But here is the good news," I said and touched the doorknob to the closet again. "You ready?"

She nodded hesitantly.

I opened the closet door all the way to reveal a four-foot statue sitting in the middle of my closet.

Avery's hand went to her mouth.

I spoke again while she continued to tear up. "All the art collectors had no clue what it was. To them, it was more of an abstract piece. For people that didn't know Rebecca Sampson's history with you, they just thought the statues that Rebecca sculpted in Colorado were some kind of angelic being. A nice reprieve from the ominous animals Rebecca was said to have hidden from view back in Galveston."

Avery still didn't speak, but her and I both knew what the statue depicted.

Avery dropped to her knees and softly said, "It's a nun."

I watched her reach out and touch the wood.

After a moment, I added, "Yes. She made tons of these. All sold off to families in Colorado. I managed to find one at auction for you."

"Thank you," Avery said. "Thank you so much."

I turned towards her and lifted her to her feet. Her watery eyes were still on the statue. I held her and said, "Don't write off who you are because you think it will negatively impact your new life. Rebecca must have found something in you that she couldn't shake. You were, in a sense, her muse. You were very special to her. Just like you were and are to me, and to your son."

She slowly nodded in gratitude. "Trey, what else did you find out about her?"

"Just that she had two more children after they came to Colorado. Her husband died a few years later with her endlessly by his side. From what I read, she died less than a year after that. Many say from a broken heart."

"So, she healed her marriage?"

"I didn't realize there was anything wrong."

Avery inhaled and exhaled. "There was. But if she mended it that well, it must have meant that she was able to reach him and help him. What a beautiful love story it was then."

I squeezed her hands. "Can we be a beautiful love story, too?" I pleaded. "Because Avery Weeks, I … I love you."

Avery shook her head and had a distant gaze. "This doesn't make sense but in a way it does." She looked up at me. "Trey, I do, too. As Margaret, I loved you and now as Avery…" She paused.

Before I let my heart get too excited, I asked, "What?"

"I love you, too, Trey."

"You do?"

"Yes!" She exclaimed and smiled brightly.

I kissed her and pulled her in for a tight hug. "Really?"

"Yes!"

We just stood there hugging as many more moments passed. It felt so nice to find a woman that I knew would never hurt me. I squeezed her tightly and kissed the top of her head. I wasn't letting her or Ralph go.

After we held each other for what seemed like an hour, I asked, "So, what are we going to do now?"

"Now?" she asked and smiled even bigger. "It's so freeing."

I hugged her again and we both sat down on my bed embracing each other even longer. Her sweet vanilla scent and warm embrace ignited that familiar inertia of peace that I had when I could only talk to her through a diary.

I kissed her forehead. "I meant, now what do *we* do?"

She pulled back and squeezed my hands. "Why don't you just sit here with me and enjoy," she said coyly, which was such an Avery thing to say and do.

"Enjoy what?"

She crinkled up her nose. "Enjoy the fact that you were able to win the heart of not one woman… but two."

"But they are both you."

"Not really if you think about it. They both had their own lives that impacted their choices. In that way, they were both different."

I shook my head. "Whatever, that's enough of the psychological dissections. I'm just glad you figured out what I've already known."

"And what is that?" she asked as she laid her hand on my chest.

"No matter what life you were in before or who you are now, girl. *You… are… mine.*"

Avery smacked me on the shoulder and winked. "No, Marine. You are mine."

Then, she laid her head back over my heart and whispered, "But first, we belong to God."

CHAPTER 51

A few days later, I stood up on a stage in front of a few hundred people and began to give what I hoped would be the most brilliant speech ever. I had written it the night before, and it was going to be all about the literary world, how I brainstorm for my book ideas, and why I chose an old house to be the setting for my first novel.

Instead, as I began reading off my preplanned words, I went off script and started saying, "A rainbow comes before, after, and sometimes between a storm. Yet, it doesn't matter when we see one, it's the fact that it comes. I spent a lot of time after my tour in Somalia where I hated trivial things like rainbows. Or even comedy shows, or small talk with others, or any other things people here in the states enjoyed. I was numb to everything. And the anger… it would come when I didn't expect it. And sometimes I didn't notice it, but others did. I'm incredibly sorry to those that faced the brunt of that."

I looked down into the audience that filled seats in row after row inside the small Denver theatre. But there, in the row closest to the stage and smiling up at me was Avery and Ralph. But my heart was full when I saw who was sitting next to them. It was my mom, my brother and his wife. All of them flew in after Christmas to see me. And just a few seats down, I saw my new closest friend, Larry Wheeler.

I smiled down at them and continued my presentation, "Someone once told me that talking about your mistakes or your past hurts is therapeutic. However, it's like a thorn stuck in your finger when you're a child and your mom tells you it's not going to hurt when she pulls it out. But then she has to dig into your finger deep, so naturally it does hurt. You see, if you leave that splinter in, it will get way worse and infected. So, it would be better to get it out with a few minutes of pain than to wait days with tremendous pain. Writing in general did that for me. It got a lot out of me. I was hurting deeply. Writing helped me heal. So, I decided to begin this book after I came out of the aftermath of my own self destruction from my time at war. I wrote this book because of a true-life story and some amazing women involved. Their story spoke to me at a time when I needed it the most. But theirs is a real story of tragedy caused by another form of devastation… a hurricane. It was not because of a war between men. This one was caused by something we had no control over. You see, hurricanes come and do what they do as do rainbows. However, now to me, I'm glad for those rainbows because they symbolize love. As it did on that day after September 8, 1900 when the most destructive hurricane the nation had ever seen took parents from children and children from parents. It took brothers from brothers and sisters from sisters. It separated friends from friends and pets from their owners.

'And on that day, it took 90 precious orphans and 10 beautiful nuns from the world. But a rainbow still graced the sky the next day and the people of Galveston saw it. They also saw other signs of love, like the reality of the sacrifice the nuns had made in an attempt to save the orphans, all of which moved them to rise up with hope. Because in the aftermath of a horrible storm, under that rainbow, people found in strangers what they never would have found if not for that tragedy. What did they find? They found love. Because on that day, everyone worked together and helped each other. They picked up the fallen, fed the hungry, and comforted the sad. They buried body after body of people they didn't even know, but stopped long enough to say a prayer for them. That is love.

'If the nuns that we lost that day could come back and talk to us, how would they feel about the survivors and their descendants? I think the nuns would be happy because their sacrifice was remembered and honored. They set the example for all of us and they would be proud we followed it. And I think that's what that rainbow signified on that next morning after the hurricane. It reminded us of God's love and that we should love one another the same. No matter someone's faults or what they may have done to you, you should love them. If you do that, then no one really died on that day as no one in your family who you may have lost had really died either. If you love one another, all your loved ones live on.

'I wrote this book because of those nuns. And I finally followed what their memory inspired in me. I, myself, have forgiven others and chose to love them despite what I had thought of them. Because of that miracle, I honor and remember the little boy, Webster, who I lost in Somalia but who continues to live in my heart. Because of that miracle, I also found out that I had had a son that now also lives on in my heart. But more importantly, because of that miracle, I can finally do the same. I can finally live…"

Surprisingly, the crowd stood up and began to clap before I could finish. Cheers filled the room. Instead of continuing with my speech, I walked down the steps to Avery. Her eyes were full of tears. I pulled her in to hold her. Everyone seemed to clap louder around us. "Was it okay? Did I mess up anywhere?"

Larry came over and patted me on the back. "It was horrible. That accent, buddy. I don't know how you kept everyone listening."

We both laughed.

Instead of a comeback, I leaned in and gave him a hug. "Thank you for coming."

"You're welcome, but now it's time to find a bar. That flight got me crazy."

"Well, you go on ahead and get your White Russian. We'll meet you there."

"Sure thing." Then, he smiled. "I'm proud of you."

I nodded and watched him tell my family bye, too, as he walked out. My mom and brother with his wife came over and gave me hugs too and said they were going to go ahead and follow Larry to the bar. They said they'd see us in a bit.

After they walked off, I turned to Avery. She smiled. "Worried about how you sounded, huh? So now it's you, the Marine, that is lacking in confidence?"

I laughed and stared down at her seat where she had placed the dozen roses I gave her when we first arrived. "At least I got you liking flowers again."

Avery looked down at them. "Hmmm, they'll do." Then, she smirked. "But one thing that won't."

"What is that, babe?"

"We have to live in Galveston. This snow and rare sunlight in Colorado is killing me."

I pulled her in again for a hug while laughing louder. "Ha, I guess the ocean life is what works best for you."

"Yeah, as a former London girl, I now appreciate the sun I enjoyed as a Texan. However, if a hurricane comes, we're getting the heck out of dodge, and Denver it is."

"Deal."

She pushed herself back off my chest and smiled up at me. "Yup, I knew you'd see it my way, Mr. Reynolds."

I drew her back in. "Come here, future Mrs. Reynolds." I held her tight and kissed her with everything I had.

EPILOGUE

Galveston
Present Day

And that was how my crazy story went. No, I didn't plan on meeting a nun, writing a book about renovating historic homes and including inspirational elements, or even meeting the love of my life who came from another time and then popped in again in my time. That turn of events was surely unexpected, but God is funny like that. He proved to me that *anything* was possible. Heck, I was just trying to survive before all that happened. However, as Sister Margaret had told me before, I needed to "enjoy the journey." And that was exactly what I began doing. No more surviving. Just living.

The waves out in front of me started coming in stronger and more fiercely. I stopped my trip down memory lane and headed up the stairs of the sea wall to get back on my bike. As I put on my helmet, I continued to watch the ocean. That water not only took away happiness but it gave it back, too.

I drove away from the sea wall down a few blocks while watching people finishing the boarding up of their windows with lumber from the local hardware store. A few more blocks down, I pulled into the driveway of the old tenant's house that I bought from the Gaines years ago.

As I always did, I exited my bike and stared up at the old soul that was now painted in a pale yellow with white shutters and a white porch. "I'm home," I said to it. The wind picked up behind me, so I started moving quickly to the new stairs and through the front door. The sun had begun to set, so I turned on the recessed lighting and admired my handy work in the parlor and living areas. I was extremely thankful that I went with the lighter stained floors and light powder blue painted walls.

My cell went off in my pocket. I moved to the couch and pulled out my phone. It was a Facetime call. The face that popped up was of a Marine. All dressed in combat gear with his helmet and rifle sitting next to him. A small smile crossed his face. "Hey, Dad."

I leaned back on the couch. "Hey, Ralph. How is it in Afghan land?"

His eyes seemed distant on the small screen of my phone. It was hard to ascertain what Ralph was feeling. Then again, Marines wouldn't show it anyway, would they? Ralph leaned forward. "I took your advice."

"Which one?"

"About perspectives. You warned me of what I was going to face and even though you knew everyone handles combat differently, you said something that stands out in my mind."

I touched the screen on my phone as if feeling like I was touching his face in person. The option of seeing our family and speaking to them in real time was not something my generation was able to do when we went to war. So much had changed. Still, the pain hidden behind the technology was always the same. Ralph was doubting why he was there in another country fighting a war that seemed world's away from what he loved.

Clearing my throat, I nodded. "I think I remember. Remind me because sometimes when you say things aloud, it helps. I learned that from your mom, Ralph."

Ralph sucked in his lips. He leaned forward. "I'll never forget the quote, '*Only two people were willing to die for you, the American soldier and Jesus*'." Then, he crossed his arms over his chest. "But I never wanted to be a hero, Dad. I just wanted to help people like you did, but I don't see that I'm helping anyone here. They hate us."

"Many hated us in Somalia, too. To bring order, there has to be chaos first."

"Like the hurricane?"

I frowned. "Which hurricane?"

"You and mom never told me everything, but I filled in the pieces."

"The pieces?"

Ralph turned his head to a voice off to his side. "I gotta go, Dad. Don't stay there too much longer. They say that's a Cat 4 out in the Gulf."

"It's not gonna hit us. It's headed to Corpus."

"Still, you're on the wet side."

I sat up uneasily. Avery and I never told Ralph the whole truth. I promised her I wouldn't. That couldn't have been what he meant. I dropped it. "Okay, Son. I love you. You be safe out there and remember, you are there for a reason. God put it into your heart to be a Marine. Trust in that."

"Now, you sound like Mom," he said and then he laughed. "Okay, bye. I love you."

Before I could add another thought, his beautiful face disappeared off the screen of my phone. I squeezed the phone, lowered my head, and said a prayer for Ralph and the other Marines that were beginning another morning of patrolling.

I forced my eyes shut and fought through my worries and regrets for supporting Ralph when he came to me after college saying he wanted to enlist. He gave me the whole, "I'm going to be an officer quickly since I'm already degreed. This is my chance, Dad. I've always felt that I needed to do this."

Below my feet, I stared at the same floor where Ralph's shoes would leave sand every time we visited here in the summer to get away from our other home in Houston. He would track it in after a full day of playing volleyball on the beach with his old classmates. My how time has flown. He was once a boy. Now he's a man. I had to have faith in God and in Ralph's choices. But it was hard. Would he one day face the trauma that I endured and had to fight back when I came home from war? Has he already experienced it and isn't showing it yet? And my biggest worry, would I be able to help him if he does? I then said aloud, "I'm all he has."

Above me and almost like a ghost with an angel's voice, I heard, "No, you are not."

My eyes left the floor and traveled up the still slender figure of my wife. Avery was smiling down at me. I gasped. "How long have you been here? I thought you were in Dallas with your cousin."

"Not as of this morning when you told me you hadn't left Galveston yet. And I see the weather outside. I would like to think that my crazy Marine husband would get it together before he drowns on this island, but not looking so good."

"I told you I was coming home tomorrow."

She turned and pointed outside. "On a bike in that weather? Time to go now."

"Don't smart mouth me, woman."

Avery laughed. "I wouldn't dream of it. But you are coming."

I began thinking of how much her more formal language disappeared the longer she was exposed to our modern times. After fifteen years, she sounded like Avery did before her memories came back.

As she sat down, I eyed her. "Ralph was upset. I could tell."

She sighed. "Well, at least he talks to you. He hardly calls me."

"You're the mom. He doesn't want to worry you."

"Trey, I died and was brought back for a second life. Matters of life and death don't worry me."

"I'm not talking about that."

"I know. But you also know what I told him when he said he wanted to join."

I just nodded. "About that whole quote, '*Live by the sword, die by the sword*'?"

"Jesus' words. But that wasn't why I told Ralph that."

"Then why?" I asked, almost pleading to know why she would say something like that to him.

She sat down next to me. Her long hair was pulled back in a low bun but I could still smell the coconut shampoo she used every morning. "Like that storm brewing off the coast, you of all people know what comes after your time at war. Trauma that intense is like a hurricane dumping the whole entire ocean on you. God's biggest fear is how that heartache is more damaging to a soldier's soul than a soldier simply dying on the battlefield. It's all about getting us back home, Trey. I mean, look at what He orchestrated in your life to bring you back to Him."

"I know."

"The good news is, God is capable of anything. It will be up to Ralph to decide if he wants God's help."

The rain began to pour down outside. Avery took my hands and kissed my forehead. "Don't worry. We have a lot of praying to do, but we got this."

My eyes watered up. "Yes, we do. I love you so much."

"And I, you. But let's get going, okay? You're too old to be on a bike in the rain."

"Who says I'm old?

She stood up. "I did. Let's go."

****

It took about an hour to finish the hurricane preparations on the house. After that, Avery and I said a prayer over the house and for the safety of the people staying behind in Galveston. As I walked to the front door to follow Avery out, I paused at the foyer table and looked down at the picture of Ralph in his dress Marine uniform. He was posing as a tough Marine, but his eyes had a sweet childlike innocence.

I was extremely proud of Ralph, but as any parent would do, we always think we can handle things better than our children can. Therefore, I was genuinely scared for him. But I knew, from the last fifteen years of my own life, that some things are out of our hands. I needed to continue to have faith. Just like when I renovated the house to survive even the harshest of storms, I also raised Ralph the best I could to survive. I had to have faith that it was enough since he was out there seeing *and* being a part of the worst of society. As God helps where He can, parents do the same for their children. And that's all I could do.

I closed the door and locked it behind me. When I turned around to head to Avery's car, I heard His voice say, "Storms always have an end and the sun always comes after."

THE END

ABOUT THE AUTHOR

Jackie Hovorka has been an obsessed reader and lover of all fiction, ranging from drama... to sci-fi... to historical, all her life. As a young adult growing up in Louisiana, she never missed an X-Files or Stargate show and her favorite movies are Shawshank Redemption, Pride & Prejudice, and Terminator. Her favorite books are Little Women, Devolution, Omega Man, and War of the Worlds. I know... big difference in genres, right? But that's why she loves what she does!!

Jackie is an award-winning author (some works published under Jackie Anders), award-winning screenwriter for film, and an award-winning songwriter. She is a mom of three teenagers and is married to the man of her dreams, Robert "Johnny" Hovorka, who is a combat Marine veteran. They all live in Texas with their dog and two cats!

Visit her at jandersbooks.com

Subscribe to our mailing list at
www.JJRanchProductions.com and receive FREE writing
classes, daily deals, and stay current with news on our movie
and book productions.

Thank you so much for reading one of Jackie
Hovorka's novels and visit www.JJRanchProductions.com to
purchase more of our books from award-winning authors.